Not the
Girl You
Marry

Not the Girl You Marry

ANDIE J. CHRISTOPHER

JOVE
New York

A JOVE BOOK
Published by Berkley
An imprint of Penguin Random House LLC
penguinrandomhouse.com

Library of Congress Cataloging-in-Publication Data

Names: Christopher, Andie J., author.
Title: Not the girl you marry / Andie J. Christopher.
Description: First Edition. | New York: Jove, 2019.
Identifiers: LCCN 2019001227| ISBN 9781984802682 (pbk.) | ISBN 9781984802699 (ebook)
Subjects: | GSAFD: Love stories.
Classification: LCC PS3603.H7628 N68 2019 | DDC 813/.6—dc23
LC record available at https://lccn.loc.gov/2019001227

First Edition: November 2019

Printed in the United States of America
1 3 5 7 9 10 8 6 4 2

Cover art and design by Colleen Reinhart
Book design by Alison Cnockaert

To Bud Manka,
the prototype for the Nolan men.

AUTHOR'S NOTE

I started writing *Not the Girl You Marry* in late 2017. Blasted by the bleak state of the world whenever I turned on the news, I was craving some of the lightness, humor, and hope of my favorite romantic comedy films. And I wanted to see myself—a biracial woman who has been through the wringer when it comes to dating—coaxed into believing in love again. I wanted to write the kind of hero that I would fall in love with if he walked off the pages—someone kind, considerate, smart, aware of his privilege, and with enough of an edge so as not to be a pushover. (I'm still waiting, by the way.)

But despite my intention to write a light, frothy tale centered on a biracial woman, I ended up writing a book about love and belonging—about a woman who never believed she could have that for herself realizing that she could make a space where she truly felt at home.

Despite my close-knit, loving family, like Hannah, I've struggled with feeling worthy of love and belonging. At least while I was being unapologetically myself. I am part of the "Loving Generation," the cohort of children born to mixed-race couples shortly after the 1967

Loving v. Virginia Supreme Court decision, which struck down state laws that previously outlawed interracial marriage.

Growing up in Minnesota, with my mother's white family, surrounded by mostly white classmates, my racial identity always felt like a slippery, vexing thing. And even though my parents thought of me as "mixed," plenty of other people viewed me as "black." But I never felt black enough to call myself black. This made the pernicious, frequent, rude question that biracial people face ("What are you?") extremely fraught to me. If I said I was mixed or biracial, would black people take that as a sign that I thought there was something wrong with being black? If said I was black, would someone ask why I wasn't like what they thought a black person should be?

I came to dread the question until it came from a six-year-old child I was tutoring as part of a mentoring program in college. She looked me over carefully and said, "You're not white, but you're not black. What are you?" Simply knowing that she saw me as *me*, not a projection of her own ideas—her curiosity made my answer easy.

I'm both—black and white. I'm mixed.

That exchange didn't mark the last time I felt awkward answering questions about my race or felt like my otherness prevented me from feeling like I truly belonged anywhere. But that moment did mark a turning point in my determination to define myself for myself.

Hannah is similarly determined at the moment she meets Jack. She's much more secure than I am in her racial identity, but her atrocious dating experiences have led her to define herself as not the kind of girl men want to marry. In relationships, she's felt intense pressure to subsume her own desires to those of her partners, but she just can't seem to do it. But the moment she meets Jack, she feels seen for who she is. And even though they both spend most of the book pretending and obfuscating, Hannah finds a place with Jack, and with his family, where she belongs.

I want readers to find lightness and joy in Hannah and Jack's story. And, more importantly, I hope that my readers see themselves in Hannah, whether in terms of race, personality, career goals, or even her bleak outlook on dating. If just one person identifies with her, then I know I'll have done my job.

CHAPTER ONE

ON THE THIRD DAY of ninth grade, Jack Nolan asked Maggie Doonan to be his date to the Leo Catholic freshman dance. He blackmailed his older brother, Michael, into dressing up as a chauffeur and driving them in their father's baby-shit-colored Lincoln Town Car. Then he sweet-talked Mrs. Jankowski at the flower shop into finding lilacs in Chicago, in September, just because Maggie's sister had told him that they were Maggie's favorite flower.

After that, Maggie Doonan hadn't needed any more convincing that he was the perfect half-formed man for her. And the fact that he was an actual, honest-to-God choirboy had convinced Maggie's father not to even bother threatening him with the shotgun that still resided in the Doonans' front closet.

At the time, Jack had no idea what kind of power he had unlocked.

Two years later, he and Maggie had sullied the back seat of the baby-shit-colored Lincoln Town Car in unspeakable ways. And, two years of near constant shagging after that, he'd watched her get in her parents' SUV to leave him for Harvard.

Watching Maggie's tearstained face drive into the distance had broken Jack's heart. But he'd been the only guy in his high school friend group to leave for college with valuable sexual experience not involving his right hand.

Still, he'd been sad.

Until he met Katie Leong during the third hour of freshman orientation at the University of Michigan. She'd winked at him while they'd learned the fight song at some stupid mixer for first-year students. That wink had hooked straight into Jack's dick and driven him to be the best college boyfriend ever—midnight burritos, romantic two a.m. walks to and from the library, and oral sex at least three times a week—six times during finals. Hell, he'd even started working for the school paper because Katie was going to be a journalist when she grew up.

The only thing about his relationship with Katie that had stuck past her semester in Paris, and her subsequent new relationship with some French douche named Julian, was his career in journalism and a broken heart.

But the broken heart had lasted only a few months—until he'd met Lauren James, his favorite ex-girlfriend. She was off-the-wall funny and could suck the chrome off a trailer hitch.

He and Lauren had lasted through their senior year at Michigan and a shitty apartment with six roommates in the Bronx while he'd studied for his master's at Columbia and she'd waited tables at a craptastic Midtown tourist trap and raced to and from off-off-Broadway auditions.

Lauren hadn't even dumped him when he'd moved home to Chicago for a shiny new job. She'd saved her tips and flown out twice a month until she'd met a British director who wanted to cast her in an all-female West End production of *Waiting for Godot*.

You're the best man I know, Jack. Such a great guy. I'll never have another boyfriend like you.

No, she wouldn't. Because she married the prick director after the very brief run of the show. That British guy hadn't been a Boy Scout, and he for sure didn't know all the best sex knots to tie.

As he stood at the bar of a speakeasy in Wicker Park, after waiting fifteen minutes for an artisanal old-fashioned made with, like, artisanal cherries and orange peels scraped off with the bartender's artisanal hipster fingernails or some shit, he'd been without a girlfriend for six months. It was the longest he'd ever gone, and that was why his buddies had thought it was a good idea for him to leave his couch and the Michigan Notre Dame game—to sit around and talk to them in public.

He *should* be working tonight. In addition to not having a girlfriend, he didn't have the illustrious journalism career he'd dreamed of. In a recent pivot to video, he'd become the online magazine's how-to guy. His boss told him he was "too handsome to break real news," but more important, he would be laid off if he didn't shift with the times.

Now his father grumbled about him "not having a real job" every time he saw him, and Jack kept his mouth shut because he was living in a condo his family owned. If he lost his not-real job, not only would he have to hold his tongue around dear old Dad, he would have to wear a sandwich board on the corner. Or worse, work with his dad. While his father could deal with his working a job outside of the family construction business, he wouldn't be underwriting Jack's lifestyle if he got fired.

He loved his father—looked up to him—but they would kill each other if they had to work together.

So, he was here with his buddies, trolling for ideas for his next bullshit column. Chris and Joey could be his guinea pigs for whatever he came up with. He'd grown up with them; they'd all graduated from Leo together. Unlike him, they were knuckleheads about women. The idea that they would need to stage some sort of intervention with him over the nonexistent state of his love life was freaking preposterous. As demonstrated by the fact that they were wearing suits for a Saturday night out in the hipster hell that was Wicker Park, so they could stand around a bar that served overpriced, fussy drinks while looking at their phones and not talking to any of the women actually in the room.

Neither of them understood that for the first time since Maggie Doonan had put her hand down his pants under the bleachers at the freshman dance, he was kind of happy being alone. He could finally do the kind of shit that he liked—watch the game with a beer or five, sleep until noon, bring bread into the house without ruining someone's gluten-free cleanse.

For the first time in his adult life, he was figuring out what he liked instead of contorting himself into the kind of guy Maggie, Katie, or Lauren needed. And he meant to go on that way.

Just the other day, he'd been thinking about getting a dog. Some slobbery beast—like a mastiff or a Saint Bernard. Lauren hated dogs. Which probably should have been his first clue that the relationship was doomed.

Still, he scanned the dark bar to see whatever other unfortunate souls found themselves ripped from the warm embrace of their college sports or Netflix queues. No one looked quite as miserable as him, though. Not a single one of the long-bearded hipsters littering the red leather couches and old-timey booths looked like he'd flash a nun for a beer on tap.

Looking around, he thought maybe his next video could be *How to Not Ruin a Saturday Night Paying for $15 Drinks at a Douche-Magnet Bar.* Name needed work.

His gaze stopped right next to Chris and Joey on the ass of a woman in a tiny black dress that didn't match her gray moccasins. He didn't give a shit about her sartorial choices because there was so much velvet-soft-looking light-brown skin between the shoes, which looked as though they'd seen better days, and the bottom of that dress, which made Jack's lungs feel like they were going to combust. He hadn't even seen her face yet, but he knew that she was like whisky in woman form; he felt his judgment cloud and high-minded ideas about bachelorhood vacate the premises. In his head, she was already like the first puff of a cigar. Just her gorgeous legs made his throat itch and burn. Forty or so inches of skin had him choking on lust.

Thank freaking Christ the bartender showed up again with his drink. Jack knocked twice on the bar and, not taking his eyes off Legs, said, "Put it on Chris Dooley's tab." Jack was about to lose his wits to a woman, and it was all his friends' fault for making him leave the house. They were buying his drinks for the rest of the night.

He made his way back to Chris and Joey, still looking at their goddamned phones and not at the beauty next to them. No wonder they were constantly swiping and never actually meeting any of the bots populating most dating apps face-to-face. And no wonder Chris had been single since dumping Jack's sister, Bridget, a year and a half ago. They didn't pay attention.

Considering the sister dumping, maybe Jack should have drowned Chris in the kiddie pool when they were five.

But if they were aware of their surroundings, maybe Chris or Joey would be the guy getting to talk to Legs, and Jack would be left holding his dick. So, thank Christ his friends were idiots.

It wasn't until he was a few feet away that he noticed the other women with Legs. Both of the other women were knockouts, but they didn't rate for him. Jack had homed in on Legs, and he would not be deterred.

Maybe he could figure out how to keep things casual with Legs for the first three months or so. He doubted it. Once he'd tasted a little bit of a girl's magic, Jack didn't like to date around. He enjoyed flirting as much as the next guy, but he was—in essence—a commitment-phile. He liked having a girlfriend.

Maybe he and Legs could get a dog. He could compromise and live with a French bulldog. Small and cute, but still a real dog.

"Are you guys both swiping?"

"Yeah." Joey swiped left. "But I'm coming up empty."

"What the hell does that mean?" Because of his affinity for having one lady for years at a time, Jack had never been on a dating app. He didn't see the appeal. If he'd met Maggie on an app, he wouldn't have been able to figure out that the lotion she wore smelled like lilacs. He wouldn't have known that Katie's singing voice rivaled that of an angry tomcat, but that it was so charming he didn't care. He'd never have clocked Lauren's sassy walk across the stage in the production of *Hello, Dolly!* that he'd been reviewing for the *Michigan Daily* when he'd first seen her.

And he would have seen Legs's face first. To be honest, a picture of her face might be the only thing in the "pro" column for online dating. He needed to see if her face would captivate him as much as her rocking body did.

"It means he's not matching with any of the hot girls," Chris piped in as he swiped right multiple times. "I swipe right on everyone so that I get more matches."

"But he matches with mostly dogs," Joey said. "I'm not looking to get caught up with a girl so ugly I gotta put a bag over her head."

Yeah, he definitely should have drowned both Chris and Joey twenty years ago. Instead of clocking both of them, he pointed an angry finger in their faces. "Both of you are nothing to look at yourselves so you get what you get."

He ran his finger under his collar, longing for his worn Michigan football T-shirt instead of a stupid button-down. It was damn sweaty in this goddamned hole of a bar that didn't have decent beer or a television.

"Yeah, you'll eat your words when you're forced to swim in the waters of Tinder, loser." Chris pointed back at him, finally looking up from his phone. "Then you'll realize that it's kill or be killed. The women on here are either bots or butt ugly."

That had to be the moment when Legs turned around. Jack could tell by the look on her—*beautiful, gorgeous, absolutely perfect*—face that she'd heard every word that his asshole, knuckle-dragging squad of buffoons had just said. Her eyes were so narrowly squinted that he couldn't tell what color they were. Her nose wrinkled up and her red-lacquered lips compressed with anger. Couldn't hide the fact that she was a knockout from all the angles. Not even with a raised middle finger partially obscuring her face.

She was like a sexy, rabid raccoon. And he was a goner.

SOME DIPSHIT WITH TWINKLING green eyes wasn't going to stop Hannah Mayfield from raining holy hell on the bros swiping left on the girls standing right next to them. *Two of whom happened to be her best friends.*

His tousled dirty-blond hair and the muscles straining his shirt's buttons didn't make her want to throw a drink in his face any less, and they weren't about to stop her from curb stomping his buddies. Didn't matter that the goofy fucking smile on his face said he couldn't read the room. She was about to de-ball all three of these assholes, and he was *smiling*. Maybe he was missing more brain cells than the average young professional man in Chicago—which is to say all of them.

"What the hell is your problem?"

Stupid-Sexy Green Eyes answered even though she'd turned her glare on his two bozo friends. "I didn't say anything."

No, his deep voice, which rolled over her with the subtlety of a Mack truck, wasn't one that had been calling all the women on Tinder, including her friends, dogs. But that didn't stop her from saying, "Well, then. Keep yourself busy sucking a bag of dicks while I disembowel your two friends here."

Although that was a harsh statement to lob at an innocent bystander, she couldn't risk showing any weakness in the face of the enemy. And all men were the enemy. Especially the pretty ones who looked at her like she was their favorite slice of cake. Those were the especially dangerous ones: the ones who could seep into her heart, which made it much harder when they left. And they always left—usually because they *just didn't want anything serious right now.*

"Why are you so angry?" He seemed genuinely perplexed, and honestly, she didn't know why she was so angry, either. It wasn't like she was on dating apps anymore. She'd given it the college try, but every petty humiliation suffered on those apps felt like a stab to the gut. And even when she'd met a few guys for drinks, she'd felt like she'd been at the worst audition for the worst reality show in the world. She didn't understand how people ever actually made it to sex with someone they'd never met before.

Probably drinks. Lots and lots of drinks.

"I'm pissed because they"—she pointed at Sasha and Kelly—"forced me to come to this hipster nightmare for drinks after I'd been working all damned day." She'd only been guilted into it because Kelly, a management consultant, was in town for the first time in months.

"The shoes." Green Eyes's gaze dipped to her feet.

"Not your business." She hated how warm his slow perusal of her made her feel, as though he'd already seen her naked. It was creepy, and she ought to have called him out. And the warmth melted some of her righteous indignation on behalf of her friends. *Not the plan here.*

"Working on a Saturday?"

"Event planner."

"Spent all day dealing with a bridezilla?" He took a sip of his drink, and she didn't roll her eyes at his stupid, sexist comment. The amber liquid rolling from the glass to his mouth was much more fascinating.

"That's a dumb, sexist thing to say when I'm already pissed." As if the only thing that event planners did was plan weddings. True, she wanted to plan weddings because that was where the money was, but she did so much more.

Then the stupid asshole smiled at her again. "Back to that."

She was surprised that at least half the panties in the room didn't incinerate under the force of his grin. *Good God*. He was so pretty that it hurt. Features cut from stone and stubble not quite artful enough to be on purpose. Drinking bourbon with his shirtsleeves rolled up. He was citified masculinity that wasn't quite civilized. A contradiction, and the kind of thing Hannah went crazy for. The dimples that bisected the stubble had a feral quality that made her want to touch him.

He'd moved a little closer since she'd turned around ready to tear his buddies apart. They'd retreated, but he'd advanced. It was kind of sexy that he wasn't afraid of her, that he didn't buy her pains-takingly cultivated bitchy exterior. His lack of fear was working on her in a major way, and that terrified her. After Noah, she'd sworn to herself that she wouldn't be foolish enough to believe that some-one could want her for something other than a few rolls between the sheets, and a *Hey, babe, that was fun, but I'm just not looking for a girlfriend right now.*

Because they were never looking for a girlfriend, especially not *her* as a girlfriend.

That didn't hurt anymore. *It didn't*. She'd accepted that she was just not the kind of girl men romanced. With her ethnically am-biguous looks, bawdy sense of humor, and filthy mind, men wanted to have sex with her. And then—once they realized that she wasn't entirely domesticated—they wanted her to disappear.

She had to remind herself of this, make it her mantra whenever this man was near. Never forget that men were the enemy, regardless of how friggin' sexy his smile was.

He stepped even closer, leaving only half a foot of space between them. Hannah clocked Kelly and Sasha in her peripheral vision. They'd moved over to one of the stand-up tables.

Great. Neither of them believed her when she said that she was done with dating and romance and men for good. Their seeing her charmed by the prime cut of Chicago man-meat in front of her would not do at all. And yet, she couldn't seem to turn around and run away.

Maybe she should slap him. He hadn't done anything slap-worthy, but he had her cornered. In the middle of a crowded bar, with multiple options for egress, she was pinned in place because he'd *smiled* at her.

"What's your name?" His voice softened, and she broke eye contact.

She looked around; his friends had made themselves scarce as well. "Hannah." She looked at his chest when she told him. Meeting his gaze was too intimate and it made her cheeks flush.

"I'm Jack."

That was a very good name. It made her think of hard liquor and sex.

"Of course you are." Damn, he smelled delicious. Like freshly showered man draped in freshly laundered shirt. With a little bit of citrus and bourbon on his breath. It was like a lethal dose of bro, but it appealed to her despite her struggle to maintain her antipathy along with her dignity.

His laugh surprised her. "Hannah, tell me something."

She didn't respond but made eye contact again. *Mistake.*

"Can I get you another drink?"

She looked down to the mostly melted ice and rye in her glass. It would be stupid to have a drink with him. If she spent any more time in his aura of good-natured all-American Chicago boy, she would think about him for months. She'd wonder if she'd been too harsh and why he didn't call. Because if she didn't leave right now, she was going to give him her number.

Green-eyed Jack was looking at her as though he was starved for her. He would ask for her number so he could try to sweet-talk her into no-strings-attached sex—if he didn't come right out and ask her if she wanted to bone that night. That was probably what he would do. If he did, he was so tempting to look at, and so not fooled into thinking that she was ready to hate him solely because he was a man, she would do it.

Then he still wouldn't call, and it would be even worse than if he was just some guy she'd talked to in a bar one night.

If she left now, she could be home in time and sober enough to pretend he was attached to her favorite vibrator. His tongue swept over his lower lip, and he must have taken her silence for assent. Large, blunt fingertips brushed her smaller ones as he took her glass.

He motioned to the bartender for another round without leaving her side. Probably sensing that she would leave if he gave her an iota of the space that she ought to crave.

"I don't date." It was only fair to warn him that she was done—so done.

He looked back at her. "Neither do I."

"I mean, seriously. I don't—um—" She just had to tell him that she didn't date, and she also didn't do the random hookup thing. Wouldn't be going home tonight and feeling his skin against hers. She hadn't clocked the light dusting of chest hair through the small opening at the collar of his shirt.

"We're just having a drink, Hannah." He smiled again when he passed her a fresh tumbler of rye. "Think of it as an apology from my friends."

"Why are you apologizing for them?"

"I don't talk like that about women."

But she was sure that he thought that way about women. He was young, handsome, and well built. His watch and the quality of his clothes said he wasn't obscenely wealthy, but he probably lived relatively well. His straight white teeth said that his parents had been able to afford braces. So while he was smart enough not to seem like an asshole whose interest in her would be limited to a one-night stand or a string of booty calls, there was no way that he saw someone who would bust his balls every day at the end of his dating tunnel. Too bad she would really enjoy busting his balls.

"But I'm sure you think that way."

"No." His face hardened, and he took a drink. "I don't. My friends are assholes, but I think those apps make it easy to be."

"They turn people into commodities."

"Exactly." One cheek muscle flexed, and the dimple was back. She wondered what he'd do if she put her fingertip in it. "You shouldn't shop for a partner like you shop for groceries."

Advice wasted on her. "I don't do that. I told you, I don't date."

"I don't do the apps, either."

That surprised her. But then again, he'd never be standing here with her if he did. With the face and the muscles and the nice-guy veneer, he could have been getting a half-decent blow job instead of shooting his shot with her. "Why not? You'd do well."

Although she'd hoped she'd kept her voice neutral enough that he wouldn't take her genuine desire to know why he wasn't on Tinder as a compliment, he totally did. "Are you saying I'm handsome, Hannah?"

She really liked the way her name sounded coming out of his

mouth. Way too much for her own good. "You know what you look like, Jack."

The audacity of his wink had her fighting to keep from smiling at him. Even if he wasn't a total jerk, there wasn't room for both her and his easily stroked ego in this dank basement meat market. She drained her drink and put the glass on the bar. Reaching inside her purse, she pulled out a twenty and held it out to him.

"What's that?"

"For the drink."

"The drink was an apology."

"But that apology came with strings."

"No strings."

Then she did roll her eyes. "You're wasting your time."

"I don't see it as a waste."

She'd just bet he didn't. He liked that she was a challenge. "We're not going to"—she lowered her voice and leaned into him—"you know, do it."

He choked on his cocktail, and she barely fought the desire to bump his back until his windpipe cleared. Let him drown in his old-fashioned. If he died ignominiously, she wouldn't have to think about him tomorrow or next week and wonder if he wasn't a shit-head of the same brand as every other man in this city.

Unfortunately for future Hannah, he caught his breath. "I never asked you for sex."

Her cheeks flushed. Maybe he really was just apologizing. "I'm sorry."

"For what?" His hand cupped her upper arm, good humor back on his face. "I'm flattered that you were thinking about getting naked with me."

"I wasn't." She shook her head and looked down at her shoes. The gray moccasins she'd thrown on after the last of the Lurie Children's Hospital people had left the event she'd thrown today for some local NFL players who had wanted to give a whole boatload of money to kids with cancer. They were terribly ugly, but her feet would have fallen off had she kept her heels on for ten more seconds. "I didn't think about that at all."

"I must be losing my touch, then." He wasn't. One smile and he'd melted part of her shell. A touch on her arm burned her skin through her dress. "I just wanted to apologize and share a drink with someone not staring at their phone."

"Oh." He couldn't seem to stop surprising her.

"But I was definitely thinking that I'd be lucky to get naked time with someone like you."

There it was. Jack was lethally sexy, dangerous to her equilibrium. The flutter in her lower belly just from being near him would lay waste to her inner peace, such as it was.

"I don't do that, either." Part of her hoped that he would argue with her. Try to convince her. She waited a beat for him to respond. When he didn't, she adjusted her over-the-shoulder bag and shifted away from him. "I've got to go."

He swigged back the rest of his drink and winced. It was kind of adorable on him—this totally gorgeous, seemingly self-contained man not used to the burn of bourbon in his throat. The contrast between his manly appearance and that slight show of weakness attracted her even more. Her hesitation at this point was pure self-preservation.

"I'll walk you out."

"There's really no need."

He took her arm again, and she was sorely tempted to shake him off and maybe stomp on his foot. She was just about to, she swore, when he said, "There's a taco truck outside, and my stomach will hate me tomorrow if I don't eat something."

"That many drinks?" No wonder he was flirting with her. In her experience, guys like him did not flirt with women like her unless they were drunk or trying to slake their curiosity about dating a biracial girl.

Like Joe Osborne, the insanely good-looking but profoundly lazy stoner she'd dated sophomore year. He'd been into new experiences in general—mostly drugs, loose women, and never finishing a paper on time—but she'd mistaken his curiosity about her for genuine interest. Too bad that curiosity had never extended to whether she'd enjoyed their hookups. A few dozen orgasms might have made the shocked look on his mother's face when he'd introduced them over parents' weekend a little bit worth it.

Since her father had evaporated as soon as the pregnancy test came back positive, and her mother had been busy working to pay for her education, she'd been on her own with Joe's family. For two days, she was subjected to the *I'm Trying to Prove I'm Not Racist* variety show. At multiple points, she'd wanted to stop Mr. and Mrs. Osborne from talking about all their black friends and tell them she believed them. But that would have made them even more uncomfortable. Considering their son's lack of sexual prowess and the fact that he was probably going to flunk out once Hannah stopped pressing send on his papers, she spared them and broke up with Joe as they were driving away.

Which brought her to Jack. He was probably just drunk enough to step outside of his comfort zone to hit on her. Once he sobered up and/or figured out that she was pretty much just like the white girls he dated, only she would make his parents feel weird, she'd never hear from him again.

"Nope." He bent down close enough that his breath touched her ear when he said, "I just want to spend more time with you. Buy you a taco and see if you'll give me your number."

CHAPTER TWO

JACK HAD NO CLUE why he was taking a girl who'd looked at him as though she'd wanted to filet him for half of their half hour of acquaintance out for late-night tacos. Sure, she was beautiful. But he'd had beautiful, and the pretty that came with nice was a whole lot easier to be around. His stupid dick just didn't like it as well.

He had only a minute to wonder why his penis hated him, while she said goodbye to her friends. Their looks and hand signals amused him, but he was careful not to show it on his face. He stood there trying to look as much like the choirboy he once was as possible. Might have even made the sign of the cross to seem more innocent, but he just knew he needed a little more time with the lovely Hannah and her lovely legs. Maybe he'd say something dumb and she'd roll her eyes at him again. Or flip him off with her black-tipped fingers.

His sister, Bridget, had gone through a Goth phase in elementary school, around the time their parents had split up. Mom moving out had been rough on everyone, particularly the only other girl in the family. So she'd clothed and adorned herself all in black for several months. Like she wanted to wear her anger and confusion on the outside.

The final straw had been when she'd dyed her auburn hair black and stained the entire bathroom. Their dad had lost it and forbade Bridge from dyeing her hair after that. And his sister had decided that she looked too much like a cartoon witch without the dye job.

Hannah should look kind of like a witch in all black, but she didn't. It suited her, as though the real woman under the clothes was so intertwined with what she wore that they couldn't be separated. There was nothing soft about her at first glance. And even though he was sure she was leaving with him only so she could shake him off, he didn't really care.

He was a desperate man. If the only thing she wanted to give him was a one-finger salute as she got in a car, he'd take it. In the six months that he'd been single, he'd been figuring out what he liked on his own, but he hadn't been this amped about a girl since long before Lauren moved to London.

Hannah was as exciting as she was beautiful. And thrilling and mean beat pretty and nice with him every time. As clear as day, a picture of Hannah all soft and sated after he'd had his way with her popped into his brain. The satisfaction he'd feel if he could get her to let him in was almost palpable.

A part of him knew he should just walk out now because Hannah could wreck him. All the telltale signs of him falling hard were there—the clammy skin, pounding heart, and racing thoughts. If he knew what was good for him, he would leave her wondering where he'd gone. Nah, he'd be a curious footnote on what had been an unremarkable night for her. She'd sneer when she thought of him tomorrow, if she thought of him at all.

Jack was a twisted man to be so torn up over a girl who showed every sign of being even less open to a relationship right now than he was. She was like a soldier on her umpteenth tour of duty, hunkered down behind her sandbags of attitude, M16 at the ready, cynicism resting heavy on her shoulders, like armor she couldn't put down.

Still, the flash of uncertainty he'd glimpsed in her hazel eyes after he'd lied—bald-faced lied—about not angling to sleep with her kept him in the game. He tried to tell himself that the pull he felt deep in his gut was not the recognition that she was going to be his next best mistake. Talking to her was not pulling her essence under his skin, forcing him to pursue her. He didn't enjoy being around her so much that he'd lied about needing tacos in order to stave off a hangover. That flush under the lovely brown of her cheeks did not make him want to take care of her and make sure she had everything she needed.

He definitely didn't want to do a little dance for joy when he saw that his favorite taco truck was still a block away from the bar. And he absolutely didn't become uncomfortably aroused when she made a little moan in the back of her throat.

"This is my favorite truck!" She looked at him with bright eyes and lips curved into a smile, the first he'd seen on her. It wasn't even about him, but it knocked him flat on his ass. She slapped his shoulder with the back of her hand and he barely suppressed the need to catch her fingers between his own.

"Because you have great taste."

"You don't know that about me." She picked up one foot and pointed to her shoes. "I could think that these look really neat."

"Nope. You said you were working earlier. Guessing the shoes you wore to work were killing your feet." And he was sure the shoes she'd been wearing to work were sexy as hell. If she'd been wearing stilettoes when they'd met, she might as well have stuck one pointy heel right into his heart. Her legs were devastating as they were; heels would almost be too much.

"You were paying attention." She sounded surprised, and he hated that.

"Of course I was. Who wouldn't pay attention to you?" She was captivating, at least to him. But she didn't seem to see it. As soon as she'd turned, ready to commit heinous acts on behalf of her friends, he'd been caught up in her. Maybe her favorite tacos would give him some insight as to why.

"What's wrong with you?" Her question caught him off guard only a little.

"What do you mean?"

"I mean—and don't let this go to your head—you're good looking, probably not broke, and you don't seem stupid right off the bat." She stopped and ran a hand through her dark brown hair. He couldn't help but look where the strands nuzzled her breast. "Why are you even talking to me? Are you a glutton for punishment?"

In addition to being superhot, she was definitely a pill, but the superhot part was winning. Plus, there had to be a reason she was giving him such a hard time. He'd chalk it up to journalistic instinct that he wanted to know what was up with her. "Definitely a masochist."

"Figures." She rolled her eyes at him, and—hand to God—it made his heart race.

"You're seriously not going to cut me any breaks, are you?"

"Why should I?"

He hated that she was likely lumping him in with some douchebro who'd done her wrong, but he could understand. He knew what kind of shit men pulled when they were trying to dip their wicks. He'd been friends with Chris and Joey for two decades.

"My winning smile?" He crossed his arms over his chest, and she mirrored him as though she wasn't going to give him an answer. When she said nothing, he raised an eyebrow.

"Just a nice boy from a good family, just making conversation. Aren't you?" She shook her head.

Her voice sounded world-weary, and he felt empathy with that. But *good family*? His family was just fine, normal for his block. But after his parents split up, the kids had kind of been left to fend for themselves. And things with his mother still weren't the same. She'd wanted more than her husband and kids. Gone back to school, got a job at the Museum of Contemporary Art, found another husband. By the time she'd tried to make her way back into her kids' lives, they'd all sort of moved on. Michael to their family contracting business, Jack to school and his various girlfriends, and Bridget to being the very best at everything all at once.

A shard of anger worked through the lust that Hannah had kicked up in his gut. How dare she peg him as some idiot bro? He knew what he looked like, but that didn't give her the right to toss her baggage at his feet.

Someone had clearly done a number on her. It wasn't his job to clean it up. She didn't want him; she'd made that clear. He didn't walk away, though, because the anger wasn't enough to overpower the lust and the growing tenderness she'd reached into him and pulled out.

"Who hurt you?"

She snorted, and her face contorted into as close as it could get to ugly. Still pretty. "Who hasn't?"

He reached out his hand to her, waited for her to take it. "I haven't hurt you, and I promise I won't."

"You won't." She shrugged, still not reaching for him. "We're just getting tacos."

"Shake on it?" He threw in a smile, which softened her up like it had inside the bar.

She grabbed his hand, and he liked how her soft skin felt against his palm.

He didn't let her go but tucked her hand under his arm and escorted her to the taco truck.

He didn't laugh out loud when they both ordered the same thing—carnitas. Once they found a seat at a picnic table under a streetlamp, he started on the questions. "So, where'd you grow up, Hannah?" He couldn't stop saying her name. "Where were people such assholes?"

"Outside of Minneapolis."

"Aren't people from Minneapolis supposed to be nice?"

"I was born in LA."

"Figures." Hannah narrowed her gaze at him, and God help him. "I just meant—LA face."

The side of her mouth quirked up. "But I don't have the Oakland booty to go with it. And that doesn't save it." *Damn*, she wasn't going to let him get away with *anything*. "You're from Chicago?"

"That obvious?"

She smiled again, for real this time, and he savored it as though it was something crazy-precious. And frightening. "The accent gives it away." She took a deep breath, as though she was thinking hard about whether to continue talking. He couldn't breathe until she opened her mouth again. "You also walk like you have a big dick. I've noticed that a lot of guys in Chicago do that, regardless of what they're packing."

So, she was calling him a cocky bastard, and he wouldn't disabuse her of that. Not if the decent-but-cocky-guy thing would get him laid—not tonight, but eventually.

"I'm not walking like that because I'm putting on airs, Duchess." He winked at her. She'd opened the door to this conversation when she'd mentioned his cock.

She rolled her eyes again, and it was even more of a turn-on because he didn't think she wasted the energy to roll her eyes at guys she didn't like just a little. "I'm not angling to find out."

She'd demolished her taco in a fashion that was kind of scary but mostly impressive. His instincts told him that she was going to bolt, and he didn't want that. He wasn't about to throw her over his shoulder caveman style—that wasn't him—but he didn't meet a girl he sparked with like this every day. Or even every six months. Though he wasn't looking for anything serious, he couldn't help hoping for more than a taco.

"Can I have your number?"

She shook her head and leveled him with a look that would make a lesser man run in the other direction. When she wiped an errant drop of crema off the side of her wide, lush mouth, he quaked a little in his boots. Instead of showing weakness, he pushed the remains of his food aside so he could lean over the table. To get closer.

"Why would I give you my number?" There was an unmistakable breathy hitch in her voice.

"So I can use it."

She leaned back, and that's when he knew he was going to get it. She was just as affected by being close to him as he was by her. "How good's your memory?"

"Damned good." Had to be when deadlines were tight and news stories came fast.

NOT THE GIRL YOU MARRY

She rattled off ten numbers, and he fumbled with his phone to enter them. Just as he got the last one in the phone app, she stood up. "Thanks for the drink. And the food."

The few seconds of hesitation before she grabbed her phone, something expectant about it, gave him the chance to stand up and get next to her. He glanced at her screen, where it looked like she was booking a car. They were close—close enough to kiss. But he wouldn't kiss her without permission. So he just waited.

Her breaths were little gasps as she looked up at him. "I told you that I don't date."

"Then why'd you give me your number?"

She shrugged, but it was more trying to be cool than actually being cool. "You amuse me."

"Bullshit." That made her break eye contact with him. He was losing her, and he had to get her back. Although he'd been benched for a minute, he was still a world-champion suitor. That had to be why watching her leave right now would physically hurt him. "You feel this *thing* between us too. Just admit it, and I won't pester you for a date."

"I just have to admit it?"

He nodded and gave her his most winning grin. Even though she looked as though she wanted to slap him, he could feel something about the invisible ten-foot concrete barrier she had around her crumble a little bit. He wanted to pump his fist in the air. But he was about to have something infinitely better to do with his hands. "Admit you like me. And then you're off the hook for a date."

"Okay." And then she had the audacity to look *bored*.

Because of the blasé look on her face, he didn't expect it when she pressed her mouth to his. Everything in him froze with the feel of her mouth against his. The press of her hands against his chest. His hands hovered over her shoulders, as though repelled by the electromagnetic field of *holy hell sweet baby Jesus yes* surrounding this kiss.

He didn't react, couldn't. He was so surprised that it took him a beat to really make the most of this opportunity before she ripped it away. But when he remembered himself, he pulled her close and took her mouth with his.

And she let him get away with it, softened under his kiss. It was perfect. She was perfect. In a split second, he knew he would crave the feeling of this woman dissolving into a puddle under his lips forevermore.

He almost broke away from her then; it was simply more than either of them had bargained for. She'd seemed to freeze up, too. Knowing he'd have to give up on the feeling of her soft mouth under his pained him.

Just as he was about to pull out of the death spiral, she grabbed ahold of him. And the way she wound her arms around his neck and pulled him close told him that—even if kissing had been impulsive—she definitely wanted more. Flames of need worked their way through his whole body, no chance of banking them as she pressed her body close. Her curves molded to every inch of him.

Damn, she might not date or be down for a one-night stand, but she could kiss. His arms around her waist, she let a breathy moan loose into his mouth. When he put his hand on the back of her neck and took the kiss deeper, she bit his bottom lip. It was as though a crack of thunder went off in his body. The way they kissed, he knew that everything with her would be a battle of wills, a fight that made his cock hard. Little whimpers into his mouth sounded like victory. He ran his fingers through her hair and gathered the strands at the back of her neck to pull her closer, to angle her head so that he had all the access to her witchy mouth.

The text tone of her phone, which she clutched to the back of his head, made her pull back. Still, her gaze was hazy, bewildered. Looking as though he'd stolen her puppy. Jack was much more interested in her kitty, finding out how it tasted. He groaned, imagining how she'd look at him after he'd spent time between her thighs.

"My car's here."

Jack nodded, still satisfied by how stunned she seemed to be by their kiss, even though she'd initiated it. It didn't affect him any less. This time, when he grabbed her hand and walked with her over to the Kia with its blinkers flashing on the corner, she didn't even try to pull away. He might have been imagining things, but he thought he felt her squeeze his hand before releasing it to get in the car.

He kept his smile at bay until he'd shut the door and the car had driven away.

CHAPTER THREE

HANNAH'S WORK WIFE, ROOMMATE, best friend since freshman year, and all-around platonic soul mate, Sasha, came into her office and closed the door. This was never a sign that all was well with Sasha, but it was especially bad ten minutes before their Friday morning staff meeting. Sasha's meltdowns generally took at least fifteen minutes to clean up, and—judging by the smudged mascara around her eyes—this was a twenty-minute tantrum. Nay, a *mantrum*.

"What did this one do?" Hannah passed over a wad of tissues and a mirror she'd gotten as swag for an event they'd done for a best-selling romance author last month. She made a motion under both of her eyes to indicate that Sasha needed to get her shit cleaned up.

"He sent me a dick pic." Sasha's voice came out as a watery wail, and Hannah could barely keep herself from rolling her eyes. "This morning on my way to work, my phone pings. And it's a dick pic."

She honestly couldn't comprehend why her best friend continued to subject herself to loser after loser on dating app after dating app. *This* app was always going to be different; she was always on the verge of meeting "the one" at the next singles event. Or at least they would be if Hannah didn't go along with Sasha to speed-dating events just for the drinks and snacks and end up heckling the feckless douchebags.

And it always ended in tears Hannah had to clean up. The last one, Mitchell, Sasha had dated for nine months. He'd been promising as a life partner, if boring in bed. But then, on the way to meet her parents, he'd told her that they couldn't continue seeing each other unless they "opened up" the relationship.

Hey, Hannah was a live-and-let-live kind of gal, but ol' Mitch was a moron if he looked at Sasha and thought she was down to share. No judgment for people who that worked for, but it just wasn't her best friend. Sasha was a perfect Catholic pearl, from her skin-care-ad complexion to her curtain of shiny black hair. Sasha was basically a Disney princess.

Half her closet was pink, for Christ's sake. She had more than one floral dress. Sasha was not the kind of girl to get a second boyfriend because her first boyfriend couldn't live without dipping his wick all over town.

It would have been understandable for douchebag Mitch to assume that *Hannah* was into OPP. He wouldn't have been the first, and he wouldn't be the last. Like Miguel Contreras, the guy she'd dated for six months before she'd met her last serious boyfriend. She'd liked him because he wanted to talk about feminist theory until the wee hours of the morning. He'd really seemed to get it. Until one night when he'd taken hours trying to explain to her that monogamy was merely a tool of the patriarchy and she was subjugating herself by insisting on exclusivity. She hadn't bothered to explain that her philosophy—*if I lick it, it's mine*—worked just fine for her feminism.

Miguel had shown his ass when he called her a stuck-up c-word on his way out the door. After that, she'd started to suspect that all straight, cis-gendered men were utter trash. But after Noah, she'd confirmed it.

And her image and demeanor had sort of transformed until she was the hard-ass bitch sitting in her office right now. The all-black, all-the-time wardrobe was easy—but it was also a warning. Her eyeliner was always perfectly winged because she did not have mascara-smudging meltdowns at work. Not anymore. Nor did she have eyeliner-obliterating make-out sessions. At least not usually.

She wore lipstick as red as the blood of her enemies to warn any unwary souls who might wander into her sight line that she was not to be fucked with. It also made it less likely that anyone would try to kiss her. And it mostly worked.

Until she'd stolen a kiss from Jack.

Jack, who hadn't taken her firm suggestion that he piss off for an answer. Not yet. On the other hand, he hadn't faltered in the face of her rage at his friends. He'd soothed her with a drink, the best carnitas in town, and a kiss that she could still feel imprinted on her lips.

In the six days since the night they'd met, he'd been texting her almost every day. Not dick pics, but it didn't make her wish she'd given him a wrong number any less.

The problem was, Jack was charming her. He'd kept his promise and he hadn't asked her out, as though he knew that would be too much. But he was enticing her with each street-taco picture, and every snap of a happy dog he met on his morning run melted her resistance. His texts were so chatty and disarming that *she* was closer to asking *him* out with each random question he asked.

Lou Holtz or Ara Parseghian?

It was definitely Coach Parseghian. The fact that he'd asked about her team, even though they were sworn enemies because he was a Michigan alum, touched her in a previously icy spot in her heart. It seemed as though he actually wanted to get to know her.

But she was still waiting for the other, perverted and/or misogynist shoe to drop.

It didn't help that her Goth-girl, power-bitch look had the unfortunate side effect of making some guys think that she would screw them and that they didn't have to take care with her feelings. But that was a problem for a different day.

Today's problem was getting Sasha to see that none of these guys she was dating were worth her tears. If they couldn't see the real, tender heart of her best friend, they didn't deserve her, and they certainly didn't deserve for her to risk losing her job because she cried through the mandatory staff meeting. Of course, eventually Sasha would marry someone, but Hannah knew that she'd probably be replaced by a married girlfriend at that point. Someone who could understand what it was like to get bored with the person she'd pledged to love forever.

Sasha blew her nose in the tissue, and Hannah pulled out a foundation sample from last week's cosmetics party.

"I've told you about giving them your phone number." As she looked at her friend, so broken, Hannah ruthlessly suppressed the twinge in her heart and the guilt she felt for not telling her about Jack's texts. If Sasha would just listen to her good advice and give up on finding "the one," she wouldn't have these periodic breakdowns. Muddying the waters with her inability to adhere to her own best practices would not be helpful here.

Maybe she'd drag Sasha to a dog adoption event or something this weekend. They'd both be more successful looking for unconditional love if they stuck to canines. Maybe there was an app for that, too. They could each swipe right on the Fido of their dreams.

"If you make them message you in the app, you can at least report the inappropriate photos and get them banned."

"But we'd gone on two dates." Sasha wiped under her eyes. "I thought the text was asking me for a third."

"You know they have sex toys that will literally suck your clit *for you* now?" Her friend was looking for a husband, but Hannah was starting to doubt the utility of a husband given the recent advancements in sex toys.

"And *you know* I like the full-body contact." They'd had this conversation before.

"Let me see the dick." Her friend handed over her phone after Hannah made a "gimme" motion. The offending photograph displayed, and Hannah's avocado toast nearly made a reappearance when she took in the sickly pink cast of the unimpressive appendage. "Has he ever heard of grooming?"

Sasha hiccupped; Hannah had been hoping for a laugh. Jesus, this was a lot of crying over one photo of a sad penis. But Hannah understood. It wasn't the single photographic assault that put her over the edge; it was the sheer number of them Sasha received by virtue of her willingness to brave the dating pool. It wasn't just dirty; it was fetid and foul. Like wading through thigh-high pig shit in knee-high boots.

Hannah'd soured on it long before her friend had, but she recognized the lost look in Sasha's mink-brown eyes. It was the same look that Hannah had had on her face after her on-again, off-again boyfriend had told her two years ago that she was "just not the kind of girl you marry."

But Noah was just the last in a long line of guys who treated her like a warm body before they had sex and yesterday's soiled socks afterward.

It would also be the last time she'd allow herself to be brought low by a man. *Ever.* Her resolve to stay single was not being eroded with every text from Jack.

It. Was. Not. Crumbling.

He only liked her because she was mean to him, anyway. The sick shit of it was that her newfound iciness drove men crazy. She'd never gotten as much interest when she was soft and vulnerable and pink-wearing as she did now. Still, she rejected all of them, because as soon as she showed a man anything that didn't jibe with her hard, cold image, he thought she actually wanted something real from him and he was out the door.

Except for Jack. That kiss.

She didn't have time to dwell on the nonexistent state of her love life. And the puppies would have to wait until tomorrow. Right now, she needed her friend to get her head straight and off this guy's sub-par schlong.

"At least you have some good information now."

"Huh? The only information I now have is that he doesn't groom." Good, her sense of humor was back.

"Also, you know his dick is too small for you."

Sasha looked at her phone, tipping it sideways and her head in the opposite direction. "It's bigger when you hold the phone horizontally."

"Honey, dudes are too plentiful and low in value for you to be wasting time on a guy who thinks that a dick pic—a shitty one at that—is romantic."

"I just can't believe he sent it to me at work." She stood up and put her hands on her hips. Her voice rose when she asked, "Seriously, who does that?"

"Guys are simpleminded and useless. We're better off without them."

"That's easy for you to say." She pouted her lips and smoothed on some gloss. "You're so independent, and you can't go two blocks without tripping over some guy with a monster member that wants to serve you. Like that guy from Saturday night."

Hannah laughed but decided that she definitely wouldn't tell Sasha about the texts. If her friend only knew how unsatisfying it was when a guy pursued her these days. Every time a guy hit on her, all she could think about was how much work he would be and how disappointed she would be when he started acting like an ass.

Except Jack. Some traitorous part of her brain wouldn't let go of the idea that Jack wasn't like the rest of the jerks and losers. Why couldn't her brain let her have her broad generalizations about an entire gender?

"Give me the phone again." Sasha handed over the phone and Hannah did a Google search for cat pictures. The guy had had the nerve to ask for pictures of her friend's pussy, and he'd be getting some angry pussy. Once she found a photo of a famous angry-looking cat, she downloaded it to the phone and sent it with the caption *Don't even think about asking me if it's wet.*

Once she handed over the phone, she picked up her notebook and favorite black and red pens. "We have to get to the staff meeting."

HANNAH WANTED TO BE her boss when she grew up. Like her, Annalise Koch had grown up as the only child of a single mother.

She'd not only pulled herself up by the bootstraps; she'd made her own freaking bootstraps. But unlike Hannah, Annalise was happily married. So maybe she only wanted to be like half of her boss.

"Sasha, how's the proposal for Senator Chapin's daughter's wedding coming?"

Koch Events was responsible for the most expensive weddings and poshest events in Chicago. But the wedding of a sitting senator's daughter was a coup in and of itself. The former president and first lady would be there, as would representatives from every lobbying firm and political action committee that had any connection to the city of Chicago, the state of Illinois—hell, the whole United States.

Hannah would kill to be the lead on that kind of event, but weddings weren't normally her thing. As the resident expert on selling sex, she handled the parties hosted by local sports teams and cosmetics companies and the risqué gallery openings. Basically, if the night was likely to end with the police showing up—either to mop up drunk and disorderlies or to arrest an artist for public indecency—Hannah was the woman in charge.

The only problem with her brand within the company was that she was never going to get the senator's-daughter's-wedding type of event on her docket. And without those types of events, she was never going to become a vice president. She rubbed the embossed words on the business card she kept in her notebook. *Lead Event Planner* just didn't have the same ring to it as *Vice President in Charge of Classy Shit*, did it?

Sasha, with her commitment to happily-ever-afters, was the go-to wedding gal. At least, she was when she was on her game. And Hannah would have no problem with Sasha being promoted before her. They were a team, and Sasha would pull Hannah up along with her.

But the newest event planner on the team, Giselle, was gunning for both of them, and she had no plans to help any of the women she worked with—especially Hannah.

Hannah had never had a nemesis before Giselle, and she wasn't yet sure if the other woman was worthy. It was as though someone took Regina George from *Mean Girls* and mixed her with Cruella de Vil in a blender, then poured the resulting concoction into a Natalie Portman skin suit.

Sasha might have a mini floral-dress wardrobe, but Giselle needed a full-on closet for her floral dresses. She needed one for every Junior League fund-raiser, all the better to rule that organization with an iron fist. Hannah might look like a bitch, but at least she had friends who liked her. Even Giselle's husband seemed afraid of her, and he was twice her size.

Hannah often wondered if flowers died whenever Giselle walked through the Garfield Park Conservatory. Certainly the animals at the Lincoln Park Zoo scurried away if she ventured too close.

But the worst thing about Giselle? Annalise loved her. Thought she could do no wrong. If she asked for an event, she got it.

With Sasha looking rough because of the weight of collective male douchery, Hannah glanced over at Giselle. She had her tongue pressed to the corner of her mouth in this predatory way that told Hannah that the senator's daughter's wedding was about to slip from Sasha's grasp.

Before Giselle could say anything, Hannah raised her hand. "I'm helping Sasha scout venues today."

"I thought she asked Sasha about the wedding, didn't she?" Giselle gave Hannah a death glare disguised as a smile. "It's her assignment."

"It is." Finally, Sasha spoke up. "But the senator's daughter has a wild past, and she wants some rather—outlandish—features for the reception. I thought that Hannah's perspective would be useful on this one."

Annalise pressed the tips of her fingers together in front of her face and squinted her eyes as she often did while making a decision. The weight of Hannah's and Sasha's professional hopes bared its neck before Giselle's sharp axe. A few seconds felt as though they stretched out into a minute. The whole time, a smile was spreading across Giselle's face and a rock of disappointment was forming in Hannah's gut.

Under the conference table, Hannah squeezed Sasha's forearm. She'd done the best she could to cover, and it wouldn't be her fault if Annalise reassigned Giselle to the event. Sasha needed to buck the hell up. It was just one dick pic, and she knew her friend could hang on until their after-work wine.

"I need to think about this." The boss's words were like scatter-shot bullets, and even Hannah's nemesis looked like she'd taken a direct hit. "Hannah, please see me after the meeting."

She slapped the table with one hand like a gavel, and the meeting was over. Hannah was out of her chair in an instant, breaking stride toward the door only to raise her fist to Sasha. She was going to save both of their asses if it killed her.

Even though she was four inches taller than Annalise, she struggled to keep up in her heels. But she maintained a furious clip for fear of being intercepted by Giselle's ass-kissing brilliance.

She only let herself take a deep breath when she and her boss were both in the relative safety of her corner office. Annalise motioned for Hannah to take a seat. Hannah lowered herself slowly, like the classy bitch she was trying to be.

"So." And then nothing. Hannah wondered for a moment if this was one of those silences she was meant to fill, or one of the ones she was meant to leave blank for the sake of her boss's sense of drama. "We have a problem."

Deep breath in. Don't seem too thirsty. "Sasha and I can handle the wedding. It's not even the highest budget that either one of us has handled on our own."

"But you don't do weddings." Annalise's ice-cold blue gaze roved over her as though she were a speck of lint on the chair. As much as Hannah hated being looked at like that, as much as she craved her boss's approval, she didn't let the hurt show. She sat up straighter. "You're my booze-and-beer-and-boobs girl."

"I do sports, too." That was her best answer? She might as well kiss her promotion goodbye. "And, in this day and age, politics is sort of like sports. This is going to be a glossy magazine event. Not just featured on Style Me Pretty or The Knot. The *New York Times* isn't just going to run an announcement; they're going to do a feature in the Style section. And maybe the magazine. Deals are going to be made at this wedding."

She mentally gave herself a high five when Annalise sat back in her chair and raised her eyebrows as though she was ready to agree internally but not ready to admit defeat.

"And Sasha and I are the perfect team for this." Hannah felt her heart beat faster, knowing that she was about to take down the gazelle. She could be just as predatory as Giselle, but she wasn't a sociopath. She *knew* that she and Sasha were the best team for this wedding—she'd known it as soon as she'd opened her mouth at the staff meeting. "I'll bring the flash and pizzazz, and Sasha will bring the class. It will be perfect."

"And it has to be." Annalise looked down in an uncharacteristic avoidance gesture.

Growing frustrated, Hannah asked, "What is it?" She would do anything to convince her boss she was the right woman for this job—and for the promotion she knew she deserved.

"You've just never shown any interest in weddings before."

"They're a big part of our business, so of course I'm interested."

"You roll your eyes whenever the other planners talk about their weddings."

"No, I don't." She thought she'd hidden her disdain for frilly shit from her boss.

Annalise leveled a look that said, *Come on.*

"Well, I've changed my mind."

"How am I supposed to believe that?" Her boss clicked on her mouse and glanced at her monitor as it came to life. Hannah knew that the blue light from the computer hitting Annalise's face was a bad sign. She was about to be dismissed. "It's not like I haven't heard about your little man embargo."

"What does that have to do with planning a wedding?"

Annalise shifted her focus back onto Hannah. "Whether it fits with your modern, feminist sentiments or not, a wedding is quite often the most important day in two people's lives together. It's monumental for the families that become joined. And it has to be perfect. I just can't trust that someone like you, who disdains the idea of weddings or commitment, can throw all your energy into making a wedding fabulous. And this is the biggest event we've ever planned." She paused, and her face softened. "I have half a mind to plan it myself."

The other woman had a point. Hannah hadn't taken enough care to hide her antipathy for the whole dating-and-mating dance. She much preferred hating from the sidelines. But that wasn't because she hated the idea of weddings or the idea of commitment.

She'd told herself that she didn't need or want those things because no one had ever offered them to her. Admitting out loud that she couldn't entirely suppress the desire to have a person of her own— one who wasn't afraid to tell the world that they belonged to each other—felt entirely too vulnerable.

So she'd started scoffing at the people who were still in the arena, clawing and grasping for love. The ones who actually deserved it and would get it someday. Even after every guy she'd ever felt anything for had dumped her.

Except for Jack.

"Things have changed, Annalise. I've met someone." Pretty sure she wasn't imagining the disbelief on her boss's face. Hannah half couldn't believe she'd said it. And that it wasn't even a white lie. "We met last weekend, and he seems kind of great, honestly."

"Really?"

"Yeah, the only thing bad about him is his taste in football teams." And because she never knew how to quit when she was ahead, she said, "He seems like the kind of guy I could marry."

Why did she say that? Before Noah—B.N.—she'd thought things like that about every guy she'd been serious about. She'd had their weddings planned before date number three. Eventually, it had become a post-breakup ritual to trash the Pinterest board for her imaginary weddings. And it had been freeing, A.N., to not have to make them anymore. Not having any hope at all had saved her a whole lot of disappointment.

Then why did it feel so good to say that she was thinking wedding bells about Jack?

She didn't have time to ponder the question any more because her boss had come to a decision. "Okay, you and Sasha will plan the engagement party at the Drake Hotel." That made sense; both of them had done extensive work with the venue. "And if you can show me that you can be appropriate, you'll get to plan the wedding, too."

"You won't regret this, Annalise." Hannah stood up to leave the room before her mercurial supervisor changed her mind.

"See that I don't." She had her hand on the door when her boss added, "I'll want to meet this young man at the company Halloween party."

About a week from now. And another week before the engagement party. She'd have to date Jack for two weeks—keep him interested for that long. He'd have to appear to be at least a little bit in love with her. She couldn't scare him away.

Fuck.

CHAPTER FOUR

JACK HAD KICKED ASS on his last how-to article. It had gone viral, and yet, he was embarrassed whenever anyone mentioned "How to Make Your Lady Scream (for More Ice Cream Because You're Going to Learn to Make It)."

If he said so himself, it was a pretty good listicle. But the mere fact that it was a listicle was a problem. He'd also had to start running twice a day so that all the homemade ice cream he'd eaten while researching the article and accompanying video hadn't shown up on his gut. But mostly, he was done with the fluff and wanted to be writing hard-hitting political pieces.

When he'd gotten his master's in journalism, he'd planned to come home and work for the *Tribune* or the *Sun-Times*. But newspapers had been consolidating or folding. He'd even been willing to work for one of the local indie papers, but none of them would pay enough to keep him from having to go work for his dad.

Haberdasher's Monthly, the storied gentlemen's magazine that was now entirely digital, had been his only option. It paid well, and it wasn't hard. His how-to videos got quite a few views from the start

because people liked to watch him try and fail and eventually suc-
ceed at stuff. Then they liked to send him links to their homemade
porn, but he could just ignore that. What he couldn't ignore was the
fact that some of the other reporters and writers at the site—ones
hired at about the same time he was—were starting to be assigned
more substantive pieces. And he wasn't because his series was so
popular. Each how-to got millions of hits on the site, but he didn't
know how much longer he could stay out of the real-news game. His
success was turning out to be a curse.

As though the universe was mocking him, he kept running into
real-news pieces. In fact, last week, he'd been hanging with his dad
and some of his buddies at the pub when a lead had practically
surfed over the head of his Guinness. A corruption scandal involving
a politician with a national profile could make his entire career.

Pop owned a contracting business—semiretired now that Michael had taken over. Now that he'd handed off most of the day-to-
day to his eldest, Jack's dad had time to go to happy hour. And since
Jack didn't have what Sean Nolan considered a real job, he got an
invite to talk shit with his dad and his buddies—most of whom were
connected at city hall.

One of them had told him that there was a rumor flying around
that a sitting senator was about to be indicted for corruption. He
didn't have very many details, but that was where Jack came in. To
fill in the details.

So today Jack was meeting with his boss to convince him that his
next how-to should be "How to Catch a Senator Red-Handed." He
knocked on Irv's door, struck by how going over the threshold was
sort of like stepping back in time. Where the rest of the office was
modern, white, and open concept—which only meant that no one
had privacy for anything—Irv's office had wood paneling, leather

furniture, and even a Tiffany lamp. Piles of newspaper clippings covered the desk, even though they didn't even publish anything on paper.

Somehow, Irv had convinced the powers that be who owned the website that he needed to have the character of a newspaper in his office in order to produce as he'd promised.

Jack liked it. Every time he came in here, he got a reminder of why he'd become a reporter. Now, if only Irv would let him do some actual reporting.

"What do you want?" Irv didn't speak; he barked. And then he usually got angry he wasn't holding a cigar in his hands.

"I want to write a political story." Best to just drop that out there with a guy like Irv. He was busy making the site the hottest thing online by doing actual editing and assigning stories that would get the clicks coming without the bait.

"Not unless you want to write the politics of splitting the check." A barked laugh as he waved one hand to clear smoke that didn't exist. "But that's been done."

"There's no politics to that, Irv. If I'm taking out a lady, I'm picking up the check."

"That's why I like you, kid." Of course he was the kind of guy who called his employees kids—men, women, didn't matter. They were all "kid." "You see things the way I do. No need to muddy up issues in a complicated world. Now—"

"About this political story—" Normally, he wouldn't dare interrupt his boss. But this was important. It burned in his gut, and he'd learned never to ignore that feeling. The previous Saturday, he'd had the same sensation of need running through his whole system before he'd kissed Hannah. Hannah who still hadn't agreed to go out with him.

NOT THE GIRL YOU MARRY

"You're not on that beat." His boss's emphatic closing of the issue wiped Hannah from his brain. He wasn't focusing on her right now. Maybe he'd focus on her later, when he had the kind of reporting assignments he wanted. After he'd gotten the kind of dog he wanted. And been on his own a while longer.

For now, he and Hannah were just friends, and he had a story to get.

"But I trained for that beat." He didn't mean to sound like a whiny asshole, but when Irv sighed, he was afraid that was the impression he was giving off.

"Your beautiful mug is the site's most popular feature."

Jack flushed. He hated feeling like a piece of meat, which was possibly why he empathized so much with the women on dating apps these days. Maybe he was just raised right—both before and after his parents' divorce. Even though his parents barely spoke, his father respected his mother and could admit that she'd been right to move on to bigger and better things. Sean had been kind of a son of a bitch in the early years of his kids' life. He hadn't seen that his wife was growing more and more unhappy.

Jack had seen that and vowed never to let his lady feel like she was less than the most important thing to him. He couldn't imagine demanding that Hannah leave a job to stay home with the kids.

Because he was never going to have kids with Hannah. He just wanted to be her friend. That's why he couldn't stop texting her cute French bulldog pictures or photos of food he thought she'd like. Maybe he needed to get a personal Instagram account. Under a name that the fans of his how-to column didn't know. Maybe if he had another outlet, he could stop trying to talk to a woman who didn't want him.

"Where are you, Nolan?"

His boss's impatient staccato was a few decibels below a bellow. *Shit. Stay focused, Jack.* "Thinking about how I can convince you to give me a shot at this lead I found."

"What lead?"

Oh no. He wasn't about to hand Irv the lead and have him hand it to one of the political reporters. He would do it himself or let the site get scooped. It didn't sit well with him because Irv had been good to him, but this was too important to miss.

He stuck his hands in his pockets and shook his head. "Not unless I get the story."

Irv collapsed in his chair. "You're going to be an asshole about this." Not a question.

"I want in on this." *And out of the how-to game.*

"I don't see why you wouldn't continue doing the how-to." Irv gestured to the bull pen. "Political editors are a dollar a dozen. You have a niche."

"I don't want to be the good-looking fluff guy." He didn't like calling himself good-looking. He thought it was weird, but he didn't have body dysmorphia. He knew how he looked.

"You should capitalize on it while you can." Irv ran a hand over his weathered face. "I can't just let you jump ship. If you're going to graduate to the big leagues, you have to go out with a bang."

Bang. He hoped he didn't have to write a sex story. He was too out of practice at this point. Plus, some of the nuns who'd taught him in grade school read all his stories. He couldn't live with the shame of being responsible for informing Sister Antoninus about what she'd been missing for sixty years.

But he couldn't write another story about dating etiquette, even though the listicles about dating got a lot more play. They hit more

Twitter and Facebook feeds. And, since he wasn't dating anymore—well, not unless texting a girl six days in a row was dating, which it could be. He didn't know, because he didn't date.

"I've got nothing."

"Come on, I've heard about you."

"You couldn't have heard anything too salacious." Jack paused to smile, knowing that his image as a rake was kind of key to his employment at the moment. "Lately."

"You can't get a girl either?"

"I can get a girl. I just don't want to." He leaned on the back of the guest chair, knowing that Irv would cut this short if he sat down. "Right now."

"Dating guys now?"

"Nope. I just want to do my own thing for a while."

Then Irv got red in the face. "What's the problem with kids these days?"

"I have no idea." Jack wasn't a part of whatever problem Irv had spotted with youths and their mating rituals. He wasn't part of the solution either; he needed to get himself solved first.

"No one dates anymore." Jack jumped when Irv pounded on his desk. He looked out at the bull pen to make sure no one was watching him get reamed out for something he didn't do.

"I date. Just not right now. Still sore from my girl leaving me for that director."

"You've got to get back out there."

"Maybe I'd meet a nice girl political reporting?" Jack shrugged. "I'd like to find a Maggie Haberman type to come home and talk shop with."

"She's already got three kids, and she would eat you alive." Irv would know. He'd been an editor for the *New York Post* while Haberman was there.

There was an awkward pause during which Jack wondered if he should leave. Irv looked like a computer buffering, and he only hoped he hadn't sparked the rainbow wheel of death by coming in here and asking for a real story.

After fifteen seconds, Irv hit the desk again. And Jack jumped. Again. "I've got it. You're going to figure out what the problem is."

No. He was not going to do another dating how-to. Not even if it was the last one. It might make him terminally stupid, but he just didn't have it in him. "Actually, I know what the problem is." He did. He'd been witness to the problem on Saturday night. He'd almost missed out on kissing Hannah because his friends were idiots. "Men are assholes."

"But you're not?"

"I'm an asshole, but in a good way." He'd been an asshole when some drunk loser at a Cubs game had grabbed Lauren's breast. She hadn't wanted to be there anyway, and she'd almost demanded to leave a playoff game. Instead of missing out on the game that would clinch the pennant, he'd given the groper a black eye. And then he'd talked his way out of getting arrested. That had been kind of an asshole move. Maybe.

"Then you can teach these schmucks something." He motioned out toward the newsroom.

"Teach them what?"

"How not to lose a girl."

That was one thing Jack had no expertise in. He'd never figured out how not to lose a girl once she saw something better on the horizon. He could convince a girl that he was a good bet right off the bat—well, every girl excepting Hannah—but he couldn't make it over the finish line.

"Listen, Irv. The only thing I have to teach is how not to behave like a total asshole."

Another wild gesture. "That's what I need you to do."

"It's pretty simple. Look up from the phone. Don't send dick pics." Jack almost laughed out loud at the face Irv pulled when he said "dick pics." "Pay attention to what the lady says."

"None of these knuckleheads know that." He put his hand on the side of his nose in a thoughtful gesture. "But you're right. That's a boring story."

"I didn't say it was boring—"

"So, I need you to do all the stupid shit."

"That seems like a terrible idea." And deeply unethical. The Catholic schoolboy inside him objected to it.

"Not on tape, of course. That would tip anyone with a brain in her head off to the whole story."

"I don't want to do it at all."

"If you do this—"

"I don't even know who I'd do this to." *Definitely not Hannah.* She would see right through him and rip his balls off. "It's really mean, don't you think?"

"You'll get to write your political story at the same time." *Dammit.* He didn't have a choice. Not if he wanted to be taken seriously as a reporter at this site. Not if he wanted to work in his hometown again. If he refused, he'd get a reputation.

Maybe he wouldn't have to do it for long. One date he could pretend to screw up. He wouldn't even have to do it with Hannah. He could go out tonight and meet someone else. Or he could just go with it for one date. He could write the story from one date. Then he'd tell Hannah, and she'd understand.

"I want five thousand words. You have two weeks." Shit. "And make sure it's a girl you like so it doesn't seem fake."

The only girl he'd liked in ages was going to kill him when she found out that he was trying to get her to *not* like him for a story.

CHAPTER FIVE

HANNAH SURVEYED HER CLOSET like a general surveying the field of battle. She hadn't been on a date in almost two years, and her fun, going-out clothes had been gradually culled from the walk-in until only daytime and nighttime work clothes remained. Just a few months ago, she'd donated everything that didn't "spark joy," and somehow everything she'd ever worn when she was with Noah had ended up in the box going to Goodwill.

Her closet purge presented a huge problem now that she had a date—one she had to impress—on this fine Friday night. Jack had texted her a few minutes after her fateful meeting with Annalise. As though the universe had heard her silent, screamed pleas not to have to ask him out herself, he asked her if she wanted to have dinner with him tonight.

On the one hand, she could have used more than one day to formulate her plan of attack. Like, instead of actually dating him, what if she just told him that she needed a fake boyfriend for a few weeks? Jack seemed like the kind of guy who would be game. But part of her resisted that idea—the same part that wanted to know what it would be like to actually be in a relationship with a guy like him. One who seemed to be thinking about her—more than about getting in her pants—a guy who seemed to care about what she thought about things.

She flipped through three nearly identical black dresses before sitting on the bright yellow rug on her closet floor.

"This is dumb," she said to no one in particular. She usually tried not to talk to herself—something her mother did all the time. Her bitter, lonely, stuck mother. The one she'd sworn she would never be like. But ever since Noah, she'd taken down bitter and was rounding the corner on lonely. The only way she would avoid stuck was if she dated Jack long enough to get a promotion. If she was professionally successful, she wouldn't have time to worry about the fact that she was going to be alone for the rest of her life. By choice. Definitely by choice.

If she didn't find something to wear, she'd end up going out with Jack in her bra and panties—definitely not nice enough for the restaurant he was taking her to. Her eyes had nearly popped out of her head when he'd suggested it, and she'd just stopped herself from asking how he would afford the Michelin star restaurant on his salary.

That was what really kept her from inviting him into her scheme. He seemed to be serious enough about her to blow a month's rent on a first date.

Not that he wasn't good at his job. She'd watched a bunch of his videos, and they were great. She just didn't know if they were being-able-to-afford-Alinea-for-a-first-date great.

His suggestion had brought up a lot of guilt, too. She was agreeing to date Jack only because she wanted a promotion. This wasn't a real romantic evening; this was the beginning of a two-week-long con. It wasn't about getting to know Jack or building intimacy.

This date was about baiting the hook so he couldn't help but bite. Too bad she wasn't in possession of any fancy lures, er, clothes that would hijack her date's hormones for the two weeks and make it so that nothing that came out of her mouth would turn him off.

She was still sitting on the floor when Sasha walked in with a vodka soda and a glass of wine. She'd had to come clean with her best friend about the previous Saturday night—the tacos, the kiss, the texts. They shared a two-bedroom condo in Bucktown, owned by Sasha's parents, and it would be impossible to keep an actual date from Sasha. Besides, right now she needed the liquid courage and a wardrobe consult.

Hannah motioned for the vodka soda. It wouldn't do to greet Jack with stained teeth.

"What's wrong?" Sasha's forehead wrinkled, so Hannah knew she must really look like a mess. "Why aren't you ready?"

"I have nothing to wear." She took a swig of the cold, fizzy drink. "Everything I own is for work."

"Want to borrow something from me?"

"I wouldn't feel comfortable in any of your clothes."

"Why not?" Sasha looked puzzled, and it made the crinkle in her forehead deeper.

"Stop doing that with your face, or it will stay that way."

Sasha smoothed out her forehead with her finger. "My clothes fit you."

"But they don't feel right." Sasha tried to look confused without making her face crinkle but failed. "I look better in my clothes, but I don't have date clothes."

Sasha picked through her nighttime work clothes until she found a tight black dress that would probably show off her hoo-ha. She'd worn it to a party after the local hockey team won the championship.

She was pretty sure a few of the players had appreciated her ass in this dress as much as they'd appreciated the vodka-luge replica of the trophy. "This one."

Hannah rose off the ground. "Really? It's not too over the top?"

"Just sexy enough."

"But I thought I wasn't going for sexy." She squinted. "I thought I was going for potential girlfriend."

"Obviously, neither of us knows how to dress for that," Sasha said, taking a big gulp of wine.

"Oh, honey." She took the dress from Sasha. "Did you hear from him after he sent you a picture of his anemic penis?"

She shook her head and took another drink of wine. Hannah's stomach sank from the pointlessness of it all. Sure, she could put on the barely there dress and play the game of making Jack think he might get laid. That might keep him chasing her for two weeks. But she had no idea how to put on the pretense anymore. She'd probably end up like her friend, in sweats and no bra, ready to settle in with Herr Netflix on a Friday night.

"It doesn't matter." Sasha sniffed, probably to suppress unshed tears. "What matters is that you have a great time tonight."

"And why does that matter?" Hannah dropped her robe and pulled on the dress her friend had chosen. "This isn't about enjoying myself. It's about getting the job I want."

"Don't do that." Sasha's voice had a firmness it didn't often have.
"Do what?"

"Pretend like you don't like him."

"I don't know him."

"You know enough to smile when he texts you."

Jesus. She thought she'd been smooth. "That's just chemistry."

"Which feels great." Sasha sounded so wistful. "Chemistry is rare."

Her friend had a point. She'd missed feeling like that since Noah had dumped her. The dopamine hit to her brain that she got every time she heard from Jack was nothing compared to how she'd felt when he'd kissed her. She'd been blown apart in those three minutes waiting for a car service, and she hadn't quite put herself back together again.

As she turned around for Sasha to zip her up, she said, "I can't afford to think about how good it feels. If I do that, I'll fall down with my legs open and his penis between them. Then he'll never call me again and I'll never get promoted to VP." As her colorful grandfather used to say, men paid attention to women who "turned up their tails and ran a little."

"That's quite a leap." Sasha walked into the bathroom and rifled around in her makeup bag. "At least wear pink lipstick. More kissable. Less angry."

"I shouldn't be kissing him if I want him to call again."

"You kissed him last week."

"But I wasn't trying to make him my boyfriend last week."

Sasha held out a light pink shade. "What do you think you do with a guy you want to be your boyfriend?"

"Like I would know." Hannah spread the lipstick on, liking the effect. Immediately, her face looked more inviting than it usually did.

"You kiss him." Her best friend's words were slow and clearly enunciated, like she was talking to a toddler or a poorly trained puppy.

Taking Sasha's advice wouldn't be a hardship, if her memory served. "I can do that." She grabbed the glass with the remaining vodka soda and melting ice cubes.

"Just, whatever you do, don't sleep with him on the first date."

"Considering the precautions I've taken against that happening, I think we're safe."

Sasha stopped in her tracks. "Precautions?"

She considered whether or not to enlighten her best friend and roommate on the truly drastic measures she'd taken to ensure that—no matter how much she might not want them to—Jack's hands and his sinful mouth would remain completely out of her knickers. "You're not going to want to hear this."

She walked into the bathroom to retouch her makeup and Sasha followed her. "Hear what?"

"I don't think your delicate ears could take it."

"Take what?" She moved to sit on the closed toilet and stared at her. If the Catholic Church ever decided to allow women priests, Sasha would be the one who got all the juicy confessions, even though she'd be utterly scandalized on a daily basis. No one could withstand the stare. "Think back to how long it's been since I've had sex."

"There was that one guy right after Noah dumped you—" She paused to do some internal calculations, and then her eyes grew as large as Magnum-sized condom packets.

"The urologist who was—ironically—sort of a twat."

"It's been two years!?" Sasha shook her head. "I knew it'd been a while, but I didn't think it had been that long."

"Yup." She hadn't made a big deal out of the fact that she wasn't having sex, and it wasn't that she didn't want sex. She just didn't want just sex with anyone who'd offered it—for the past two years. *Thank goodness for the advances in sex-toy tech.*

"How are you going to keep yourself from sleeping with Jack?"

That was a good question that Hannah had thought long and hard about, amid all of the things she was hoping were long and hard about Jack. "I haven't waxed my hoo-ha since the last time I had sex."

"So you think the power of your great seventies bush is going to keep your legs closed? I don't think it works that way."

"That's precisely how it's going to work."

"I mean, you said just him kissing you had you all hot and bothered. And it's been two years. How are you going to stop yourself from doing the nasty if he puts on the moves?"

Hannah loved her friend because she said things like "hot and bothered" and "puts on the moves," her whole old-fashioned way of encouraging her to live a little. But Sasha's brain clearly hadn't stopped shorting out over the whole two years thing because her friend just stared at her, wide-eyed, in the mirror as she applied a dusting of highlighter on her cheekbones.

"It's not like you've never gone through a dry spell." Hannah shrugged, hoping she wouldn't have to explain herself further. She'd been on dates in the past two years, though not many. But she hadn't wanted to get naked with any of them. "I'll just keep reminding myself that self-service is speedy and satisfying service."

She said it as much to convince herself as to convince Sasha. All the other guys had lacked that essential zing, the chemistry that she'd felt right away with Jack. And without the zing, it was hard to justify opening up her body to someone else. Even if her heart would stay resolutely safe. Especially if he couldn't touch it.

"I'm just kind of surprised." Sasha handed over the eyelash glue. "You sort of have this whole jaded-red-light-district-prostitute thing going on."

Hannah narrowed her gaze on her friend. Although they'd been through a lot, she thought Sasha knew that she was a lot more tender-hearted about her friends than she was about dudes.

Luckily, her friend got that she'd toed over a line. "I don't mean that you were ever promiscuous."

That was a lie. Hannah had tried not to be free with her affections, but she'd gone through dudes like tissues for a while when she'd first moved to Chicago. She'd just gotten dumped by Miguel and blown up her whole life, so she'd indulged in male attention. Until she'd met Noah and grokked the idea that he wanted her to at the very least pretend that she was a longtime resident of Stepford.

Her ability to pretend—for a while at least—spoke to the fact that she could put on a show when necessary. And Jack seemed to like her without the show, so this would be much easier than trying to learn how to make an adequate potato salad for Noah's mother, only to have her sneer from beneath her church hat.

"I think the good news is that I have a lot of practice in turning sex down." She winked at Sasha, who took a sip of wine and somehow managed to look skeptical at the same time. "And I'm not about to ask a guy I want to ask me out again to contend with my *Debbie Does Dallas*–style bush."

Sasha simply pressed her lips together, as though she wanted to say something inappropriate but was afraid her mother would pop her head into the bathroom. It was usually an endearing habit, but it was kind of annoying right now.

"Out with it."

"Well." She took another sip of her wine, as though she was bracing herself. "Some guys like the bush."

"Do I want to know how you know this?"

"Not really."

Hannah turned and smirked at her friend, who had turned as red as her favorite lip gloss. "Oh, but I think I do."

"Mitch wanted me to grow mine out."

"He was really trying to bring back the whole put-your-keys-in-a-bowl thing from the late seventies, wasn't he?"

Sasha crossed her arms over her chest, apparently done sharing. "I think the moral of the story is that you need to have good boundaries in case he's all for what you have going on down there." Sasha gestured toward her crotch.

Being unable to erect boundaries against whatever Jack offered her was exactly what she was afraid of.

CHAPTER SIX

TO LOSE A GIRL, you have to know how to get a girl in the first place." Throughout the duration of their friendship, it was the one smart thing that prodigious idiot Chris Dooley had ever told him about dating.

It was an ever-vexing mystery to Jack how his friend had gotten through law school. His best guess was that his sister, Chris's ex-girlfriend, had pulled him through by her teeth. And pulling all 185 pounds of Chris Dooley through anything would be a challenge. He knew from the experience of fireman-carrying him three blocks after he passed out during the St. Patrick's Day parade.

He didn't know why he was friends with the guy, other than their long shared history, but he was going to take his one TED Talk–worthy bit of advice and put it to good use.

Being good at dating is simple. Make a plan and follow it. Communicate. Pay attention to your date and be clear about how you feel about her without jumping the gun and ruining it by seeming too eager. Treat women like they are actual people because—news flash—they are.

That was so good, he took out his phone and jotted it down in his notes app.

Jack pulled up in a Lyft precisely on time. He never showed up early, because it interrupted makeup and hair time. He didn't care if she came out in sweatpants, but most girls liked makeup and hair time. And he never showed up late, because that could make a woman feel as though she wasn't important—and even if he was dating her for a story, Hannah should get to feel important tonight.

He'd have to learn to resist it—being the perfect-boyfriend candidate—after tonight.

The thrill he'd felt when Hannah had said yes to his invitation warred with his practical need to sabotage the nascent *thing* going on. He'd fully expected her to tell him to shove it, so he'd planned ahead and called in some favors to get reservations at the best restaurant in the country. He thought that he'd maybe have to couch it as an assignment, a culture piece, and the date as a "favor" to keep him from having to eat many courses of exquisite food—and wine pairings—all alone.

In truth, the sous chef had owed him a favor for introducing him to his girlfriend on the set of his viral *How to Do Molecular Gastronomy without Being a Douche* video. Regardless, the meal would go on an expense account and impress Hannah, the second thing being much more important.

If he was starting his campaign to lose a girl—to lose Hannah—though, he would have texted her to come down. But in order to lose her, he needed to *have* her to lose—to have her like him enough to put up with the ensuing two weeks of bullshit.

If he had thought about this—at all—he never would have picked Hannah for this bullshit stunt. He'd have gone out to another bar, hit on another girl, and found a more amenable lady to jerk around. The idea of adding to Hannah's already low opinion of men sat like noxious acid on his skin.

But he couldn't stomach the idea of dating anyone else right now. Didn't want to contemplate anyone else's lips over dessert. Maybe some part of him thought he could save the thing they had after all this was over. A very foolish part of him—the part of him that maybe wasn't fit to be a hard-hitting journalist. The part that still believed that people—some of the politicians even—could actually live up to their ideals.

He pressed the buzzer for Hannah's apartment. After a few moments, Hannah's voice sounded through the intercom. Even her staticky "Jack?" hit him below the belt.

"Expecting someone else?" He anticipated a little bit of laughter, but he got silence and a buzzer. Definitely should have chosen someone more amenable.

When he got to the top of the aged wooden staircase, Hannah stood on the landing outside the closed door to her apartment.

He must have given her a skeptical look, because she said, "Believe me, it's for your own good. My roommate might look like a cream puff, but she'd have you crying for your mother in no time."

For some reason, he wanted to tell her that his mother never would have responded to his crying, so he didn't do it—not even before his parents divorced—but he kept his mouth shut.

This wasn't about showing her his heart. This was about charming her enough to string her along for two weeks or five thousand words, whichever came first.

She was gorgeous. Dressed in a black lacy dress that worshipped the tops of her thighs, heels that his sister would likely covet, and a black trench that hid away the tantalizing skin below her collarbone. Still, she shifted from foot to foot.

Her lips, the ones that had left a streak of red across his cheek the night they'd met, were painted a dainty pink, like brand-new ballet slippers. Against the honey of her skin, the color spoke of innocence but promised sin.

Maybe she expected him to say something more, but he didn't. Couldn't find words.

So he offered her his arm and led her down the stairs, quaking a little inside from the feel of her soft palm through the arm of his jacket.

They got in the car, and she stayed silent for a long moment. He still didn't have his full capacities back. Just the flash of thigh that he'd gotten when she'd bent to get in the car had diverted blood flow from his brain. Sweat gathered on his upper lip.

He'd never been *nervous* on a date before. Even with Maggie—at fourteen—he hadn't felt like this. He'd gone after her with all the idiot gusto of youth, never expected her to say no. He'd *known*, down to his marrow, that they would fall in love.

But Hannah surprised him at every turn. Flipping him off, then kissing him. Telling him no to coffee, then agreeing to a full-on dinner date. Maybe that was why he could scarcely bear looking at her.

But he had to risk it if he wanted this gambit to work. And he did, only to find the corner of her gaze on him.

"What made you say yes?"

She bit her lip and smirked at him, and he could feel a little bit of her cynical armor slip into place over the lace and gabardine of her clothes. "Well, I always wanted to eat at Alinea, and your videos don't make you seem like a serial killer."

"What do they make me seem like?" *God, what a dumb question.* Where had he misplaced his balls?

"Different." He wanted to probe that, but they pulled up to the restaurant, and it would have to wait.

Maybe forever, because he couldn't plumb her depths and hurt her—really hurt her—and live with himself.

HANNAH HAD NEVER BEEN on a date like this. This golden retriever of a man had actually shown up at her door. She'd never had that happen before. Scratch that. Before tonight, no one had even driven a car really slow outside of her condo so she could jump in. It was too much for a first date, and she hadn't helped matters with her dumb joke about him maybe, possibly, being a serial killer.

She had to get her shit together—this was about the promotion, not hoping that this guy liked the real her.

When they entered the restaurant, they were in what looked like a long corridor. His hand on her lower back made her feel slightly less creeped out when a bit of wall that had been concealing the entrance opened to their left side.

He'd picked her up and then he'd brought her to a restaurant she hadn't ever been able to justify a trip to. Part of her had wanted to come here when she finally secured a promotion to VP, and it was poetic that her ticket to that promotion brought her to the midwestern temple of molecular gastronomy for their first date.

She'd wanted to argue that it was way too fancy, that they were just getting to know each other, but she didn't want to be argumentative. According to Noah, she didn't know when to shut her mouth and be polite—when to go along to get along—and that was why she hadn't asked about how he could afford this place. Journalists didn't make that much money and were in constant danger of getting laid off. Once a week, there was news on social media about an outlet closing down.

Curiosity gnawed at her as she took her seat across from Jack in the stark white dining room. But the need to have answers for the questions haunting her and her delight at finally getting to eat here warred with sharp lust for the man sitting across from her. She'd thought he was infuriatingly handsome the night they'd met, but she must have forgotten how sexy he was. He was cute, but there was a little bit of the devil that danced in his stupid green eyes. His gaze was sharp with something that said he was thinking all sorts of filthy things, and those telepathically expressed ideas wound their way up her spine and implanted pictures in her head of hot kisses and lots of his naked, golden skin.

Thankfully, the server arrived at the table before drool hit her lips and slipped down her chin. Jack confirmed they wanted to have the wine pairings, and that raised Hannah's hackles a little bit.

It must have shown up on her face, and he must be astonishingly perceptive, because he laid a smile on her that had probably magically disappeared panties all over town for years. She couldn't stop the smirk that hit her lips at thinking about Jack and what she wanted him to do inside her panties—after at least three dates, of course. And if he didn't stop looking at her like that, she wouldn't last the full three. At this point, she would be lucky to make it through two and half dates before going boots up on the closest available sturdy surface.

"What?"

"You're beautiful."

"You're full of shit." Despite her denial, her skin flushed, and she smiled at him. "Or, if you're trying to seduce me, you're certainly doing it the wrong way."

"Well, the thing is, I'm not trying to seduce you." She hadn't expected him to say *that*.

"You're not?" She looked around the room, at all the well-heeled and quiet couples and foursomes scattered across the ultramodern décor. "Why would you drop almost a thousand dollars on dinner if you weren't trying to seduce me?"

"I got them some coverage—viral coverage—for their reopening, and the sous chef owes me." He shrugged, but it was faux modesty. He was cocky about his influence, and—God save her—she kind of loved it.

"But you aren't trying to seduce me?"

He shook his head. "I'm trying to show you that I'm taking this seriously."

"You don't even know me." The fact that men who had known her for years couldn't take her seriously as a long-term romantic prospect rode her hard and blew her doubts up to giant-sized.

"I know you well enough to know that I like you more than a cheap seduction."

"What would you do if this was a cheap seduction?"

"You really want to know?"

She bit her lip. "Yes."

This whole dating thing was so strange, because she needed it to lead to more than sex with Jack. But sex was heavy in the air between them and would explode. She shouldn't be goading him into telling her how he would seduce her, because this thing between them couldn't go there right now. It was as though she was lactose intolerant and just popping into an ice cream shop. If only she didn't have to convince him that she was girlfriend material for the sake of her career, she'd be able to indulge.

But she wanted to hear about Jack on a mission for a one-night stand. Something she desperately wanted in that moment, but couldn't have. It wouldn't hurt to hear about it.

"I wouldn't bring you someplace this quiet."

"Hmm?"

"I'd bring you someplace loud so that we'd have to sit really close together."

She wiped the side of her mouth, checking for phantom drool. "Using the pheromones, eh?"

"Nah. I don't believe in that shit." Of course he didn't. He would only believe in the power of his own magnetism. Cocky. Sexy. He crossed his arms and leaned back. "I would want to be close enough so that I could whisper in your ear." She could almost feel his breath against the skin behind her ear, and it made her shiver. He rubbed his chin and her gaze followed; she wanted to trail over the stubbled surface with her tongue. And she hadn't even had a single wine pairing yet. She was so, *so* screwed.

"I'd have to rest my hand on your thigh so I could hear what you were saying." She could actually feel his thigh under her palm as she said it. "What would you say?" she asked.

"I'd tell you how much I wanted your hand six inches higher, and how much I wanted to kiss you."

"But you wouldn't kiss me?" She tried to keep her tone light even though her skin was hot and she felt suddenly breathless.

"Not in the loud restaurant."

"Not into PDA?"

"With you? Yeah." He paused. "But I remember the first time we kissed. I need a lot longer. I need more." Inside, she was screaming for the scenario that he'd just described. She wanted to have his hands on her more than she wanted to eat the most exquisite food on the planet—and that was saying something considering that food was extremely important to her. "It would be a short dinner."

"Not three hours and eighteen courses?" she asked.

"The only thing I'd need eighteen courses of would be you, Duchess," he said with a shit-eating grin.

"But not tonight?" She couldn't quite contain her disappointment, knew he could hear it in her voice.

"We've got time." Not enough time. The way she'd reacted to his words, the way he'd kissed her the first time, had her so messed up. Two weeks was simultaneously too much time and not enough.

"So, tell me about your family." Both a change of pace and the question she'd been dreading since they'd met. Sometime between an initial conversation on an app and the second date, the *Where are you from?* or *Tell me about your family* conversation happened. She'd never felt the need to lead with her ethnicity in the romantic arena because she didn't consider that the most important thing about herself. More important things: her love of French bulldog puppies, her loyalty and long-lasting friendships, her competence at her job, and the fact that no one got to fuck with her heart anymore. Been there. Done that.

But guys always wanted to know. Needed to know. Couldn't help but ask. And even though Jack was proving himself to be different in a myriad of ways, it wasn't like she could blame him for his curiosity. Still, she gave her first answer in the well-trod series of answers. "The usual. Divorced parents. My mom really raised me on her own. My grandpa was around a lot, too."

She smiled when she thought about her grandfather. He used to tease her that she'd gotten her good looks from him, along with his great hair. He'd been pretty good-looking, but they didn't really look alike. He'd only said those things because it made her feel good—like she belonged.

She sobered when Jack said, "Me, too," shocking the shit out of her. "Just switch it around."

Usually the next question quickly followed, and it was, *But, like, tell me where you're from.* She hadn't expected him to be actually asking about the family structure she grew up in.

"Oh, really?" She was going to give him a little more rope to hang himself; he could veer into the bad place yet.

"Yeah, you know, fifty percent of marriages and all." He motioned to the edible menu.

"So, you're a messed-up kid from divorce, like me?" She had not expected this conversation to lead to their finding common ground, but she was glad that it had.

"I mean, if messed-up is what got me here with you, then I guess we are." Dear Lord, he was charming. If his father was even half as charming, that was probably what had ended his parents' marriage. "You have any brothers or sisters?" he asked.

She decided to ignore his strangely sincere, flattering comment, and just answer his question. "No. Plenty of cousins, though—all girls but one."

"Are they all as—sharp-tongued as you?" He said it with a smile, so she didn't take offense.

"Not all of us. They're nice girls."

He grinned at her, and she melted. "Present company excluded."

"Hey, I've been extraordinarily nice to you. I'm here, and you're not even planning on seducing me."

"I see what kind of guy you think I am." Then that jerk-off had the audacity to *wink at her.* As though it wouldn't make her commitment not to go boots up for him vanish completely.

"You're not like anyone else I've ever been out with," she said, with a sigh she hoped didn't sound too dreamy. His charm had weakened her resolve not to get in too deep with him emotionally, either. She couldn't help but say what she was thinking around him.

"How so? I'm just a regular guy." He shrugged.

"You asked me about my family, and you actually wanted to know how I grew up."

His brow furrowed. "Yeah?"

"Most of the time guys ask about my race."

More furrowing followed that statement. "That seems rude."

It had always seemed that way to her. As though a guy needed to know her race in order to know which bucket to stick her in, which racist misogynistic stereotypes he could use against her. Noah had done it, and she'd expected it from Jack.

"My mom is white, and my dad was black." She looked down at her glass when she said it, not able to help but worry that it would change what Jack thought about her. "I'm biracial."

"Cool." She looked up to find Jack smiling at her. It was seriously just a piece of information about her that he thought was interesting.

He was actually perfect, and she almost wished she wasn't just using him to get a promotion.

She could have slipped into maudlin worries about how she would feel once this was over, but their first course arrived—a "salad" made of five different kinds of jellied vegetables arranged in a row across a rectangular plate. They looked like something that could have come out of some nightmare of a midcentury cookbook, and she looked at them skeptically for a moment.

Then she looked up, wanting to see Jack's reaction. She'd figured him for a meat-and-potatoes kind of guy, not necessarily up for culinary adventures. But he looked at her with mischief written across his face as he picked up a piece of the dish with a spork-like utensil and took a bite—and it made her think of him taking a bite out of *her*.

She followed suit with the green jelly square, and the flavor of an honest-to-God Caesar salad exploded in her mouth. Her eyes widened, and her gaze caught Jack's.

A total surprise. Hannah didn't normally like surprises, but both this meal and Jack promised to be full of them.

CHAPTER SEVEN

AS THEY WALKED ALONG the quiet West Loop street after dinner, Jack wanted to put his arm around Hannah despite the fact that this was a first date and a strange one at that. Even though there had been some awkward moments while they were eating—normal getting-to-know-each-other stuff—that didn't dim the connection between them.

And mostly, they'd been distracted by the food experience. It was more than just good; it was surprising and transcendent. Almost like experiencing a moving piece of art for the very first time. Each dish looked like one thing but tasted and smelled like another—everything from the jellied veggies that had started the meal to the lobster thermidor that had the protein wrapped in a bubble of sauce.

There was no one he'd rather have shared it with than Hannah. She compelled him more than any other woman he'd ever met, and he would likely die from his attraction to her before he'd finished writing this article. Because there was one thing for certain: he couldn't sleep with her while he was lying to her. He hadn't planned to, going in—he'd wanted to make sure she liked him enough to hang on for two weeks while he put her through the wringer, but he didn't want to get so intimate with her that he'd break her heart when he revealed the truth.

Before tonight, he'd thought he could walk that balance, but now he wasn't so sure. Every moment he spent with her made him like her more, made it harder for him to justify lying to her for a stupid article—even a stupid article that could totally change the trajectory of his career.

But he always did this in relationships. He found a girl he was attracted to, and then he gave her everything she asked for to make her happy. Projected his own feelings onto her. And she always left him anyway.

Hannah would be no different. It didn't matter that she turned his crank like no other woman before her. It didn't matter that the look on her face as the ravioli brittle cracked between her straight white teeth had made his cock stand up like Willis Tower. Didn't matter that her sucking on an edible sugar balloon had nearly made him need to go to the restroom and relieve some of the pressure in his groin.

She might turn him back into a fourteen-year-old boy, but he wouldn't forget the hard lessons he'd learned from every other woman he'd let in. Being in her presence might be a delight now, but her absence would surely hurt more than anything he let grow between them.

And he'd almost convinced himself that it was the truth when they got to the entrance of his building. That should have been the moment that he pivoted toward the objective of this exercise. He'd fully planned on kissing her cheek and calling her a car.

But then she turned those pretty hazel eyes up at him, and he let himself glance at her mouth. He had to stuff his hands into his pockets to keep from touching her. Everything inside him wanted to grab her by the shoulders and haul her into his body for a kiss. The vulnerability seeping out of her with every breath mixed in with his desire for her as the moment stretched long, like the cheese inside the squash blossom they'd been served an hour and a half ago had stretched as she'd taken a bite.

Her tongue darted out as she licked her bottom lip, and that put the final nail in his coffin. Just by existing, she tested his will-power and shorted out the motherboard of his better angels. "Want to come up?"

She smirked. "I thought you weren't trying to seduce me."

"I'm not." He looked down, feeling his skin get hot. "I just want to spend a little more time with you."

That was the truth. Not the one that he'd meant to come out. It would have been a good way to go about losing her to be inconsistent with what he said. He'd always found that women responded well to his general sense of personal integrity. Apparently, it was rare.

As a practice, he never said he would do something and then did the opposite. He never said he was looking for a relationship if he was really just trying to screw around. And—maybe it was just his nature—but he was never looking to just screw around.

The one-night stand had never been his thing. In fact, the whole story that he'd told Hannah about what he would do if he were try-ing to seduce her into a cheap fling was bullshit. Not the part about how he would try to seduce her, but the cheap fling part.

She was worth so much more than that. So much more than this.

That was why he hated himself a little when she stepped into his body and said, "Yes, I'd love to come up."

That was why he hated himself even more when he smiled and wove his fingers with hers before opening the door for her.

HANNAH WAS GOOD AT her job because she had a great memory. Where most people needed lists and spreadsheets to keep track of the million-item to-do list, she needed three Post-its and her own mind. The only time she displayed forgetfulness was when she was really into a guy.

If a guy warned her, as guys so often did, that he wasn't "ready for a relationship" or wasn't "looking for anything serious" on a first date, she could forget it by the third. She wouldn't remember until the only thing left of the relationship was an STD test and regret.

She could already feel her memory failing her with Jack.

As soon as she'd tasted the cellophane-clear apple pie, she'd known that her promise to Sasha—the one about not sleeping with Jack tonight—was done for. And it wasn't that she could be bought with an expensive meal, either. It was the way he'd looked at her as she'd been enjoying it, as though her pleasure in eating the food was just as important as his.

When he'd stared at her as she'd licked the last of the translucent pastry off the custom-designed pie plate, she'd felt it all the way from her toes to her scalp. Even as he ushered her through the lobby of his building toward the elevator, there was searing heat where his palm touched hers and an excitement flowing through her veins that she hadn't felt for a very long time—maybe ever.

She definitely hadn't felt like this with Noah. Even though their breakup had hurt so badly that she felt it through her entire body, had cried almost every day for six months thereafter, she hadn't felt the same kind of *need* for him as she did for Jack.

With Noah, they'd kind of floated at the edges of the same social circle for a few months, edging toward each other during group outings until the group didn't have to be there. And they'd definitely had sex on their first official date. Of course, in his Noah way, he'd made her feel like she'd made a bad decision by sleeping with him right away.

They'd had quite a bit of wine at dinner, and he'd kept saying, "You started this."

She'd forgotten all about it until much later, when Noah'd said he couldn't see a future with her. Even though they'd mutually floated together, he'd found her too overtly sexual and not the kind of woman he could truly depend on to be a good wife and mother. And not black enough to be half of the power couple he desperately wanted to be a part of.

Just remembering those cutting words made her hesitate and her steps falter.

Jack stopped beside her and looked down at her, his forehead creasing with concern that she wanted to drink up like springwater. "What's wrong?"

She couldn't tell him the truth—that she was afraid that she'd climb on top of him at the first opportunity and scare him off with her extreme horniness. So she settled for a partial version of the real story.

"I know that if we have sex tonight, you're never going to call me again because you'll think I'm just after you for the D. And I'd really like it if you'd call me again."

Her words were louder than she'd intended them to be, and he looked around before cupping her jaw with both hands and pulling her close, until their foreheads touched. "I never promise something and don't deliver." His deep voice resonated inside her, and that was before he took the swoon factor and dialed it up to about eleven.

"And I promise that no matter what happens or doesn't happen when we get up to my place, I'm going to call you."

Even though she had no reason to believe him and she half expected a camera crew to pop out and tell her that this was all some sort of elaborate prank designed to make her look foolish on some obscure streaming channel aimed at incels wanting to humiliate feminists, she believed him.

"Let's go upstairs, then." His smile made her shine from the inside out as he led her the rest of the way to the elevator. Her guard was pretty far down at this point, so after she took in the luxe finishes in the common areas of the building, she asked, "How do you afford this place on a reporter's salary?"

When he grimaced, she tried to cover. "I mean, you don't have to tell me. That was so nosy."

The door dinged, and he squeezed her hand. "I'd have been a little surprised if you hadn't asked, honestly."

"Oh?"

"Yeah, I mean, I couldn't afford this on my own," he said. "My dad owns the contracting company that built the place, and he got a unit in the deal closing because the development company didn't have enough cash to pay him."

For some reason, she felt relieved to hear that he didn't come from crazy-big money. "And dinner tonight?"

He grimaced again before looking down and reaching into his pocket, presumably for his keys. "The sous chef really did owe me a favor."

She felt bad then for allowing her nosiness to almost ruin the best date ever, in addition to feeling kind of mercenary for leading the guy on. Not knowing exactly what to do—when she always knew the right move in her professional life—made her feel vulnerable. After spending so long trying to push away any hints of vulnerability, she was unaccustomed to the sensation. It almost felt as though her chest gaped open and he could see all the broken, gross insides of her. "Big favor."

He gave her a sly grin that told her he knew she was feeling awkward, opened the door, and put his hand on her lower back again, moving her into his space and reassuring her at the same time. Some of the anxious, edgy, almost-naked feeling receded.

"I'm glad I got to share it with you." *Crap, did he always know what to say?*

"Me too." She looked down, not wanting to meet his gaze. "I had a really good time with you." She said that twice. And she couldn't seem to stop doing a lot of girly-stupid things around him that she'd thought she'd sworn off forever.

"Can I take your coat?" This gentlemanly bullshit had to stop—immediately. Maybe he thought he was slick and that she hadn't noticed how he was always pulling out chairs and opening doors and stuff. Or maybe it was all just second nature to him. What she knew for sure was that his good manners seemed to be straight-up hardwired to her clitoris.

Taking her coat and hanging it for her was practically better than getting fingered. From the way his skin had brushed hers while he was removing the trench, she knew that was a lie. If he did anything to her girl parts with his fingers, she was going to know and remember forever exactly what he did to her body.

The manners were just an aphrodisiac.

"What can I get you to drink?" He led her into an open-concept industrial living space. Exactly what she would have expected but for the meticulous cleanliness and touches of smart design. There was the de rigueur bachelor big-screen television, but he also had neutral, tasteful accent pillows and decent furniture. He definitely hadn't found any of it on the curb or bought it off of Craigslist.

"What do you have?"

He smiled, and his incredibly sexy dimple popped. She could spend years trying to make him smile so hard that his dimple popped out. Then he sauntered over to a cabinet that hugged the exposed brick wall and opened it up. "Whatever you want."

She knew in her bones that his offer extended to more than liquor, and the ideas running through her brain made her throat dry out. The wine pours with dinner hadn't been generous—basically enough for a swallow of wine with each dish—so she wasn't drunk. But she was giddy on the man smiling at her.

Just then, she was struck by the fact that she was surrounded by him—things that smelled like him, what he liked to look at and taste—and was overwhelmed. Even though she'd found herself stammering and a little awkward around him, she found that she liked being surrounded by him and his things and the way he smelled. "I'll have whatever you're having."

Her words were croaked out, and then he winked at her. He might as well have just taken the bones out of her legs right then. "Have a seat. Bourbon okay?"

"Bourbon is great." She sank onto the butter-soft leather of his couch and stared up at the ceiling when he turned to mix their drinks, extracting an orange and ice from a minifridge next to the bar.

As he worked, she had the opportunity to stare at his gorgeous, perfectly round ass as he bent and straightened and shook their cocktails. Everything he did seduced her. He didn't even have to mention sex to make her feel like he was putting moves on. She was so screwed.

If she did manage to keep him interested in her for two whole weeks, she was going to miss him when things eventually fizzled out.

The whole reason that Jack had asked her out was that she was an überconfident bitch on wheels. The more he got to know her, the less she tried to be perfect, the less he would like her. Either that, or she would get tired of the whole façade and just want to be herself: sometimes an überconfident bitch, sometimes just a girl who asked rude questions and liked bourbon on the rocks with a hot man.

For a moment, she wished that this was an entirely different scenario. Maybe that she'd met him years ago, before she'd met Noah. If they'd gone out then, she could have swaggered and told dirty jokes and captivated him with how flipping cool she was without worrying that she couldn't be herself with him.

She shook that thought out of her head. Didn't need to be thinking about what it would be like to date him for real. This whole production was for one purpose, and one purpose only—to get him to fall in love with her and secure a promotion. Whatever happened afterward didn't matter.

If he liked a bitch on wheels who flipped him off one moment and kissed the hell out of him the next, that's what she would give him.

CHAPTER EIGHT

WHEN IT HAD COME time for Sean Nolan to give a birds-and-bees talk, he hadn't wasted any time. Michael had been ten and Jack had been eight.

All three of them sat down in the family living room, Sean in his easy chair and Michael and Jack on the sofa facing him. They'd each had a beer—root for Michael and Jack.

Sean ran his work-hewn paw over the rapidly graying stubble on his face, looked them each in the eye, and said, "Ladies first."

Michael and Jack looked at each other and then back at their dad. Sean continued, "I found the porn on the computer, and you need to know that it's all bullshit. That's not how sex should work. Mostly because it's supposed to be fun for both of you. And to have it be fun for both of you . . . ladies first. Any questions?"

Jack and his brother had remained silent for a long moment. They'd telepathically decided that they were probably better off finding out more information from one of their mom's romance novels, and mostly relieved that neither of them was getting in trouble for watching porn. So they shook their heads.

Sean nodded, took a swig of beer, and added, "Also, wrap it up, for Christ's sake."

HANNAH HAD SETTLED ON her plan to remain a mercurial harpy to keep him interested, when Jack swaggered as he brought her drink over. She didn't even call him on it, and she was for sure losing her edge. The spark that passed between them when he passed her the drink might have shorted out her bitch circuits completely. And not even the cold bourbon and slight tinge of bitters and orange could bring them back.

He took a seat at the end of his couch, close enough that she could touch him if she reached out, but far enough that it was clear that he wasn't trying to crowd her.

"So." Just one word. Then he took a swallow of his drink and she watched his throat work. Over dinner they'd mostly covered pop culture and politics, so she knew that he was publicly neutral but privately liberal, that he liked *Game of Thrones* the TV show more than the books, and that he was a serious foodie. His love of tacos and choice of restaurants weren't just flukes.

"How'd you get into journalism?"

"A girl." He gave her a wry laugh and looked at her under his too-long-for-a-man lashes. "Every bit of trouble I've ever gotten into happened because of a girl."

"Oh, really?" She took a sip of her drink, trying out her words as the liquor made its fiery way down her throat. "Do you think I'm trouble?"

"Definitely." The certainty in his declarative statement combined with his smile made her feel as though they were back into flirty-first-date mode and out of the awkward swamp she'd been wading through for the past few hours.

Maybe it was the extra drink, or the ease in pressure from not being out at a superfancy restaurant. Or the intimacy of it being just the two of them. But the magic that she'd felt the first night they'd met was back in action, that feeling that she could do no wrong, that he saw her and liked what he saw.

And it was more intoxicating than an eighteen-course meal and wine pairings. "I don't want to cause you any trouble."

He scooted toward her on the couch so his bent knee touched her thigh. She fought off a moan of pleasure at the contact. First, his manners were going to get her off, and now his touching her thigh? She'd definitely been out of the sex rat race too long if this was going to be her reaction.

She was like a fourteen-year-old girl with a poster of Freddie Prinze Jr. in her room again. Except—like the current Mr. Sarah Michelle Gellar and all-around silver fox—Jack wasn't a teenage boy; he was one hundred percent, full-fledged man.

"I like the kind of trouble I could get into with you, Duchess."

"Why 'Duchess'?"

"Just popped into my head, I guess."

"No one else would have that pop into their head when thinking of me." She couldn't be further from royal material.

"You look kind of like the new one." He skimmed a fingertip, cool from holding his drink, on the exposed skin of her thigh, making eye contact to make sure she was on board with it. "But that's not why I called you that."

"Why did you?"

"That first night we met, you might have been flipping me and my buddies off, but there was something kind of classy about it."

She nearly choked on her drink. Classy? Her? Never in her life had anyone described her that way. Assertive? Yes. Mouthy? Of course. A total raging bitch? On more than one occasion.

"I can honestly say, that's the strangest thing anyone has ever said about me."

"I'm a strange guy." He waggled his eyebrows, somehow managing to be even more charming than before. "Maybe 'classy' is the wrong word. But the way you were going to stand up for your friends—with your fists, if necessary—tells me that you have something that a lot of people who would never think of using the f-word don't have."

The way he was describing her to herself was intoxicating. Perhaps her ego was out of control, but she wanted to hear more—couldn't resist it. "And what's that?"

"Loyalty."

All her plans to save anything physical for the third date flew out the window and wafted east until they floated away on the fetid waters of the Chicago River. She put down her half-full drink. Just as Jack opened his mouth—probably to ask her if she wanted something else—she kissed him.

She grabbed his face and swung her leg over his lap, pinning him to the couch. His old-fashioned sloshed in his glass, some of it spilling on her cleavage before he put it on the side table.

For the first few moments, his mouth didn't respond to hers. For a fraction of a second, she stilled and thought about pulling away. Just as she was taking in the feel of his roughened cheeks against her palms and the scent of liquor on his breath and some manly scent coming off of his skin in waves, he put his hands on her hips and pulled her fully against him. So that she could feel exactly how on board for this he was.

And then he shocked the shit out of her—again—by *taking* her mouth. She immediately realized that the kiss they'd shared the night they'd met was child's play. He'd been holding back and unsure that night, even though just his mouth against hers had been enough to invade her thoughts and plant naughty daydreams about his mouth for a week.

This kiss belied the good manners and the choirboy smiles that he put on like an intricate mask. This kiss was all lips and teeth and animalistic sounds made by two people who were practically in heat.

Without thinking, she rolled her hips against his groin, needing to feel his hardness against her, knowing that if he let her go long enough, she'd come all over him. She wouldn't even have to get rid of her panties.

For his part, Jack pressed his palms against her hips before stroking the curves of her sides and using his powerful hands and forearms to press her closer to him. It might have been eons before their lips broke apart, both of them panting.

Her total disorientation reflected back at her from his heated gaze. He trailed a finger over her bottom lip, though, melting her core even more, making her want to sink into his well-honed body.

One corner of his mouth kicked up into a lethal smirk. "If I'd known complimenting your integrity would get me a kiss like that, I would have done it the night we met."

"It was a little bit the nickname." Her voice sounded breathless, but she was too amped to beat herself up about being *that girl*. Not in that moment, looking at him, while his hands were still on her.

"Duchess." The endearment sounded like an accusation, but he kissed her again, even hungrier this time. His hand cupped the back of her skull as though she were precious to him while his mouth became well acquainted with hers, their breath mingling.

She felt like her skin was steaming as he ran one palm over and over her upper spine, as though he knew that he needed to keep her anchored to him.

He maneuvered their bodies until he was laid out on top of her, pressing between her thighs. She hadn't dry humped since early in college, and she couldn't remember it feeling this good. She couldn't remember anyone touching her feeling this good. And she'd never been kissed this long or this thoroughly before in her life.

If Jack Nolan ever did a how-to on kissing, the women of the world would be in serious trouble. Mail wouldn't be delivered, the fields would be untended, because everyone would be too busy kissing. All day, all night.

When he broke their kiss a second time, he looked just as shell-shocked as she felt. Good. Maybe it wasn't like this with every girl he kissed. He sat up on his haunches and she bit her lip, wincing because they were so swollen and all her lipstick had been rubbed off.

Speaking of rubbing off, he ran a hand up her thigh. She stopped him just before he got to the edge of her panties.

He moved his hand away to the safer territory of her thighs immediately. "Too far?"

"I mean—" It really wasn't far enough. She was practically dying for him to touch her. "There's a situation of sorts down there." When his brow furrowed in concern, she covered her face with both hands. "I want to die. I want to die, right now."

Then he did the worst thing that he could possibly do, and he laughed. "What kind of situation? Like vagina dentata or something?"

Hannah propped herself up on her forearms. "A vagina den-what-a?"

"You know, like a vagina with teeth." He inexplicably made claws with his hands.

She was *this close* to telling him to get off of her because he had clearly smoked crack when he went to the men's room just before dessert. "That's a thing?"

"There was a horror movie about it." He blushed and looked sheepish, and she was definitely not getting up.

"I just sort of have a Miss-Havisham's-attic situation in my basement." His brow furrowed in confusion. "Like, everything is the same as it's been since the last time someone had their face down there." More confusion. "There's hair, Jack. Lots of hair."

Jack shrugged and smiled and said the most perfect thing he could have said. "That's all? Seriously?"

"You don't care?"

"Not at all." He leaned so that he hovered over her, their mouths aligned again. "I would have cared about teeth, but hair—I'm fine with."

"Who are you?" She reached out and traced his mouth with one finger. He stayed still and let her.

"What do you mean?"

"It's just like—I don't know—toxic masculinity skipped you or something."

Something troubled clouded his gaze for a split second. She would have missed it if she hadn't been looking at him, examining him quite so closely. Then it passed, and his shit-eating grin was back. "So, I can keep kissing you?"

"Definitely." He laid a kiss on her neck and licked over the skin where his drink had splashed, cleaning up all the sticky residue. Such a gentleman, even when he was doing filthy things to her with his tongue.

He lifted his head, and she grabbed on to his hair in protest.

"Anywhere I want?" His hand on the inside of her thigh told her that "anywhere" was going to be "exactly where" she wanted it.

"Yes. Please."

EXCEPT FOR THAT SPLIT second when she basically made him out to be some sort of feminist hero because he didn't give a shit about whether she'd gotten a wax job, this had been the best date of his life.

Her moments of vulnerability made him want her so much more, but they amplified the guilt growing in his gut every second he spent with her. She was sharp and funny, and so beautiful it made his eyes tired—he didn't blink enough when he looked at her. He didn't want to miss a single smile or hand gesture. Didn't want to miss her looking at him. Under ordinary circumstances, he would be trying to make sure that she knew that she was *the girl for him*. It was shitty luck and shitty timing that he had to treat her exactly how she expected him to treat her.

As he kissed the tops of her gorgeous tits, he tried to justify what he was doing.

This is wrong. You'll break her heart.

She won't even remember your name in a month.

She would eventually leave you anyway.

She thought you would be kicking her out the moment you found out about her pubic hair. The least you owe her is an orgasm for the anxiety.

That last one was the one that had his hands moving up her thighs, getting her fuck-hot dress out of the way so he could dive right in. Jack had never had any qualms about going down on a woman—especially one that felt as much like *his* as Hannah.

If he wasn't using her for a story, he could imagine this being the first of many times that her breath caught when his fingers reached her panties. The commencement of the sighs she'd make when he caressed the skin of her lower belly with his tongue. One of many moments when he opened up her thighs and tasted her like she was better than anything he'd tasted during their many courses of dinner.

Because she was.

It was all he could do to stop himself when she wound her fingers through his hair and rode his face. He did a swirly thing with his tongue until she made a keening sound combined with words that didn't make sense. He kept going until he'd completed his mission and she came all over his face, nearly pulling his hair out at the ends.

He rose onto his knees and pulled her dress down, a mirrored sense of satisfaction melting through his chest. She had her forearm blocking her eyes, but he wished that she would look at him. He didn't deserve them, but he wanted her eyes.

Looking at her kiss-swollen lips and flushed skin, he couldn't help wanting more from her. His libido was certainly on board with that idea, but he had to draw a line somewhere. After all this was over and she found out that he'd lied to her, he wouldn't be able to live with the guilt of taking pleasure from her if it was based on a lie.

Over the next two weeks, he would probably wear the skin off his dick from jerking it, but he wasn't about to be *that guy*. He'd have to seem like that guy for the article, but he wasn't going to take advantage of her.

That was the only way that maybe she'd give him a real shot at being her real-life boyfriend at the end of this. If he let *her* use *him* for this whole two weeks, maybe he'd have a chance of convincing her that he wasn't a totally morally bankrupt asshole and that she could give him a shot.

In the time that it took her to recover and look at him, he'd made the decision that he wouldn't get his rocks off with Hannah until this whole farce was over. Immediately, she tested that determination when she reached for his belt. Knowing that he would break his promise to himself and to future Hannah who might want to be in a relationship with him, he twisted out of her grasp and off of the couch so quickly that he knocked into the coffee table and spilled both of their drinks.

"Shit!" He yelled louder than he intended to. His brother had made the coffee table for him out of old railroad ties, and he would get a hard glare the next time Michael came over if there were watermarks on the wood.

"I'm so sorry!" Hannah sounded horrified, and he immediately felt like a huge asshole. Even through her hard-ass exterior, he'd read some vulnerability in her wariness. She just seemed like someone very accustomed to calibrating her behavior to a situation. Even though he was using her for a story, he needed to find some way to be careful of her feelings. He had to make her realize that whatever he did to her to get her to break up with him was because of his damage, not hers.

They both rushed toward the kitchen, but he grabbed the paper towels and kept them away from her. "Not your fault, Duchess."

"Sure. Right." Didn't sound like she believed him.

He cleaned up the spilled liquor and righted the glasses before straightening. Hannah stood on the other side of the couch, worrying her bottom lip, and she made his heart skip. He hated that she felt bad, and he couldn't seem to stop wanting to make things right for her.

Part of him just wanted to tell her right now, the whole story. But he stopped himself. He'd spent his entire adult life trying to make things right for the women in his life. If he was honest with himself, he'd been trying to make things right for the women in his life since long before his mom left to follow her bliss.

And it had never worked. He'd been walking on eggshells with every woman he'd ever dated, and they always still walked away. Being the best guy they'd ever dated had never kept them from walking away from him and following their bliss. Bliss always won out, and he'd never been anyone's bliss.

No matter what he did to make Hannah happy, anything they had would be temporary. He'd be the great, solid boyfriend she deigned to be with until something more fun and shiny happened along. He would throw his whole being into giving her everything he could, and it would never be enough.

So he could throw away a chance to finally make his career happen. If he could get into the game of real journalism, maybe he wouldn't need to put so much effort into relationships. Perhaps he'd be the kind of shiny, exciting guy who didn't have to be the perfect boyfriend in order to get a woman interested in him.

"I had a lot of fun tonight," she said.

He had, too. He didn't want to end it here, but he couldn't guarantee he'd be able to resist if she went in for his fly again. "Let me get your coat."

"You sure you want me to leave?" She looked down at the front of his pants with a pouty look on her face.

He painted a smirk onto his mouth. It took a little effort, but he needed practice in the whole being-a-callous-dickstick department. Coming up with a fast, believable lie wasn't really his forte. "Yeah, I have an early-morning meeting tomorrow."

He grabbed her coat from the rack by the door and helped her into it. Hey, some habits couldn't be unlearned. She had the fall of her hair over one shoulder, and the skin on the back of her neck proved to be way too tempting.

After laying a peck on that soft stretch of skin, he said, "Sleep well," knowing that there was no way that he was going to be able to sleep tonight without a long, cold shower.

CHAPTER NINE

THE CLOSEST TO YOGA that Sasha ever got was SoulCycle, but Hannah's best friend had a mantra. Since college, whenever Hannah had a wild hair up her ass to do something crazy, which was often, Sasha said, "I'm not judging you, but are you sure that's a good idea?"

It usually made Hannah pause for at least a moment to reconsider.

As they mounted their stationary bikes at cycling class the next day, Sasha squinted at her as though she were a steely-eyed detective in a procedural drama winding up to interrogate a suspect. Hannah only hoped that she kept the I-just-had-the-best-orgasm-of-my-life glow to a minimum after her fitful night's sleep.

Luckily, her roommate had already been asleep when she'd arrived home. The debriefing she'd been spared the night before and pre-caffeine was apparently going to happen right before cycling class.

"You had sex with him, didn't you?" *What the hell!? Does Sasha have orgasm radar or something?*

Her face heated, and she thanked whatever asshole decided that putting spinning in the dark would make it a whole new, very trendy thing. Her mental gears locked for a moment, as she wondered how she could answer this without revealing how intimate she and Jack had actually gotten.

Finally, after the clock in her head resumed its ticking, she said, "He did not put his penis in my vagina." She hoped that sounded as confident as she was trying to make it seem.

After looking around to make sure that the other early-morning exercisers were not listening, Sasha quietly asked, "Finger stuff or mouth stuff?"

"Both." She could not be dishonest with her best friend, as much as it would help her seem more serious about this whole process.

Sasha pursed her lips slightly. "Well, was it at least good?"

Hannah let everything go at that point—the false confidence and the illusion that what had happened with Jack had not affected her. "It was so good that if he ghosts me after last night, and I see him months or years from now, I will give him the roundhouse high five from the homoerotic volleyball scene in *Top Gun*."

"That good?" Her best friend's eyes widened as though she'd never heard of sex that good before.

Hannah nodded.

"Like top and bottom fives?" She mimicked the motion of the high five in question.

"Top and bottom."

Sasha turned and clipped her shoes into her bike before responding. "Shit."

"Yeah."

Luckily, she was saved from spilling her guts further when the instructor walked in. It was "It's Britney, Bitch" day in class, so she was hoping that she could lose herself in the lyrics and pulsing beats. As many times as she'd replayed the events of the date over in her head, she couldn't figure out where she'd gone wrong.

As soon as he'd made her come, it was like he hadn't been able to get her out of his apartment fast enough. She'd been primed and ready to return the favor—her promise to Sasha that she wouldn't screw him on the first date be damned.

But he hadn't wanted her. Throughout the warm-up song, that thought rang through her brain, and it elevated her heart rate more than the movement of her legs. For part of last night, she'd thought that it was going to be easy to string him along for two weeks. But her attraction to him, and his reticence, complicated things. She wished she could read his mind and know exactly what he was thinking.

Maybe he'd realized that he really had a problem with pubic hair like midway through the act, and been totally turned off. The bulge in the front of his slacks told her that that wasn't the case, but what did she know?

Through the first set of hills, she puzzled over whether he had some weird thing about sex. One of Noah's many, *many* problems with her had been how much she'd liked sex—how much she'd needed it to feel like they were connecting. Combined with his strict religious upbringing and generally conservative attitudes, her wanting to jump him had been anathema to him.

In most ways, Jack seemed like a totally different kind of guy. But maybe he was suffering from some Catholic shame. She wasn't going to feel bad about what they'd done last night. He'd offered, after all. Granted, he didn't know she'd been coming off a long drought, so he may have gotten more than he bargained for. But she'd have been just as eager to take what he was offering regardless.

ANDIE J. CHRISTOPHER

This all went to why dating Jack was such a bad idea. He was way too smart, and she had the feeling that he saw things about people that people didn't want him to see. He could probably tell that she had ulterior motives for dating him. And that was what she had to think about instead of how good touching him and kissing him had felt. As soon as "Oops! . . . I Did It Again" came blaring through the speakers, she remembered why she didn't do this anymore.

On her own, she didn't have to think about anyone else or worry about what they thought of her. What she needed and wanted was between her and her small but worthy collection of sex toys and porn GIFs. Bringing someone else into it, opening up to him, was a huge mistake. It didn't matter that he was handsome, or that she liked the way he smelled, and he was a veritable savant at eating pussy.

As she sprinted through "Toxic," she realized what she needed to do to get through the next few weeks with a fake boyfriend and a promotion. Even though Jack seemed different, she had to remember that he was operating off the same fumes of toxic masculinity that wafted through every bit of this relationship shit. He might appear to be a good guy, but she didn't really know him. If she allowed for the possibility of his charm—the general sense that he was a lovely human—to be real, she would be lost.

She'd end up locked in her room again, eating cold Pop-Tarts and crying about the fact that she would definitely, for sure, die alone. And that was unacceptable. There was no way that one date—no matter how good—was going to knock her off track. She was going to kick ass, take names, and become the most sought-after event planner in Chicago.

Even if she killed the possibility of a fulfilling relationship with Jack to do it. They could never work out anyway. She just didn't have what it took to do relationships. And she'd accepted that.

96

She had.

By the time she climbed off the bike with wobbly legs, she felt . . . not exactly better. But more like herself again. The ache in her chest spread out to her well-used limbs. The echo of pleasure from having Jack between her legs the night before had dissipated.

Sasha must have seen the shift, too. As shitty as she was about seeing how guys were always going to screw her over, her best friend was perceptive. Because Hannah wasn't always great about sharing how she felt, intuition was an essential quality in her best friend.

"You feel better?"

"Much." Even though this was a lie, she couldn't tell her friend that she wasn't exactly accurate. Before sweating out her complex feelings about Jack, she'd been like a puzzle with a few pieces askew. Right now, she felt like the pieces had been clicked into place but the other ones were missing.

Thankfully, Sasha didn't pick up on the intricacies of her inner workings right then. "Mimosas?"

"Like a thousand of them should do the trick."

JACK PLAYED BASKETBALL WITH Chris, Joey, and Father Patrick Dooley—otherwise known as Chris's much less idiotic older brother—every Saturday morning on the courts outside of the church they'd all attended as children. Unlike when they were pipsqueaks, Jack, Chris, and Joey didn't return to the church on Sunday morning unless it was Easter or Christmas. Pat was kind of required to be there for every Mass—given that he was the parish priest and all.

Patrick was sort of the conscience of the group, and Chris's Irish twin at thirteen months his senior. Although he'd participated in his share of the tomfoolery they'd gotten themselves up to in their adolescence—petty acts of vandalism and minor shoplifting—he was always the first to fess up and take the punishment. Although he'd never mentioned wanting to become a priest while they were suffering through catechism classes, the role sort of fit his slightly older friend.

Still, at times, Jack felt his buddy's conflict about his calling as though it were a palpable thing. Back in college, Patrick had been a hard-partying ladies' man. With his black-Irish good looks and one dimpled cheek, Patrick hadn't had to work that hard to blow up skirts all over the Loyola Chicago campus. The few times Jack had visited his buddy in the dorms, it had been clear to him that Patrick had a reputation as a big man on campus—in more ways than one.

The shock of his mother's death had changed Patrick, though. Where Chris had grieved and clung to Bridget, Patrick had drawn into himself and become much more serious. His once-easy smiles had become hard-won and rare. Jack had worried about his older friend. Doubly so with his sudden calling to the priesthood.

Patrick threw the ball at Jack's chest with more force than necessary and said, "Check."

Jack caught the ball and started dribbling up the court, Patrick on his tail. "Kind of harsh, Father."

Arms in the air, trying to block Jack's options for passing to Joey, Patrick replied, "My idiot brother tells me you met a girl. Again."

Because of his role as conscience and confessor, Patrick knew all about the fact that he'd sworn off dating for a while. Jack had come to the conclusion after sharing some very fine scotch he'd gotten while doing a "How to Drink Scotch and Not Look Like a Pretentious Idiot" story. Hell, Patrick might have suggested his hiatus.

Jack shot a glare at Chris and used the opportunity to fake out

Patrick and dish a no-look pass to Joey. For once, Joey didn't have a thumb up his ass and got the layup.

Joey and Chris went to midcourt, and Jack looked back at his friend the priest. "It's for a story."

"Chris told me that part, too." Patrick's forehead crinkled in pastoral concern. "It seems kind of mean."

Patrick's previous way with women was one of the many reasons Jack had always looked up to him. Even though he'd dated up a storm through sophomore year, he'd never left a woman angry with him. He was still friends with most of his exes—perhaps because he'd left them behind for God rather than another girl.

That was why Jack hadn't been about to tell him about this assignment. Or Hannah and his very inconvenient feelings for her. This whole thing had every indication that it would blow up in his face. And leave Hannah hurt and even more bitter about men.

Jack sighed, frustration building. He wasn't sure if it was with himself or with his anthropomorphic conscience beating up on him about as hard as he'd been beating up on himself. After Hannah had left the night before, he'd planned to spend some quality time in the shower with his right hand. But his enthusiasm for the endeavor had deflated as soon as Hannah's disappointment and confusion had registered in his brain.

He wasn't sure he was cut out for this whole losing-a-girl-on-purpose thing. Even though he'd been decided and determined to follow through the night before, doubts dragged on him. Now, looking at Patrick and his rolled-up forehead, he was thinking that it was simply his Catholic guilt getting the best of him.

"I have to do it, Patrick." He looked over at Chris and Joey, who were dodging their morning workout by standing around and talking shit—the usual—to make sure they weren't paying attention to this conversation. They were the guys to go to when he wanted to crush a few beers, not the kind he wanted to have a heart-to-heart with. "It's the only way I'm going to get to cover politics for *the magazine*."

Patrick knew how much Jack wanted to get off the how-to beat, how much he needed to carve out his own place in the world. That was what made this so hard. By going through with the story, he felt as though he was finally making the right choice with respect to girl versus career.

And his friend must have seen the conflict on his face because he smiled and said, "Let's get back to this game. I need to win so you have to buy the beer."

CHAPTER TEN

JACK OPENED HIS NOTES app and titled a new document: "How to Lose Hannah." And then he looked at Chris and waited for him to tell him how to mess up a relationship. Being a perfectly decent but boring guy was Jack's only move when it came to losing girl-friends, and that was really more of a long game. He needed to get out of this thing with Hannah fast if he hoped to file his article on time.

"You have to send her a dick pic." Chris was probably right, but that was way further down the line. Patrick had left a little while ago—church emergency—so they were free to brainstorm about this shit. "Or, if she tells you that she feels fat or bloated, write out an exercise and diet plan for her."

Jack looked at his friend, feeling nothing but abject disgust. "Have you actually done that? To a real, live woman who didn't brain you afterward?" Still, he wrote it down because it was properly boneheaded.

Chris took a deep interest in his beer glass. "Maybe."

"Did you do it to Bridget?" Jack seriously thought about punch-

ing Chris once a week over dumping Bridget, but if he'd been sending his sweet baby sister dick pics or calling her fat, he could not be
accountable for his actions.

"No. Bridget would've taken my balls and worn them as earrings
had I called her fat."

"Did you send her a picture of your Johnson?"

His former best friend turned red from his collar to his hairline,
but Jack shook it off. He needed to shake him down for intel on how
cads treated women. He couldn't go balls-to-the-wall shithead right
away because Hannah would be wearing testicle earrings in less
than a minute. The fact that she took no bullshit was one of the
things that attracted him to her.

"I need to start with some low-grade stuff." Jack took a swig of
his beer and looked around Dooley's, the dive bar owned by Chris
and Patrick's dad, to make sure that none of the old-timers were
listening in. They were all deep in their cups by three thirty on a
Saturday afternoon, so he didn't need to worry. "Like maybe something that makes her think that I'm a little *too* interested."

"Like stalking her or some shit?" Joey always took things way
too literally. That was how he ended up in jail for a night that one
time that they didn't talk about.

"Not stalking, but maybe make her think that I'm already at
wedding bells in my head." He turned to Chris. "You know, like you
did with that first girl you dated after the second time you broke up
with Bridget—the one you took to meet Patrick without telling her
that he was your brother. She thought you were going to a Pre-Cana
class or something on your second date."

"That was definitely an unforced error." True. The girl had run
screaming and put Chris's picture up on a website that had anony-
mous reviews of dudes. The site had been taken down after a few

months because of multiple defamation claims, but it had slowed Chris's roll for a time. "But I'm not sure that Hannah is going to see you being too serious about her as a turnoff."

"What do you mean? She's the most skittish girl I've ever met. As a fellow child of divorce, she's going to see seriousness and commitment as a red flag. If I start acting like we're walking down the aisle in six months, she'll freak out—at least a little."

It wasn't until that moment that he realized how effective Hannah had been at steering their conversation toward the calm waters of the superficial—movies, food, celebrity gossip—and out of the rocky shoals of their childhoods. Maybe that's why he liked her so much. She didn't pry into his family business right away, and he hadn't been forced to confront his mommy issues on the first date.

"C'mon, Nolan." Joey motioned for another round of beers. "You're the best-looking guy out of all of us. Excepting Patrick— God rest his soul."

Chris scowled. "He's not dead."

"Might as well be." Joey and Chris had been arguing about this since Patrick had decided to enter the seminary. Despite the fact that Joey was kind of an idiot about feelings, he knew in his bones that Patrick hadn't really wanted to become a priest and had wanted to have an intervention. Chris had refused for reasons Jack still wasn't privy to.

"I don't see what my looks have to do with whether me taking Hannah wedding dress shopping on a second date is going to freak her out enough for her to break up with me—or at least think about it."

"Don't do that," Chris and Joey said simultaneously.

"Then how am I going to seem too serious?"

Chris shrugged. "Introduce her to your mother."

The air might have been sucked out of the dank bar right then.

Jack didn't like to talk about his mother, and he saw her as little as possible. Sunday brunch was a command performance, but he kept all other contact to a minimum.

Ever since she'd left and made a new life for herself—along with a fancy-pants new husband and high-society stepkids—their relationship had been about the same as his adult relationship with the Catholic Church. Even though the new husband and stepkids were no longer around, he saw her on holidays, stayed long enough for air-kisses on the cheeks, and showed up when directed to at the MCA, where she was head curator.

But he didn't tell her about his life, and he'd *never* introduced her to a woman he was seeing. If this whole thing with Hannah was really for real, he wouldn't even think about subjecting her to Molly formerly Nolan and now Simpson.

It wasn't that his mother was a bad person, but he always had the sense that she was vaguely embarrassed by him. Didn't matter that he had a master's degree in journalism from an Ivy League school or was gainfully employed in a field that had been contracting for decades. There was something vaguely blue-collar about him that he would never overcome.

That, and the fact that he was the spitting image of his dad at that age. She must see her worst mistake—getting tied down to Sean Nolan—every time she looked at him. Her disdain was unspoken, but that didn't make it any less real.

"I can't do that to Hannah."

"You gotta be all in with this or it ain't gonna work." Joey had started dropping consonants, which meant Jack was in for a South Side truth bomb. "You like this girl too much, man. And she's like every otha girl you've eva liked—too fancy and shit for you." He held his hands up. "No offense."

"She gave me the finger when we met." A weak defense of Hannah's down-to-earth nature to be sure. She'd been much more at home at the best restaurant in the United States than anyone sitting at this table would have been. "Not that fancy."

"Would you want her on your team in a back-alley knife fight?" Chris offered the ultimate test for whether a girl was tough enough. The one they'd come up with while still in grade school.

Truth was that Hannah was probably perfect for him. She was whip smart and witty in a way that none of his exes had been, they were interested in the same things, and he couldn't stop thinking about the way she tasted and smelled. She didn't suffer fools, and she'd probably withstand the back-alley knife fight of an evening with his mother with minimal bruising. He didn't want to give the right answer—that Hannah just might be the perfect combination of South Side tough and inside-the-Loop class—so he shrugged.

"Introduce her to your mother." Chris was firm on this as the next step in the plan. Even though his friend was awful with women, he was probably right.

He did have that exhibit opening that his mother had left him multiple messages about. His fingers itched to text Hannah about it right now, but he knew he had to wait until the day of to spring it on her. By the end of the evening, with his mother air-kissing and name-dropping, Hannah would probably be about twenty percent turned off, which was right where he needed her to be.

"IF THOSE SWAN-SHAPED VODKA luges do not show up on time and in good condition, I swear that I will"—Hannah listened for a hot millisecond to her ice vendor's bullshit excuses before continuing—"end your worthless life."

After a few useless excuses and her escalating threat to rip his balls off and serve them as hors d'oeuvres, he agreed to the terms of the contract she'd signed with his firm for a local professional football team's benefit the following week. She hated that everybody always wanted ice sculptures. She *despised* the things.

Hannah didn't even bother looking around to see if any of her coworkers had heard her tirade. They were used to it, as it happened at least once a week. In fact, most of her coworkers—with the glaring exception of Giselle—came to her when they had very serious issues with vendors because the vendors were all afraid of her wrath and went out of their way to placate her.

She lived by the motto that her good regard was very cheap and her anger was very expensive. It was easy for the people she worked with to earn her good regard—all they had to do was their jobs. Well, if they didn't, they paid the price and then they did their jobs. And Annalise liked having her as an employee / secret weapon. So did everyone she worked with—excepting Giselle.

Her rants were entirely mundane, part of the background noise of the office. Except today someone had heard. Noah—someone who never wanted to hear her when she was on a tear.

Although she didn't gasp when he entered the office, she sucked just enough air in to ensure that she could breathe through what was about to happen. Whatever Noah had to say to her was sure to suck all the oxygen out of her tiny—and shrinking—glass office.

"You know you catch more flies with honey."

She felt her face heat even though she snapped back, "Next time I'm trying to catch flies, I'll try that. For now, I'm doing my job."

He smiled at her, and she remembered why she'd dated him for so long even though they were woefully mismatched from the start.

That was a lie; she never forgot the cursed dimple in the side of his deep brown cheek that popped whenever she said something challenging to him.

Always with the dimple. She needed to learn to hate dimples, or they would be the death of her. She just needed to remember the why of this particular dimple: he'd always thought it was cute when she challenged him.

Her face stayed hot, but not because of how good Noah still looked in a suit. He was six feet four inches of perfectly tailored man. Not a loose string or a line out of place on his closely shaved head. He filled her office with the scent of his aftershave, and she could almost remember sinking into that smell on her sheets.

The only thing that kept her in that room and firmly out of fantasyland was the way he'd always thought she was cute. He'd always thought it was cute when she did her job well, or when she had a new idea, or when she got angry. He never took her seriously, and that had always enraged her, which he subsequently thought was *cute*.

Until he'd dismissed her.

Hannah tried not to think too much about the fact that her parents' relationship would have been illegal less than three decades before she was born. It was depressing, and it made her chest feel tight. And it reminded her that a lot of people still didn't know what to make of her.

When asked about her racial identity, she always told people that she was biracial. This tended to bother black people—it had certainly bothered Noah and his parents—because they thought that she was trying to deny or downplay her blackness. That wasn't the thing at all. It just didn't sit right with her to deny her whiteness, either. There was privilege inherent in having a white parent—an acceptance in certain white spaces that Noah didn't have. To deny that would be denying half of herself.

Hannah had the sneaking suspicion that Noah had put her in the category of Not the Kind of Girl You Marry the moment she'd told his mother that she was biracial. The woman looked as though Hannah had slapped her in the face. Before seeing Noah again, she'd regretted that. But now she felt as though she'd dodged a lifetime of pretending that half her family didn't exist for the benefit of his.

White people tended to be curious about her race and then ignore the fact that she was half-black until it became inconvenient for them. For the white guys she'd dated, it usually became inconvenient around the time that it seemed natural to date exclusively or introduce her to their parents.

So, no. She wasn't going to take herself on a walk down memory lane back to the time when he'd had his criminally lush mouth all over her skin, back to the time when she'd thought that he was the only man she'd ever be with again for the rest of her life. Or the time after he'd dropped her like last week's takeout into the trash. Because, of course, it was her fault that she hadn't been able to keep him in her bed. Because she was such a raging bitch—even though it was only in service to her coworkers, her clients, and the people she cared about.

Under Noah's strict rubric, she was not the sort of girl you married. And Noah was looking to get married.

"What are you doing here, Noah?"

"I work for Senator Chapin."

Her thoughts about the past went away, and she was happy for him. Noah had always wanted to work in DC. He'd always been miserable in advertising. And she was beginning to suspect that he'd chastised her frequently because he'd needed to spread that misery around. After their breakup, she'd erased any trace of him from her social media, but she knew through friends who wanted her not to worry about seeing him around town that he'd taken the foreign service exam and gone off to the Middle East for two years.

He must have done well in his post to score a job with the ranking member of the Foreign Relations Committee in the Senate. And it meant he was here on business—probably to fire her—instead of out of some desire to see her again and apologize for destroying her self-esteem.

"I see."

"I'm his press secretary." Again, she couldn't help but be impressed. He'd found a way to join up his skill with spin and his interest in the wider world. "And I'm concerned that if you're planning the wedding, it could cause the senator embarrassment."

There it was. She was gauche and embarrassing because she'd declined her acceptance at law school and decided to do something fun with her life. He thought she was trashy because of the job she did and the way she did it—and because of who she was.

Before she could stop herself, she was standing and leaning across her desk. "I understand that a political wedding is a different kind of thing than the first-string quarterback's booze cruise."

"I know you do, and that was why I was surprised to hear about you planning Madison's wedding." The way he said the senator's daughter's name made her suspicious. It sounded almost—wistful. "You're smart enough to know where your talent lies, and it isn't with marriage."

Screw him.

Instead of contradicting him, which would just lead to his explaining her and her talents to her, she forced a one-sided grin and said, "I'm working with Sasha on the event." A look of mild relief crossed his face; he'd always liked Sasha. He'd once asked her how she and Sasha could possibly be friends because they were such opposites—herself being the opposite of good-girl, quiet-girl Sasha. But she wanted to probe the way he said Madison's name. She hadn't known him for almost a decade for nothing. If he tripped over a word, it meant something. "And Madison has somewhat eclectic tastes, so I'm on as a sort of consultant." She skipped the part about how planning the engagement party was just a trial run for the wedding. He didn't need to know that. And the slightly ashen tone his face had taken when she'd said "Madison" was sort of delightful.

She'd always liked Noah best when he was back on his heels. Right in that moment, she was almost tempted to mention Jack, the fact that she had a man in her life who seemed to like her for her, but something stopped her. She didn't want to share about Jack, because it was temporary—not something that was real and solid. It was just some faux relationship for the benefit of her career.

So she didn't mention Jack because he wasn't worth mentioning. She was dating him for a job, and she would go out with him for two weeks. As much as it would feel good to see Noah jealous of what Jack temporarily had, she would keep her mouth shut. Maybe she'd matured since their breakup and during her period of self-enforced singledom after all.

"This is important for me." Noah was emphatic, but he wasn't making any sense. Senator Chapin's daughter's wedding shouldn't really be any of his business. She was getting married, not announcing any policy initiatives.

But Hannah didn't have time to dwell on that cryptic statement, because Sasha walked into her office after a wide-eyed rubberneck past the glass wall. Ever the professional, she schooled her face before Noah turned to greet her. "Such a surprise, Noah."

"Noah works for Senator Chapin, and he came here to make sure we don't have strippers at Madison's wedding." Noah flinched at the woman's name. Something was definitely up.

By the time Sasha had assured Noah that they weren't going to humiliate the senator with a wedding theme of nudism, Jack had texted her. Her hopefully sly glance at the screen determined that he'd asked her to an event at the Museum of Contemporary Art—fancy.

Maybe they were turning into a thing after all.

CHAPTER ELEVEN

THE MUSEUM OF CONTEMPORARY Art was chock-full of people for the opening of a new exhibit. Hannah was excited to be there because she'd formed a friendship with the artist due to an unfortunate and serendipitous incident a few years ago during which they'd shared a holding cell after being arrested on charges of public indecency.

Not her proudest moment, but there had been a minor miscommunication between the artist and the gallery owner regarding the content of the show. Artemesia "Artie" Valencia was known for throwing her paint-slathered naked body up against canvases. The fateful night when Hannah had gone from planning her first party for a major gallery to wearing handcuffs—and not in a fun way—she'd made the erroneous assumption that the gallery owner would be excited for the artist to create a canvas live.

She hadn't known that the very conservative gallery owner's assistant had planned the show as revenge directly before she quit by going outside to move her car and never coming back.

Artie had been naked and covered in black and pink paint in front of an audience of mildly liquored-up patrons when the cops showed up to arrest her. And then Hannah had ended up spending a night in jail for "resisting arrest," which was total bullshit. She had just enough white privilege and Artie had enough charm that things didn't turn too ugly. And the desk sergeant had actually cowered in fear when Annalise's lawyer husband showed up to bail them out. For her part, Annalise had laughed it off and said that it would make both Hannah's and Artie's careers.

Since then, Artie had moved on to the big leagues, a solo show at one of the country's greatest museums. But Hannah was still waiting for her shot.

Hannah had met Jack at the bottom of the steps to the entrance of the museum, since they'd both had to work that day. Though he'd been enthusiastic about asking her for the date, he seemed a lot more aloof that night. She hadn't even detected a dimple through his stubble when he'd smiled at her. And the mischief in his twinkling eyes, the ones she'd been thinking about all sex-glazed since their first date, was completely banked.

Part of her wanted to find out what the hell his deal was. She'd hated this hot-and-cold bullshit when Noah had done it. To be honest, it had turned her into an insecure mess and probably contributed to his dumping her. She was determined not to be that girl with Jack, even if she had to white-knuckle it for two weeks before letting it rip and revealing her crazy.

The guy she was *dating to get a promotion* led her through the crowds with a purpose. They moved so quickly that she didn't even get a chance to pause and check out the exhibit. Or get a glass of champagne. He'd seemed distracted when he'd met her at the entrance, kind of sweaty and twitchy. When she'd asked him what was wrong, he'd gotten all stiff—and not in the fun way.

Other than the inherent awkwardness of being on a second date and trying to impress Jack, this was kind of her element—shaking hands, talking to rich people, and making them feel important. She was never so pushy that she slipped them a card. If she made just enough of an impression, they would find her.

For his part, Jack stayed close. To anyone who looked, it would be clear that they were together-together. Somehow, this felt even less casual than their overly fancy first date had been. Maybe she was imagining the tight, possessive grip of his palm against her waist or the way he seemed to pull her closer whenever she introduced him to any of her friends or acquaintances. But instead of a date, she was starting to feel like a safety blanket.

Regardless, she couldn't think about this with the noise echoing off the white walls and the museum patrons milling around. That night, there were cater waiters circulating with champagne and hors d'oeuvres.

Hannah grabbed a flute of bubbly off one passing waiter's tray and some sort of crispy meat pie off of another. The moment she did it, it dawned on her that she should have probably waited for Jack to get her a champagne, or at least asked him if he wanted anything. That would have been the ladylike thing girlfriend material would do.

She'd shoved half the canapé in her mouth when she said, "Oops," compounding her lapse in manners. Jesus, you really couldn't take her anywhere. Maybe this was because she was always behind the scenes, shoving leftovers in her face at the end of the night before collapsing in bed and doing it all over again the next day.

Instead of the disapproving look she'd probably have gotten from Noah, Jack gave her the first genuine smile he'd flashed the whole night. And then he got his own drink. "No problem."

They tapped their glasses together.

"You're sure you're okay?" She'd gotten used to his easy smiles and wanted more of them. Not because she actually cared but because she needed to convince Annalise that he was in love with her. It would help for him to look happy.

"Not really." She could feel the flush of embarrassment filling her face until he deflated it with "Not because of you."

Why was he acting so weird? "Tough day at work?"

If it was just his job, maybe she could take his mind off things. He leaned in as though there were spies all over the room listening in. "Terrible."

She took a gulp of champagne. "We're going to need more of this, then."

That earned her another smirk, with a wink this time. "I'll go run some down at the bar."

She wanted to ask him what was wrong, but she didn't want to pry. She was pretending to be his girlfriend, not his therapist. For all she knew, he didn't like parties.

She never had before. She'd started planning parties as a way to ameliorate her social anxiety in college. She'd always figured that if she was in charge of the food, the drinks, the invite list, the décor, and the music, she would always be invited to the party instead of sitting at home, eating pints of ice cream and wondering why nobody invited her out.

She'd gotten so good at it that several of the residence halls had hired her to plan dances and social events. Although she hadn't realized that it was her calling until a few years later, she'd been grateful for the cover of being a planner instead of a guest.

Her social anxiety had faded away, and now everyone wanted to be at an event that she planned, and she didn't stay in eating ice cream unless she wanted to.

Bonus, at parties she planned, she was usually too busy for anyone to pin her in a corner to talk about the weather.

Instead of risking eye contact with anyone and falling into a small-talk trap, she looked at the art. Artemesia had grown as an artist in the past few years and gotten a lot of publicity with all the arrests. From the looks of her new works, displayed next to the great American women painters of the twentieth century, she'd matured quite a bit in her subject matter.

Hannah was lost in one particularly phallic representation of an herb garden when slim arms wrapped around her waist from behind. She stiffened because it definitely wasn't Jack, not that she was looking for PDA from him anyway.

As soon as she heard the husky Italian accent—*"Bella"*—she relaxed and turned, hugging her erstwhile cellmate.

"Artie!"

"I did not know you were coming; otherwise I would have put you on a VIP list." When Artie talked, she did so with her whole body—she did everything with her whole being. She floated from project to project, continent to continent, lover to lover, as though she knew that everything would turn out in her favor at all times.

Hannah admired that about her. She could never live like that herself—planning was too much a part of her DNA—but she could admire it in her artistic friend.

"I'm here with a guy."

Artie wrapped her bony fingers around Hannah's upper arms and shook her, taking in the very low-cut dress she wore. "You. Look. Gorgeous." A shake for every word. "Of course you are here with a man."

Compliments had always made Hannah feel uncomfortable. There was a distinct difference between knowing intellectually that she was attractive and really feeling like it was the truth.

Growing up an ugly duckling with frizzy hair and darker skin than any of her classmates in suburban Minneapolis hadn't been the best way to feel like a great beauty. The bullying she'd endured from a few vicious classmates had been enough to make her wary of a compliment. A "Your hair is so curly!" could easily turn into "Have you ever thought about straightening it?" And that was just a hairsbreadth away from "You look like a mangy lion" and everyone roaring at said curly-haired adolescent in the hallway. For a year.

So, yeah, Hannah deflected compliments like a damned ninja.

Artie knew all of this because they'd gotten into superdeep childhood shit during their brief incarceration. "Just say *grazie, bella*."

Determined to steer the conversation into a lighter place, Hannah curtsied to her friend. *"Grazie."*

Her friend was gracious enough to laugh. "Who are you here with?"

Even though the room was chock-full of people, Jack stood out like a beacon. He was just leaning on the bar but looking deeply fine in a pair of wool pants that looked they had been blessed in a previous life to be spending their time perfectly tailored to just such an ass and a white shirt that draped his broad shoulders like a blessing.

ANDIE J. CHRISTOPHER

She couldn't keep a sigh in, and she knew Artie would notice that she was bordering on moony-eyed over this guy. And, since the artist was utterly lacking in subtlety, she pointed at him with glee. "That one? He is very good-looking, so good-looking he must be stupid, no?"

Hannah sort of wished that Jack was stupid. She'd feel less bad about tricking him into liking her. "He's not. He's a journalist for *Haberdasher's Monthly.* Funny, too."

"So, a very dangerous man, then?" Though it was phrased as a question, her friend meant it as a statement.

As they watched Jack wait for their drinks, a woman approached him. She wore a black tunic over black pants and had thick, black-framed glasses. She was tall—almost as tall as Hannah. Her gray hair was brushed into a gleaming chin-length bob. She smiled at Artie as though she knew her.

The woman intercepted Jack as he made his way back to Hannah. She put her hand on his upper arm and Hannah couldn't help but notice that he stiffened for a moment before seeming to will himself into relaxation.

That was when it clicked into place. She had the same face shape as Jack. And the adoring look of someone who'd changed the diapers of the grown man next to her. There was only one person she could be—Jack's mother.

"Does he have a taste for much older women?" Artie joked. "That's Molly Simpson. She's the curator of the *Twentieth-Century Women's Collection*, and she is utterly terrifying. I love her."

"She must be Jack's mother," Hannah said with dawning horror. Suddenly, the low-cut dress designed to drive Jack out of his ever-loving mind didn't seem like the best idea. She couldn't believe that he'd sprung this on her.

Who did that?

She didn't do the whole meet-the-parents thing. Not anymore. She'd met Noah's parents by accident. They'd dropped by one morning before he'd had a chance to shuffle her out so that he could walk past the church he told his parents that he attended just to check in on social media before heading to a buddy's house to watch the Bears game. His Sunday routine.

Needless to say, his parents had not been impressed by her—full-on bedhead and wearing one of Noah's shirts. Hannah was pretty sure that his mother's pursed lips would haunt her nightmares for years to come.

Meeting Jack's mother was even worse because he'd knowingly sprung this on her. He'd arranged it and everything. When he'd texted, about seventy-one hours after their first date, just as she was about to go out to a bar and pick up another guy as insurance, he'd known that he was going to do this to her. And he hadn't said a damned word.

Hannah's palms were sweating and she rubbed them on her thighs. She forced herself to stop biting her bottom lip so she wouldn't wear her scarlet lipstick off.

She thought she was going to throw up champagne and a mini beef empanada all over this nice woman's outfit. This is why "meeting the parents" didn't happen on the second date.

By the time she'd had enough opportunity to freak out, Jack and his mother were almost in front of her. Thankfully, he was carrying two drinks over to them, wearing a strained smile. Hannah tried to keep her attention on her date but didn't miss the way that Jack's mother examined her as though she was a possible acquisition for an exhibit of women not good enough to date her son. By the time Jack made the introductions, Hannah had it clear in her head that Jack's mother's approval would be crucial in making this fake relationship last long enough for her to secure a promotion.

The realization that Jack was putting her through some sort of test washed over her, and she felt as though someone was sticking pins and needles under her fingernails. She girded her loins for the kind of unpleasantness she'd suffered at the hands of Noah's parents that first and only time they'd met.

To her surprise, there was none of it. After keeping her in suspense, Molly offered her a smile that seemed genuine. Even more so when Artie began regaling Jack's mother with the tale of their night in the slammer. Although her heart had lodged somewhere in the vicinity of her throat when her friend had started telling the story and she might have punctured the skin in Artie's forearm once she got to the part about living-nude sushi trays, Hannah's dread vanished the second or third time Molly laughed.

By contrast, Jack's tension ratcheted up every time his mother laughed. Hannah reacted by instinct and took his hand in hers, offering it a squeeze. The heat from his palm radiated through her body, never letting her forget the connection they shared. Their gazes met, and a spark of electricity arced between the two of them.

This was going to be fine. It was a jerk move, but maybe he hadn't meant anything by it. Or maybe he was already so into her that he was *ready* to introduce her to his mother.

It was just her luck that the only guy she'd met in years whom she could actually see herself falling in love with was the one guy whose heart she was going to have to break.

Because after this was all over, and he found out that she'd been lying to him, there was no way he'd still want to be with her.

IF HIS BROTHER, MICHAEL, were here, he would have been making lots of derisive snorts. He'd never played along with their mother's shift from their neighborhood, which boasted a dive bar and a church on every block, to what Chicago thought of as "high society."

The change had made Jack twitchy at first, but he'd gotten used to it. Maybe too used to it. Not as twitchy as it was making him that his mother seemed to adore Hannah.

"Did you always want to be an event planner, Hannah?" Jack's mother's question bit into his gut and twisted things up. He hated that, even though she was clearly impressed, she was still interrogating Hannah. As though she would know what kind of woman would be best for him. She didn't even know him.

This was all a huge mistake. Hannah didn't even look pissed off. She answered his mother's question and then complimented her on the event. His mother actually preened.

Sometimes, he had no clue how his parents had actually stayed together long enough to have three kids. They couldn't be more dissimilar.

Sean Nolan was a man of few words and a single routine that he followed without fail. Even though it had thrown all of their lives into chaos when she'd left, Jack could understand how his mother must have felt as though she was dying a slow death eating the same meals on the same day of the week. Every week for years on end. Going to the same church service with the same priest; playing cards over beers with the same friends.

Jack remembered the first time his mother had brought him to a museum. She'd passed baby Bridget off to one of their church friends and Michael was off riding his bike with some of his buddies. So it had been just the two of them walking up the stairs of the Art Institute, past the lions and into the echoing halls. Halls filled with art from across the known world.

Before that day, he hadn't known that his mother could truly be excited about anything. She certainly never spoke with hushed tones of wonder about any of the new meat loaf recipes she'd tried and his father had rejected. That day, Jack realized that his mother had an inner life of her very own, separate from what he and his siblings and her husband had access to. Although he could never have predicted that his mother would leave them a few years later, first to move to New York for school and then to return to Chicago with a new husband and stepkids who seemed to fit her a whole lot better than her own kids, he had kind of understood it.

But watching his mother chat with Hannah, liking her more and more and getting her to reveal things that Jack didn't know about her, made him realize that he always chose women who were a little unknowable to him. He always tried to figure out what would make them stay, but he was never very successful at it.

"I sort of fell into it, actually." Hannah's voice didn't have the high, nervous quality it had had when they'd walked in that night. He wasn't sure if it was his mother's warmth toward her or the champagne that had loosened her up, but this ploy—the one to get Hannah to think he was doing too much too soon—wasn't having the intended effect. "I just realized I had a natural talent for being at the center of mayhem, I guess."

One of the many things Jack hadn't realized about Hannah was that—like his mother—she was friends with famous artists. The only artist being featured in this exhibit who wasn't too infirm or too dead to show up to the show was hanging off of Hannah's shoulder.

Something about the similarities between his mother and Hannah crawled inside him and pulled out some things that he didn't want to feel. Hannah laughed at something his mother said, and he was transformed into a teen boy again—and not just because her laugh gave him an inappropriate hard-on. Just seeing them together made him acutely aware that Hannah was not someone he should depend on to stay in his life. She would leave, and she wasn't going to be his person.

In a way, it made what he had to do next—sabotage this date—much easier. He'd hoped that introducing Hannah to his mother would do the trick, and that, while he was dropping her off, she would grab on to his upper arm and tell him that "things are moving too fast" and she "hoped that we can stay friends."

He'd much rather have to convince her that he could take things slower and that she should give him another chance than have her and his mother become besties.

She might still think this was too much, but it seemed less likely now that Hannah had formed some sort of witchy triumvirate with his mother and Artemesia Valencia. Every time one of them made a joke and the other two cackled, Jack felt as though his balls were in a vise. His mother had never liked any of his real girlfriends, but she liked the one girl he was actually trying to get rid of? The irony made his stomach hurt.

Introducing Hannah to his mother on the second date was an abject failure. And he was almost five days into the two weeks allotted for completing his article. So far, he'd given her a mind-blowing dinner—and his best oral sex performance—and made his mother fall in love with her. He was as bad at losing a girl—during the first few weeks of a romance—as Chris and Joey were at keeping a lady interested. But they were also quitters, unlike him. He would turn himself into a human red flag tonight, come hell or high water.

So, he'd have to move on to Plan B, who was currently circulating among guests and pouring champagne. He caught her eye and winked. After hesitating for a moment to fight his instinct to tell Hannah he'd be right back, he walked toward Plan B.

ARTIE GRABBED THE FAT on the back of Hannah's arm and squeezed. That was just plain rude. "What?"

"Your man." She nodded toward their left. "He is flirting with another woman."

"He's not my man." Hannah's gaze followed her friend's. Sure enough, Jack was holding a drink and close-talking a waitress. "He's probably just being friendly."

They watched for a few moments, and the server threw her head back in a fit of audacious laughter and put her hand inside his jacket as though she was about to stroke his left moob.

Hannah gasped, and a spark of anger made the champagne turn over in her stomach. She was the only one who currently got to grab either of his moobs, and that was the way it would stay for the next two weeks.

Artie made a little grunt that conveyed her lack of approval. Hannah wanted to do a whole lot more—like run over there and bust her empty champagne flute over that woman's head. She'd always prided herself on not being the jealous type—it wasn't very enlightened—but something about Jack made her want to bust a cap in the ass of any woman who touched him like that. This wasn't even rational. Jack wasn't her real boyfriend, and she wouldn't have the right to get jealous over him, even if he was. This was a second date.

She was in the midst of chanting *This is fake. This is fake. This is all fake*, in her head when Jack's mother noticed that they were no longer paying attention to her story about the sculptor she'd slept with while doing her thesis project in Spain. She looked over her shoulder to where Jack was *still letting that woman touch him* and snorted.

"You don't have to worry about her."

"I'm not worried." Hannah's attention snapped back to Molly. "Who's worried?"

Molly motioned toward Hannah's face with one slim finger. "You're bright red, dear."

Shit. "We've only just started dating." Molly raised one brow, and Artie started looking for more drinks or for people with less family drama to talk to. "He can do whatever he wants."

Jack's mom shrugged. "My point is that there's no point in being angry—"

"Can we just pretend we never saw this?" Hannah asked. "Can we maybe pretend that this portion of the conversation never happened?"

"I'm not going to tell him anything, Hannah." Molly held up one hand, and Artie—godsend that she was—replaced her empty champagne with a full one. "My point is that you don't have to be angry, because she's not into Jack."

"How do you know that?" Any woman who was stroking Jack underneath his clothes, in a public place, while she was working, was into him. "It certainly looks—"

"Oh, for Christ's sake." Molly shook her head and finished her drink in one gulp. "That's Darcy McGinnis; she grew up on our block. She also came out years ago. They dated in kindergarten, but then it was most definitely over."

"Well, what's going on, then?"

"My son is being a man—an idiot man."

"Aah." Apparently, Artie knew what was going on, but Hannah was still woefully in the dark.

"What the heck is going on?" Hannah had been *this close* to avoiding cursing in front of Jack's mother until now.

"He's trying to make you jealous."

Hannah was about to argue, but she guessed that was the only thing that made sense. Except it didn't make sense at all. Why would Jack be trying to make her jealous on their second date?

"Why would he do that?" she asked, not necessarily expecting an answer.

"He's a man." Artie had turned into a parrot of Molly, and nothing was any clearer. She looked down at her half-full glass, wondering if maybe she'd had too much champagne. But too much champagne wasn't actually a thing in her world.

"You have to nip this in"—Artie appeared to search for words—"the bud." She was getting much better at her American idioms.

"I'm not going to say anything about it." What *could* she say about it? If Jack were any other guy, she'd shrug it off and move the hell on. Alone.

But if she even mentioned his talking to another woman, he would think she was absolutely nuts. They were on a second date. They weren't exclusive, and she hadn't even given him an orgasm yet. She had no right to be jealous, even if he was trying to elicit some sort of response from her.

She wouldn't give him the satisfaction of saying anything. It was too bad that he'd ruined the evening.

Unexpectedly, she'd liked meeting his mother. She enjoyed feeling like she could fit with people in Jack's family. Molly was lovely, and her first thought on meeting her was that she was the explanation for why Jack was such a lovely man. She was elegant and feminist and crazy-funny.

But she couldn't do that. She would have to grin and bear any stupid man behavior that he dished out for the next eleven days.

CHAPTER TWELVE

SEAN NOLAN DIDN'T RAISE children who gave up. The worst thing one of them could do as a kid was to show up after failing at something without a plan of action for starting over again. It was just about the only thing that could get Jack grounded as a teenager. If he wasn't going to win, he had to try his best.

Jack struggled not to let down the Nolan family name as he sat at his desk staring at a blank page, wondering what to write about his night at the museum. Because he had thousands of words to go, he was glad that Hannah hadn't broken things off after he'd flirted with Darcy for a good hour. But the fact that she hadn't even mentioned his outrageously uncomfortable tête-à-tête with Darcy at the museum on the way home irked him. He thought for sure that Hannah was the kind of woman who would call him out for flirting with someone else in front of her, but for the whole ride to her place she hadn't said a word about that or how strange it was to introduce her to his mother on a second date.

He'd even wondered if she hadn't seen him flirting. But she'd seemed smug, and dammit if that didn't make him want her.

But she hadn't invited him up to her place. She'd just kissed him on the cheek and smiled at him, spitting back his line about an early-morning meeting with a new client that she had to rest up for.

He felt as though he'd called in a favor from Darcy for absolutely nothing. Although they'd been friends since shortly after Darcy had punched him out on the first day of kindergarten because he'd asked her to be his girlfriend, he didn't really love asking his lesbian childhood friend to feel him up in public.

Darcy was cool about it, though. In fact, her laughing at him made it all the more believable.

Fat lot of good that did him. Although he didn't want Hannah to break up with him yet, he at least expected her to say something. In fact, he had to come up with another date pronto so that he could make this poor woman think that all men were scum even more than she already did. That had to be the explanation for why she'd taken his flirting with Darcy in stride—she expected that kind of behavior from all men.

But he was someone who prided himself on being the good guy, and that pissed him off. Even more than Hannah's instant connection with his mother had the night before.

The thought occurred to him that Hannah might ghost him, that there was no early-morning meeting and that she was just trying to let him down easy. Besides the problems that would cause for him in finishing the story—he'd have to start from scratch—he didn't want last night to be the last time he saw Hannah.

Even though he was wary of any woman who hit it off with his cold, standoffish mother and what that might mean about his Oedipal issues, he really liked Hannah and still wanted to see where things could go between the two of them after this farcical story got over with.

All of his jumbled thoughts and contradictory emotions weren't going to help him figure out what kinds of words he should put on the page *right now*, though.

Maybe he'd start with the premise that an eighteen-course tasting menu was a better way to get and keep a woman interested than introducing a woman to one's mother and flirting with another woman in front of her. It was common sense, but apparently at least the men in Hannah's experience lacked that in spades.

If men had common sense, there would be no way he would have had the opportunity to touch Hannah, kiss her, and see her go all soft and vulnerable under his touch. If men had common sense, there was no way a girl like Hannah Mayfield would still be on the market. There would be no way he would still have a chance with her.

So he got down to writing about why he didn't stand a chance with her anyway.

LATER THAT AFTERNOON, JACK walked into a darkened bar looking for his uncle—but not really his uncle—Lou. Lou Bernardi was one of Sean Nolan's oldest friends, and that wasn't just because Lou was the guy to get building permits from at city hall, though that was part of it. Uncle Lou had won over the Nolan kids because he always had the best candy in his office.

Even that day, Uncle Lou passed Jack a Little Debbie snack with his beer. "Not necessary, but thanks."

"Your dad said you want to know about Senator Chapin and the new federal building." Aside from the candy, the other good thing about Uncle Lou was that he was always right to the point.

"Yeah, as you know, earmarks are illegal—"

"Bribes are illegal, too. But those are barely news anymore." Lou took a swig of his pilsner. "This is beyond the pale, though. I've never seen anyone with the nerve—not since that filthy mobster who threatened to fit me with cement shoes."

Jack knew that this was going to take forever and a day if he let Uncle Lou start in on the stories, so he said, "Do you have any documents?"

"Yeah, I'll have them after one or two more beers." Lou smirked at him. "It's not a bribe—it's two old friends catching up."

Jack tipped his beer toward Lou and started the voice recorder on his phone.

CHAPTER THIRTEEN

"IT WAS BAFFLING," HANNAH said. "I have no idea where the confident, charming dude who ate me out like he'd been training for it went."

"Shhhh." Sasha placed her finger over her mouth.

Hannah was still Catholic enough to know that talking about cunnilingus in a church sanctuary was a ticket straight to hell, so she whispered, "It's like someone drained all that big-dick energy he had going on."

Sasha just looked at her with her big, rounded eyes—her expression a prayer that a new best friend, one without a filthy trash mouth, would suddenly appear at her side.

"They can't hear us." They were sitting at the back of Fourth Presbyterian Church, waiting for the senator's daughter and her fiancé—some finance bro—to finish talking with the pastor. They'd all met over coffee at five minutes past dawn this morning because they had a big day of venue visits to get through.

As soon as Madison pushed a hot-pink binder across the table toward them, Hannah knew that she'd made a grave error trying to start planning weddings. With her events—especially the sports ones—she had almost full creative control. No one had been planning their Hall of Fame induction party since they were four. As long as plenty of high-end booze was involved, she could do pretty much whatever she wanted.

But weddings were different, and hearing Sasha talk to Madison about hers—Hannah mostly listened—she felt a pang in her chest about her own long-suppressed desire to get married. When she and Noah had dated, she'd dreamed of getting married in the old church in downtown Minneapolis where her great-grandmother had gone to Mass every Sunday until she'd gone into the hospital two weeks before her death.

That had been a pipe dream. Not just because Noah had later clarified, in great detail, the reasons why he would never marry her and why she would have a hard time finding anyone willing to take her on, but because he hadn't even been Catholic.

Jack is Catholic.

Jesus Christ, her mind was a traitor. She shook her head to purge it of the idea that she and Jack were headed for anything but an awkward head nod on the train platform about a year from now after they'd been broken up for fifty and a half weeks.

A tap on her shoulder interrupted her disturbing thoughts, and the sight that assaulted her was even more worrisome than her musings about possible marriage to Jack Nolan—none other than Noah sliding into the pew behind them.

Sasha gasped, and Hannah bit out, "What the hell are you doing here?" She'd entirely forgotten how to whisper, and her voice echoed off the walls and vaulted ceilings. Madison looked back, and Hannah somehow gathered herself to smile as though the ground hadn't just crumbled beneath her.

Noah's white teeth flashed against his dark skin as he released a muted chuckle that made her feel small. Whenever she'd had an idea or shared a dream with him, she got the muted chuckle. It had become her nemesis over the year or so that they were together, and she'd heard it in her own head since they'd broken up.

Every time she tried to step out of her comfort zone, there, over her shoulder, was the muted chuckle, laced with the sentiment that she was *cute* and ought to be patted on her head and sent on her way, soaked in the feeling that she wasn't smart enough or good enough or strong enough to be taken seriously.

Except now it was real—her ex-boyfriend, as though all of her most painful insecurities were made manifest, sitting behind her in a church, just as she was trying something new.

He'd always had a sixth sense for people he should hitch his wagon to, and he was here to make sure his wagon train was still on time. Noah liked to have all of his ducks in a row before he made any move, and he was afraid that Hannah was going to kick some ducks out of their place. It was the source of all the tension between them.

She felt it now.

Before Jack, she would have been pulled in again by him. He hadn't just been blessed with stellar looks—like a young Idris Elba—he could make anyone feel like the most important person in the world. His shrewdness had been the bulk of his charm.

When they'd first started dating, she had thought it meant something that he'd chosen to be with her. The fact that this man, who knew everyone who was anyone in this town, thought that spending time with her was worthwhile had made her feel like she was worthwhile.

"You look good." The way his gaze raked over her belied the

compliment. Hannah rather liked the black-and-white mixed-media wrap dress she'd thrown on today. It was easy and fun, and she'd felt sexy but professional when she'd put it on. But Noah's disapproving tone and look came from the fact that it was from a fast-casual brand. In contrast to his suit, which he'd likely had custom made.

It draped over his body like a lover—like she'd once draped herself all over him. She interrupted her own inventory of his tweedy yet modern-looking sexiness and met his gaze. She knew that he knew that every atom of her being remembered the attraction that she'd always had to him. Even though he'd always behaved as though their chemistry was inconvenient for him. The fact that he wanted her despite the fact that her family wasn't good enough, her language was crass, and she didn't have the capacity to sprinkle the kind of bullshit that was his area of expertise had tortured him.

A slim sense of satisfaction slithered through her veins that a spark in his eye said that it still tortured him now.

That sense was shattered when he said, "You still think that it's a good idea to do this wedding?"

"Yes. Especially now that I know how much it bothers you."

Sasha had stayed silent, as though if she wasn't careful her words could detonate the highly delicate Mexican standoff in the back of the church, until she said, "I need Hannah's help on this one. She is the best at high-profile events."

Hannah sent her friend a telepathic high five. Although Sasha could be frustratingly naïve when it came to dating apps, she was intensely and unfailingly loyal. Once they'd broken up, and it had wrecked her self-confidence, he'd died in Sasha's view. And that was why Sasha was the kind of friend Hannah would call if she ever needed to bury a body. They might look like complete opposites from the outside, but they shared a burning devotion to their friends.

Hannah could trust Sasha with anything because they'd been through so many things.

Her best friend's metaphorical sword at her back was the only thing keeping Hannah in that church. Every bit of work she'd done over the past two years to make sure she would never be destroyed by a man again, every brick in the wall she'd built around her heart, was going to topple to the ground. The mortar had disintegrated; she could feel the stones teeter and start to give way under Noah's appraisal.

This was why letting Jack in had been so risky. At the time, it had felt like a calculated risk, but now she knew it was simply foolhardy to believe that she could open herself up just a little bit. She'd been lying to herself when she'd thought she could walk away from Jack and feel nothing.

Other than the flirting-with-another-girl thing, he'd been so wonderful that she'd forgotten how bad she'd felt when Noah had flipped the switch. Seeing him now, smelling his familiar cologne and all the memories that clean, manly scent evoked, reminded her that she couldn't fall too deeply with Jack.

"I trust that you're not going to make this more difficult, Noah." Hannah thought it was best to put a professional boundary between them. He wouldn't mess up his job just to screw with hers, of that Hannah was certain.

Yet his mouth flattened at her cold declaration of armistice. "I won't."

"This is important to me, and I won't stand for you making it more difficult," she said, wanting to make herself perfectly clear.

"I'm not going to do anything to hurt you." The *anymore* remained unspoken.

They looked at each other for a long beat. And now that she

wasn't shocked at seeing him again, she realized that she didn't really feel anything for him anymore. She used to have to catch her breath whenever he walked into a room. Now there was only an echo. When the surprise washed away, just the memories remained. And they didn't move her the way she would expect them to.

Hannah turned around to see the happy couple walking back into the sanctuary, but not soon enough to miss the look of pure longing fall over Noah's face like a veil when he set his gaze on Madison.

Noah had never looked at her that way, and she wasn't sure how to feel about it. She didn't want him to look at her that way, but she couldn't help but worry that Noah wasn't going to be able to keep his promise not to interfere with this wedding, even if he had no intention of muddying up her life.

CHAPTER FOURTEEN

AS HANNAH SMILED AT Jack's doorman, she recalled the words of a song by Meat Loaf that was nebulously about what the long-haired singer would do for love. Her mom had liked to play it as they drove up the interstate to the family lake cabin. And then they used to talk about what they would individually be willing to do for love.

I would do anything for you, sweetie.

What about for Dad?

For him, I might *slow down if he ran in front of the car right now.*

Her parents had had a seriously acrimonious divorce, after which Hannah hadn't seen much of her father. He'd decided that he would rather avoid his child support obligations than spend time with her. The last time she'd seen him had been at her college graduation, where he'd lectured her about her choice in career. He thought she should have gone to law school instead of going straight to work.

When he'd died three years ago, he still thought her career was just a little break from school. And the last e-mail exchange they'd had was all about how she wasn't living up to the family name but how Noah sounded like her first good choice in years.

Two of the most important men in her life had been just alike, and they'd been equally disappointed in her.

Anyhow, that song was on her mind while she was trying to sweet-talk Jack's doorman into letting her up. She really should have called in Sasha for this. Sasha was great at flirting, and she would have been upstairs and back down—mission accomplished—by now. Hannah, on the other hand, had never been adept at flirting to get what she wanted. In fact, during college she'd had one grocery store clerk ask her if she was having a seizure when she'd batted her lashes in hopes of getting him to take an expired coupon—without which she wouldn't have been able to afford an additional bag of cheese puffs.

This was going better than that, but not by much.

"You're not on the list." The older, stocky man crossed his arms resolutely.

"Listen." She looked down at the name tag on his chest. "Earl, I know I'm not on the list, but I've been here before, and I promise that Mr. Nolan won't be mad about what I'm doing in his apartment."

Her strategy was to delight and surprise Jack with something she knew he would like. He was a hockey fan, and she had a client whom she would call a friend in the front office of the local hockey team— the unlikely one that had won the championship the previous year. It was early in the season, but the tickets were at center ice.

If Jack wasn't already halfway into falling in love with her— introducing her to his mother and attempting to make her jealous— he would be all the way there once he saw the tickets, or the ticket, since she wasn't above forcing him to attend the game with her.

"Please." Her flirting might not be very good, but her begging had always been on point. She'd never been too proud to beg— another one of her mother's favorite tunes.

She could see him softening. "You're not going to do something freaky, like pee on the bed?"

"Has that actually happened?" she said, trying to contain her laughter. "To Jack?"

"Nah, Jack hangs around nice girls." He looked her up and down, the implication being that Hannah didn't look like a nice girl and wasn't Jack's usual type. This should not have come as news to her, as she didn't seem to be anyone's usual type. But, by some miracle, the paragon of manliness sans toxic masculinity that was Jack seemed to be into her right when she needed a guy to be seriously into her. And she desperately needed to clinch it.

"I just need to leave something for him." Earl softened further. One corner of his mouth tipped up, and he actually smiled at her. Though his arms stayed crossed. "Something he'll really like."

"Your panties." *Gross.* She didn't even want to know if that had happened before.

Of course he would think that, and Hannah barely—barely— kept herself from rolling her eyes. Maybe she wasn't so terrible at flirting to get her way after all. Earl was thinking about her panties. That was something. "Unfortunately, no. But I think he'll like these even more than my panties."

Earl gave her an incredulous look. "You can leave whatever it is with me."

That wasn't a terrible idea. Now that she thought about it, it was even better than sneaking into his apartment to leave the ticket. That might make her seem like a crazy stalker type. Leaving the ticket with Earl had the benefit of showing that she was willing to go out of her way for him but that she didn't want to sneak into his apartment and rifle through his stuff.

NOT THE GIRL YOU MARRY

It was actually quite brilliant.

"Deal." Then she winked at Earl for good measure, much more confident in her ability to flirt for persuasion than she had been before. At least he didn't ask her if she needed medical attention.

HANNAH STRUGGLED NOT TO roll her eyes when she caught a glimpse of herself in the glass doors of the hockey arena. She wore painted-on jeans and a jersey so tight her nipples were likely to bust through at the first hint of a breeze off the ice.

"The same reasoning from the seminal film *Clueless* stands today," Sasha had said. "You want to make him think as much of sex as possible, but not give him the sex, so that he has to keep calling you if he thinks he can get to the sex. And to get him to think of sex, you need to be as close to naked as possible."

"Why wouldn't he just get on an app and swipe?" Hannah had asked.

"You have to give yourself more credit." Her best friend appeared to get a little bit exasperated with her. "He has a taste—like, literally—for you. But he hasn't dipped his wick yet. As long as you make him wait, he's not going to be on the hunt for anyone but you."

Hannah thought the whole thing was entirely too complicated, which was one of the main reasons she'd opted out of dating after Noah and the subsequent false starts. One of the things she'd liked about Jack was that he seemed unpretentious, and he wore his emotions on his face. All of this overthinking about him, the fact that she'd raised the stakes by trying to manipulate him into sticking around, was making her think that maybe Jack's unguarded emotions and the easy way he had about him were all part of his game. And that perhaps he was an especially adept liar and manipulator.

But she had to set all that aside and implement the strategy she and Sasha had devised after the whole oral-sex-on-the-first-date thing. Because Jack hadn't actually gotten off, the damage was probably minimal. The smiley face and multiple thumbs-up emoticons that Jack had sent her along with a picture of his ticket to the game conveyed that he wasn't going to be weird about the fact that she'd come all over his face after one—admittedly very nice—dinner and then skipped out after meeting his mother.

This time, she'd come prepared. She was wearing super-uncomfortable clothes to the game, which would make her so self-conscious that even Jack's annoying habit of being sort of perfect would not get her in the mood. And she'd rubbed one—well several ones—out in the days since their first date, including a couple of times after the very weird second date. She wasn't going to trip up again and end up riding his five-o'clock shadow like a pony at the state fair.

She felt fairly confident as she walked through the turnstile and had her ticket scanned and her purse searched. Her plan seemed foolproof when the guy checking her purse for weapons or contraband snacks called her boobs "ma'am." She was positively jaunty, and her body thrilled with power as she walked to the spot where she'd told Jack to meet her.

And then she saw him standing next to the concession stand with two beers and a giant tray of nachos. He wore a T-shirt with a thermal underneath, and jeans that had a dick print that she'd need to scrub out of her memory methodically, over years, from this day forward.

That wasn't even the worst part. The way he looked at her, under his lashes, with a smirk on his face that said he knew where all the buttons to drive her wild were located, made her have to lock out her knees and stop a few feet away from him.

Even from three feet away, with people rushing past and a couple of them bumping into her—seeing as she was standing in a busy spot and the game was going to start any minute—she could smell that he was freshly showered. And then she couldn't stop thinking about him in the shower. Not getting into the shower with him. Couples showers were awkward and never sexy, but she would pay good money to watch that man shower. Although she hadn't borne witness to his abs, he must be going by the same wardrobe edicts she was, because he was definitely operating by a similar rule—tighter is better.

And she was here for it.

Like an idiot, she raised a hand and might have danced around on her feet like a little girl. "Hi."

"'S'up?" His smirk grew into a full-on grin. He totally had her number.

She didn't even care as she approached him and the din of their surroundings disappeared around them. When she got near him, something clicked into place and gave her the kind of calm she'd been looking for her whole life. A voice inside her, the small, soft one she endeavored not to listen to because it was her heart—and her heart had only ever gotten her in trouble—was telling her that he was special and different and wouldn't break her.

"I hope beer and nachos is okay."

Her stomach rumbled at the smell of processed cheese and hops, although she probably had about three gulps of beer and one chip before her jeans popped. "Better than okay. Beer and nachos are fantastic."

She was glad he found it in him to break the moment, because she would have been content to stand on the concourse of the arena looking at him, smelling him, and grinning at him like an idiot the whole night. They made their way to their seats shortly before the puck dropped.

There was this way that couples sat together that Hannah had always craved. As though they could just barely tolerate being out of contact, but still had their minds on propriety. She'd never had that. But the way Jack was sitting, as close to her as he could get without her sitting in his lap, was that kind of sitting. The whole side of her body was warm, and she took a sip of beer to cool off and marshal the wherewithal not to look at him and giggle. His nearness made her giddy.

The only thing that burst her bubble of smittenness was when he started talking. "So, that guy is the center—" He pointed at the guy poised for the face-off.

She knew that, but another part of her strategy was not being a bitch to Jack for the next few weeks. And correcting his misconception that he might know even a scintilla of what she knew about hockey would be off-putting.

If playing dumb so Jack could feel good about himself kept him asking her out until her company Halloween party, she'd do it. She gritted her teeth and said, "You're so smart, Jack."

"What they're doing right now is called the face-off."

"Where did you learn so much about hockey, Jack?" *Oh dear Lord give me strength.* She bit her lip to keep from telling him that she'd learned everything there was to know about hockey and most of the things she knew about blow jobs from the captain of the high school hockey team. They'd been study buddies and then friends with benefits—as long as it had stayed secret that he was having his sexual needs met by the weird smart girl in his AP European history class.

When she'd gotten a five on the exam, and he'd gotten a three, he'd called things off. He hadn't been able to deal with hard evidence that she was smarter than him. Jack and his condescension about hockey were doing a good job of reminding her that— however much she liked him and his naughty mouth—he was just another dude.

And it might even be a good thing that a little bit of his perfect, woke-bae façade was slipping. That way, every time the way he smirked at her in a tight T-shirt crept into her mind, she could simply think about him mansplaining a game she'd been watching since she was four years old.

"So, the point of the game is for them to get that flat black disk into the other team's net, which is called a goal."

"Mmmm-hmmmm." She tried to remember Sasha's admonishment that guys like to be the expert on things and tend to gravitate toward women who make them feel smart, but she was so close to turning the corner into Bitchville that she didn't have it in her to gush about his frankly elementary hockey tutorial.

"And hockey is played in three periods, not four quarters, like football."

At that point, she was either going to kill him or find a way to make him shut up. But doing so in a way that wouldn't make him dump her immediately would require some finesse. Which she didn't have because she'd never found a use for it until now.

If only he had an off switch of some sort.

An idea so inappropriate and diabolical popped into her head that she couldn't resist giving it a shot. It would abide by the theme of the night—offering sex without delivering it—and it would either confuse or turn him on so much that it would break the cycle of mansplaining.

Thinking about it any more would probably yield a reason why she shouldn't do it, so she went ahead and rested her hand gently over Jack's cock. She didn't even take her eyes off the ice because the puck had dropped, and she wanted to pay attention to the game.

During the first break, she looked over at him. His mouth was open, and he stared straight at her, then glanced down to her hand and back to her face. He opened his mouth to say something, but then she squeezed a little bit. She smiled at him, diverted her eyes back to the ice, and went back to her gentle cupping.

JACK HATED HIMSELF. HE was a slimeball and a creep. He'd hoped he wouldn't have to resort to mansplaining. He'd certainly been aware of the astonishingly effective technique for alienating the fairer sex, but he'd never partaken before tonight. One of the only totally awesome gifts of his radical feminist mother and whip-smart little sister. Oh, and the nuns who'd taught him in grade school. Sister Antoninus would have boxed his ears had he tried to explain a face-off to her; she'd been all-American in women's hockey before entering the convent.

But he'd been desperate. Not only was she drop-dead gorgeous and honey-sweet to the taste, but she left him center-ice hockey tickets? Fuck him, it was going to be hard to take a dive on this one, regardless of strategy. And he'd had no idea how to mess up this date enough that she'd still keep him around for a few more days. Even though she'd left him with blue balls after he'd introduced her to his mom and flirted with another woman in front of her.

But then she'd totally surprised him with her frankly genius method for getting him to shut his trap. The method that had her hand over his Johnson—Sister Antoninus forgive him—and royal blue balls. He couldn't think with her hand that close, and he definitely wasn't about to move because then there would be friction. And he couldn't be subjecting himself to friction in public.

Jesus Christ, they were in public. Granted, she was turned toward him and they were kind of in a corner, so no one could see where her hand was. But the fact that she was just staring at him calmly while her hand was where he'd wanted her hand to be since the night they first met—as though she wasn't affected by it at all—was disconcerting. To say the least.

The move had been effective, because he couldn't speak. It didn't help that every time he opened his mouth, she put gentle pressure on his sack. He was too mixed up with his conflicting shame and desperate horniness to say anything.

"I've been watching hockey since I was a kid." Her voice was the kind of dead quiet that women got when they were about to commit bloody murder. "You don't need to explain what a puck is. Understand?"

He nodded when she gave his cock another slight squeeze.

"If I take my hand off of your dick, are you going to keep acting like one?"

Although he shook his head, that wasn't a promise he could be making. He felt as though he was a walking dick—what with all the blood that ought to be going to his brain flowing straight toward her palm.

"Okay." She smirked and pulled her hand away. He had to bite his lip to stop himself from making a distinctly unmanly noise. "Now I'm going to need you to flag down one of the concessions folks for more beers so that we can enjoy the game."

He opened his mouth and immediately shut it again. Still terrified. And turned on.

CHAPTER FIFTEEN

JACK WASN'T SURE WHAT to make of his father's phone call. There'd been so much loaded into Sean Nolan's edict: "I want to meet this girl your mother told me about."

First of all, why were his parents actually speaking to each other? As far as he knew, they hadn't even set eyes on each other since Bridget's law school graduation. Second, Jack had to reckon with the fact that he'd had no plans to subject Hannah to the rest of his family. Although he'd thought that introducing her to his mother would be off-putting, he'd gravely miscalculated that one. He hadn't even been able to figure out a new way to lose a girl in the days since, and he was seriously considering scrapping the whole plan.

The only thing he could think to do was head up to the gym in his building and pound his feet against the treadmill until the pieces of his mind came together like Tetris and he knew exactly what to do.

Sweat dripped off his brow and landed on the display. He absently wiped it away with his towel but kept running. He'd run until he figured out how to make Hannah discount him as a romantic partner. The fact that she'd seen him flirting with another woman and hadn't even thrown it into a conversation obliquely still puzzled him. Maybe he didn't know how to lose a girl in the same way that his friends seemed to.

He'd certainly figured out how to lose every other girl in his life. It hadn't even started with Maggie Doonan. The first woman who'd abandoned him had been his mother. And, sure, she'd been around after divorcing his father, but she hadn't been interested in her children anymore. As much as she and his father cultivated an image of an amicably divorced couple, Jack knew that his father had never remarried because he was still in love with his ex-wife. Always would be.

That might be why Hannah's similarities to his mother terrified him. It was certainly something to run a few more miles about.

Even though Jack didn't follow in his father's footsteps and work with his hands, but instead had a job that his father had to financially underwrite—for the time being—Jack was more like his father than he would ever admit out loud. Beyond his gruff exterior, Sean felt things deeply. There was some deeply maudlin strain of emotionality that they shared—something passed down through thousands of years of Celtic ancestors. Maybe all Irishmen had a bit of Yeats in them. Perhaps it was just a family curse.

He didn't want to introduce Hannah to his father—not because he wouldn't like her; he would love her. She was sharp and beautiful and laughed easily. Just the sort of woman a sentimental Nolan man fell for and never got up from.

With his other girlfriends, Sean had winked and flirted and welcomed with his natural charm. Something in Jack's gut told him that his father would be in awe of Hannah. Sean never mentioned the names of Jack's exes after they were gone, sort of like Jack never mentioned his mother to his father. Jack knew that, if his father met her, he'd never hear the end of "that Hannah girl you let get away."

But if anything was going to scare Hannah, it would be a snapshot of where she'd be and whom she'd be living with in thirty years. And that was what finally made planning easy for him.

By the time he was done, his lungs ached. More important, his mind was empty and his next step with Hannah was clear.

AS SHE RODE DOWN to a working-class, mostly Irish American South Side neighborhood she'd never been to, Hannah couldn't figure out why Jack Nolan wanted her to meet his whole family. She hadn't even had his dick in her mouth yet, and he was vetting her for wife material. At least, that was what he seemed to be doing. Unless it was some jealous, twitchy thing he was doing—like the night at the museum. Maybe the full cast of his ex-girlfriends would be there to surprise her. Or just one. If this was a sign that he was really into her, it would be easy to keep him on the hook for about six more days. If it was more insecure bullshit, she wasn't sure she could stand one more day of it without her head exploding.

All she had to do was remind herself that Jack Nolan, in the long run, didn't matter here. Sure, he was deadly sexy and gave great head. But he was a man—a highly educated white cis-gendered dude who presented as heterosexual. If she was going to make him believe that she was the kind of girl he could settle down with, she would have to do any amount of ego stroking he required. And now she would have to impress his entire family.

She was still concerned that Jack wasn't seeing the full picture of things that could go wrong here, though. Sean Nolan sounded very old-school, which in her experience often meant low-key racist.

As delightful as she found it that Jack hadn't asked her where she was *from*—the most-often-asked question on all of her first dates—she was pretty sure that her being biracial would be a big freaking deal to his baby boomer father.

This was why it was so strange that Jack was ready to introduce her to his parents on dates two and four.

Again, she hadn't even had his dick in her mouth, and he was ready to risk a disappointed parental look and oblique racist comments. He either had the largest set of brass balls in history, or there was more going on here than she knew about.

All of those thoughts crowded her head as she walked up the newly poured walkway to the well-kept, stately Chicago bungalow. Her hand felt shaky as she pushed the button for the doorbell and waited. Her heart sped up as slow, heavy footsteps sounded across the entryway.

And she almost choked on air when the door opened and a man who shared Jack's devastating green eyes and stupid dimples—with three decades of added depth—opened the door and said, "Finally, my idiot son decided to get some taste in women."

And then he *winked* at her.

Hannah didn't know what to say to that, and her mouth gaped open for a few moments. Jack's father gave her some grace and waved her into the foyer. By the time she slipped off her shoes, she'd gathered her wits. "It's a pleasure to meet you, Mr. Nolan."

He took her hand in his giant sun-spotted one and shook it. "It's Sean."

"Okay." She took her hand back and wiped her sweaty palm on her conservative black sweaterdress. "It's nice to meet you, Sean."

When his brow furrowed, she thought she'd made a mistake. But then he turned and motioned for her to follow. "We'll get you a beer. The game's about to start."

It was a Friday night, so he couldn't mean the football game. That was a relief, because she would do a lot of things to keep Jack on the hook, but rooting for Michigan was a step too far. "Is Jack here yet?"

"He's out back with his brother." They walked into the kitchen, and Sean pulled out a Miller beer, cracked the top, and handed it to her.

Parched from her freak-out, she took a long gulp. The malty liquid reminded her of her grandfather, who had driven a truck for a beer distributor for thirty years. A lot of things about this place reminded her of her grandparents' home. The décor was way more updated than the orange Formica countertops and hand-embroidered towels of her grandmother's kitchen had been. Only to be expected given the family business. But there were piles of mail and pictures of a man who had to be Jack's brother along with an attractive brunette and a young girl who hadn't grown into her toothy smile yet.

The walls mostly had beer and sports posters, denoting that this was the domain of men. Again, something that reminded her of her grandfather, though his paraphernalia had been relegated to the garage.

Sean sat down at the table after pulling out a chair for her, and Hannah's nervousness came back a bit. Even though his gruffness was probably a veneer that belied a softy underneath—like her grandfather's had been—she hadn't gotten a full briefing from Jack before coming here.

"I heard you met my wife." Hannah noticed that he skipped the "ex" part of that equation.

Hannah nodded. "Yep."

"How'd she look?" She had not been expecting that question and wasn't sure how to answer. If he hated his ex-wife, then maybe he wanted her to say that she looked awful. If he was still in love with her, he'd want her to affirm that his decades of longing for the mother of his children was warranted.

The secret, romantic part of her soul decided that it was the latter. "She's lovely. Smart, elegant. Knows her shit." Despite her internal pep talk about manners in the car, she thought Sean would appreciate a well-placed curse. Just a little something to let him know that she didn't have a stick up her ass.

He smirked enough that his dimple creased deeper than Jack's deepest dimple, and he let out a pleased grunt. She immediately liked Sean Nolan.

Jack entered the room, followed by the man from the pictures on the fridge. Before introducing her to his brother, he swooped in and kissed her on the mouth. She felt her face heat as his lips touched hers and his freshly sweaty smell hit her nostrils. His hand at the back of her neck made the rest of the room disappear, and thoughts about what she would do to him if they weren't in his father's house crowded out the fact that they were in his father's house until Sean's smoke-roughened laugh interrupted them.

"Act like you weren't raised in a barn and introduce her to your brother."

Still, Jack took his time withdrawing from her mouth, as though it pained him to do so. Hannah pressed her fingers to her lips and looked at the skin exposed by the undone buttons on Jack's shirt for a beat before she could look up at his brother.

The brother smiled at her, apparently not fazed by the PDA. Hannah stood up and offered her hand again.

"I'm Michael, the better-looking Nolan brother."

Hannah laughed and nodded because that was polite. But it was totally untrue. And even if it was true, her judgment was impaired by Jack's kisses. He would always be the good-looking Nolan brother to her.

Like his father, Michael stared at her for a long beat. She would have turned tail and run but for Jack cupping the back of her neck. Jesus, she'd never liked to be publicly claimed by any other boyfriend. On anyone else, it would seem like a petty pissing contest. On Jack, it worked for her in a major way. Like, made her knees weak enough that she needed the touch to stay standing.

With him touching her like that, she was liable to forget that this was all a pretend game so she could prove to her boss that she wasn't allergic to romance and get a promotion.

"And this is Hannah."

"I figured that." Michael Nolan shared the same smirk with his father and younger brother. He took her hand and gave it a firm shake before letting it go. She liked the way the Nolan men shook hands. Their skin was dry, and they didn't posture or grip too tightly.

"It's a pleasure to meet you."

"Same here." Michael winked at her. "You need another beer?" Apparently, that was the sign that the Nolan men approved of someone.

Hannah shook her head. "I'm good."

JACK WAS GLAD THAT he hadn't told his father or brother about the story. They would have given away the whole game because they were shit liars, and he liked that they seemed to like her. He'd really liked walking into his father's kitchen and seeing her there, sitting with the old man. As though she belonged there and belonged with him.

When he saw her there, swathed in something soft and cashmere, sipping a cheap, domestic beer with his dad, he'd had to admit to himself that this wasn't entirely about the story. This was about him wanting to spend time with this woman. Sure, if she got comfortable with him, she'd be sure to say something that would give him a clue as how to best repulse her, but he was self-aware enough to know that he didn't want to do that tonight.

He was going to lose her; that was a given. In the meantime, he wanted to savor her.

"Did you order pizza?"

His dad slapped the table sharply and said, "Yep."

Jack put his hand on Hannah's lower back, intending to lead her into the living room, but Michael stopped them. "You're not a vegetarian, are you?"

Hannah choked on her beer a little bit. "Is pepperoni a vegetable?"

Michael laughed. "Funny, too. How'd you end up with my loser brother?"

Her spine stiffened under Jack's hand. "He's not a loser."

Warmth spread through his chest at her defending him, but his growing tenderness toward Hannah didn't stop him from saying, "Yeah, says the guy getting the divorce."

Michael had no room to comment on Jack's relationships. His brother might have gotten married right out of college and settled down into the family business like a good son, but he hadn't chosen well. Karen had made Michael's life miserable with her insane jealousy when they'd started dating, and he'd thought it would get better once they got married. Jack couldn't remember a holiday when Karen wasn't sulking about Michael allegedly flirting with someone in front of her.

That was where Jack's idea to flirt with Darcy had actually come from. But, like most things, emulating his brother's habits didn't work for him.

"Come on up to my room." He tugged on Hannah's hand and led her toward the stairs. "I want to show you my baseball cards."

"Is that what they're calling it nowadays?"

JACK'S SISTER AND THE pizza arrived at around the same time. Bridget Nolan, with her thick acres of auburn hair combined with her mother's gray-blue eyes and a feminine version of the Nolan smirk, was absolutely stunning.

Shortly after they'd gathered around the kitchen table, fresh beers at hand and plates piled high, Hannah realized that she and Bridget would get along just fine. "You're definitely not as much of a twat as Jack's last girlfriend."

"Watch your mouth." Sean's words held little charge.

Bridget motioned around the room. "I didn't use the c-word, Dad."

Sean grumbled, and both Michael and Jack snickered.

"Well, I love hearing that I'm doing better than the competition." Hannah immediately wanted to claw the words back. Competition? What the hell was she thinking? It was like all of her feminist solidarity with other women had gotten swallowed up by her lust for Jack. She normally wasn't the jealous type, but she'd probably have a *Dynasty*-style catfight with a woman who'd been with Jack.

Except then, Jack nuzzled—*nuzzled*—her neck and said,

"There's no competition." The only thing that kept her from melting on the spot into a pool of Jell-O was Bridget rolling her eyes and scoffing.

Hannah turned to Jack and said, "You're ridiculous."

"We need to play Cards Against Humanity so that I don't have to see them canoodling anymore." That was Sean, and everyone laughed at the idea that he'd read enough gossip columns to know the word "canoodling."

"Dad, we have to get you a better hobby."

Hannah wasn't sure how this was going to go. She was a stellar Cards Against Humanity player, and she was fairly certain that those skills would go over well in the Nolan household. But she also thought it might be a good idea to let Jack win. She wanted to keep him in a good mood, and winning might do that.

She didn't think Jack would be like Miguel, who'd slammed doors in her apartment when he'd almost lost a game of Scrabble. But she didn't want to risk it.

It turned out that she didn't have anything to worry about. Even if she had been giving it her best shot, Sean Nolan would have bested all of them. And, competitive as she was, she kind of liked it. She was cuddled next to Jack and full of pizza. His siblings seemed to like her. At the very least, they'd each shot her knowing smiles while they thought that Jack wasn't looking.

And Mr. Nolan—er, Sean—patted her arm when she won a round.

That was why it came as a surprise when Michael said, "I thought this one was different, Jack-off. But outclassed again."

Hannah wasn't sure what she was expecting Jack to do, but it wasn't standing up and tackling his brother so hard that Michael fell off his chair. And she gasped when Jack pounced on top of his brother and gave him a noogie that might leave a mark.

She looked to Sean, who picked up both of their beers and nodded over to the living room. "Last time they took down the table, and I hate to waste beer."

"They do this a lot?" Hannah wasn't sure what to think as an only child; she knew that siblings fought. But she hadn't expected it to be so sudden and violent. Jack's other relatives seemed nonplussed, more worried about getting her out of the line of fire than stopping their sons and brothers from killing each other.

"It's Michael's turn to get his ass kicked."

"They take turns?" She looked over at them. Jack had Michael in some sort of wrestling hold. His older brother's face was red, and he was trying to tap the ground with one hand. "I think Michael's giving up."

But Jack wouldn't let him go. Not until Sean kicked him, hard, in the side. "That's enough, boys. You've scared her plenty."

He had that right. She was a little bit terrified as both of them slowly got up from the ground. Michael's joints cracked so loudly that Hannah winced on his behalf. She pursed her lips to keep from saying anything.

She might have dated some real losers, but she'd never been with anyone who'd hit someone—even if it was a smartass brother. What Michael had said hadn't even been that bad, and Jack had just freaked out.

But it was too late to find another guy to bring to the Halloween party, and having Jack show what appeared to be his true colors now would make things a lot easier when it ended. She was stuck with him for a few more days.

No one else seemed to think an after-dinner fight over something as trivial as a stupid comment and an offensive nickname was a big deal. And when Michael slapped his brother on the back of the head and Jack laughed, she wondered if she was making a mountain out of an intersibling-violence molehill.

Michael looked at her with a toothy grin, not missing any teeth, and said, "Congratulations, he really likes you."

"What?" She was so very confused.

Bridget piped in. "They beat each other down at least once a month. And usually, when Jack likes a girl, he gets his ass kicked. But you really add something to his right hook."

"I had to defend your honor, Duchess." Hannah looked at Jack, still perplexed. He was flexing and bunching his hand, inspecting his bruised knuckles. "If I hadn't, he would have jumped me on the way to the car and jeopardized my good-night kiss."

The way he smiled at her made her soften, just a smidge. She could probably hang in for a few more days.

CHAPTER SIXTEEN

EVEN THOUGH THIS PART of the plan would have Jack pushing Hannah out of the Lyft as it slow-rolled past her door—or making her take her own car and pay for it herself—he wasn't about to end this night before securing a kiss. It just didn't seem right considering that his heart was full of her laughing at his dad's terrible jokes and paying close attention to his sister's complaints about some douche at work.

Not to mention that none of his other girlfriends had ever beat him at Cards Against Humanity. She hadn't beat his dad or Bridget, but no one could beat them. They were savants. None of the other women he'd dated had ever fit so seamlessly into his family. She hadn't even run out the door after he and his brother had tried to beat each other up. Clever, kind, and beautiful Hannah fit everything about the Nolans. And he wanted her to be all his. For real.

If not for the story and the threat of losing his job, he would brush her hair aside and tell her that under the floodlight at the door to her building. He'd tell her the truth and let her go inside and think about whether she was willing to give him a second chance.

As it was, he was prepared to leave her at the door. When she looked up at him with the doe-soft gaze that he knew she saved only for him, he couldn't help but touch her. Even though he was still lying to her, he couldn't help but get as much of her imprinted on his skin as possible. He'd never been so wound up in a woman before. And even though he was the one who was supposed to do the hurting this time, he knew that her walking out the door would cut much more than his ego.

If he wasn't careful, he would turn into the crusty husk of man his father was, and he wouldn't even have the three kids and eighteen years of marriage to show for it. Less than two weeks, and he could feel it in his bones that Hannah was it for him. She was everything that he'd been trying to force with Maggie, Katie, and Lauren.

Instead of following his instincts and spilling his guts, he kissed her. After just a split second of hesitation that told him that his plan to lose her was working, a little bit, she opened her mouth and kissed him back. Just like every other time before, her scent and taste wound their way into his blood, making his heart pump faster and his dick try to punch out of his pants.

She grasped the sides of his jacket and pulled him closer, biting his bottom lip as though she wanted to brand him as hers. Her hard edges made him even more desperate for her. He settled his hands on her hips and pulled her close so that she could feel how much he wanted to sink into her softness.

If this farce were real, it would be the right time for them to get it on, and only a thread of decency was keeping him from giving in and asking her if she would show him her etchings upstairs.

As it was, her mouth invited him to take a taste, and he complied.

Even more than making time with her, he wanted to wake up with Hannah. As compelling as all her sharp elbows and rough edges were, soft Hannah made him feel as though he had access to something rare and precious that no one else could touch. He wanted to bathe in the way she sighed when opening her lips for his tongue. Wanted to pump his fist in the air when she went soft against him. Because he knew that she didn't give that to just anyone, knew that she gave it only to him right now, in this moment between the two of them.

She pulled back and looked down at the front of his pants, biting her swollen lower lip. "Want to come up?"

When he hesitated for a moment, he somehow knew that she was about to claw back her invitation. That was how well he could see her. He felt like she was made for him. Enough pushback to call him on his shit, but open and genuine and vulnerable in exactly the way he needed.

You can just keep it to kissing and heavy petting. If you make this all about her, you'll both know it's real when the shit hits the fan.

The shit had already hit the fan for him—he was most of the way in love with her—and he couldn't seem to say no to it. "Yeah, I'd love to come up."

HANNAH WAS SHAKING WHEN Jack took her hand as she led him up the stairs to her apartment. Sasha was visiting her parents back east this weekend, so they had the place to themselves. Her best friend probably wouldn't approve of her sleeping with Jack right now, but Hannah didn't have it in her to care one bit about whether she was following "the rules," or whether Jack would respect her in the morning.

She'd always thought any rules, other than basic respect, were stupid when it came to dating anyway. And the way Jack clutched her hand and looked at her like he couldn't wait to hear what she was going to say next made her feel like the only rules that applied to them were the ones they made up.

If she'd followed any other set of rules for her life, she would be married by now. Probably have a baby. But the rules, even when she'd tried to follow them, had never seemed to fit right. They were a little tight in the crotch, to be quite honest.

And if she'd followed the rules, Jack wouldn't be in her apartment. She wouldn't be about to have sex with him. Sex that was sure to be awesome because the things he could do with his mouth made great promises about the things he could do with his hands and all his other pertinent parts.

It felt right to have him in her space, and she didn't try to explain all of the pictures of her and Sasha and their other school friends sprinkled on the walls and shelves. All she had to do was look at his face to see the amusement and curiosity. The way he took his time in taking in where she lived told her so much about him. He wasn't here to judge her; he was curious about her, as hungry to *know her* as he was to get naked with her.

Jack was different from any other man she'd ever known, and that was why it was so easy to let him in when everything in her conditioning told her to shut him out and push him away. He was perfect, and she struggled to believe she deserved him. But here she was. Here they were.

She sort of trailed after him, not so close that he would think she was hiding something, but close enough to reach out and touch. Until he suddenly turned, and he was right in her face. The heat of his body blanketed her front and she had a hard time using her legs for their intended purpose of standing.

She must have leaned into him, because he grasped her upper arms and nearly incinerated her skin beneath the sweaterdress. A drop of sweat wound its way between her shoulder blades, and the collar felt as though it would block off all her air. She was so turned on that her body was feverish, and the only thing that would make the fever break was his hands and mouth all over her.

She looked up at him, and his gaze had gone molten. His teeth dug into his bottom lip as though he was trying to stop himself from saying something. She didn't want him to censor himself around her—she certainly didn't watch what she said around him.

"Kiss me," she ordered.

He lowered his head and pressed his lips against hers, pulling her close. She wound her arms around his neck and went up on tiptoes, licking the seam of his lips until he opened up for her. Her heart picked up speed, and she whimpered. She wiggled against him, nestling closer, and felt how turned on he was. But his hands didn't wander below her upper back. She wanted him to palm her ass, maybe pick her up and drop her on the couch. She just wanted more of him.

"Touch me," she said when he pulled back for a moment to get a breath.

"I shouldn't." That was *not* what she'd expected him to say. In fact, she expected him to just do what he was told.

Indignation rose inside her. "Why the hell not?"

"I should go." And then he *actually* pulled away from her. *Unbelievable.*

She grabbed two fistfuls of his sweater and pulled him closer. She must have caught him off guard because he stumbled close enough that their thighs were touching. She felt as though she was on fire from her quads to her lower belly. And one part of him definitely didn't want to leave. When he stayed close, she said, "You should stay."

"It's really soon."

She might have felt shamed by that. With anyone else, she definitely would have. But not with Jack. Fisticuffs with his brother aside, he was too good a guy to deny her for any other reason than he thought he would be protecting her. She simply had to show him that the best thing for her in this moment was for him to kiss her and touch her and do all the things that she'd wanted him to do since the first night they'd met.

Even though she should be keeping the walls up because this would all be over within a few days, she wanted to get naked with Jack. More than any other guy she'd been with, he'd shown her who he was. She didn't like everything, but the fact that he'd been less than perfect made her trust him more somehow. She wanted to go soft for him in a way that she hadn't ever wanted with any other man.

She'd never felt this way about anyone else. And she needed to show him how she felt about him because she didn't have the words yet. That need was what made her go up on her tippy-toes and press her mouth to his.

His grip on her upper arms tightened for a moment, as though he was going to push her away, and she internally braced for the hot spray of that humiliation shower. Only she would go from shunning all romantic relationships to throwing herself at a man in less than a week.

But he surprised her when he pulled her closer and took over the kiss. One of his hands moved to cup the back of her head, and that same sense of security she'd felt when he'd introduced her to his brother washed over her again.

This was how she'd always wanted to feel in a relationship. Although she'd never been able to explain it, she'd never felt the mix of attraction and utter safety with anyone else that she felt with Jack.

Actions spoke louder than words in this case, and they could talk about everything later—much later. After they'd stopped breathing like one being. Post everyone's clothes coming off and everyone coming.

Jack pulled back. "Dammit, Hannah. I promised myself I wasn't going to do this with you."

"Why?" What they'd been doing until he'd stopped kissing her was set to become her most favorite hobby, and she only wanted more of it. More than any conversation they were going to have about this being too soon. That kind of conversation would remind her of Noah and how the timing for moving their relationship forward had never been right until the time had been right to dump her. She couldn't take that kind of shit from Jack—it would hurt so much more from him.

He gripped the sides of her face, and she could see and feel his conflict by the way his touch was sort of desperate and his eyes wild. Lust and pragmatism warred there, and she wanted to tell him that that's what made him wonderful.

"It's really soon."

She placed a kiss on his stubbled chin. "This is like date four, and you've already gone down on me." Another kiss. "I think this is plenty slow."

"I promised my priest that I would wait until I got married." She froze and backed away slowly. He shifted on his feet and stuffed his hands in his pockets. For a second, she wasn't entirely sure if he was joking. But then his face turned bright red. A clipped hysterical laugh came out of her mouth before she could clap a hand over it.

Once she calmed down, she decided to try reasoning with him. "But going down on me was sex, Jack."

He shrugged. "We've been on the 'everything but' track."

"So, you're—like—a virgin?"

He pointed a finger up in the air for emphasis. "Not exactly, but P-in-V sex is for marriage."

"What?" Hannah turned away from him and walked toward the window. "You know they made up that rule so that they could control *female* sexuality, right?"

"We can do other stuff," he said as she felt him approach her from behind. And she was tempted to take him up on his offer. He'd broken the seal on her celibacy after all, and just being in the vicinity of his pheromones made her unbearably horny.

Combined with the fighting-with-his-brother thing, his virginity pledge put the kibosh on her desire to stay in a relationship with him after the engagement party. So she might as well enjoy what she had while she had it.

She turned to look at him and smiled. "All right. Let's do this."

Once they were in the bedroom, Hannah became preoccupied with how she just couldn't get a read on Jack. The night they'd met and on their first date, she'd thought him charming and confident. She'd actually felt a little bit bad because it had seemed like he liked her and she had an ulterior motive for dating him. But now he was a super-religious virgin who observed plenty of loopholes to his vow of chastity?

Trying to square who he'd been with who he was acting like now distracted her as he kissed down the side of her neck. It felt great enough that she wasn't going to stop him, no matter how much she wanted to interrogate him on his little living room proclamation.

It almost took her back to college, when she'd made out with a seminary student for the better part of a semester. It was kind of thrilling—that he'd found her so attractive that he'd been willing to cheat on God with her.

But this—he'd let her sit on his face, but his penis was sacred?

He kissed his way down her belly, and that felt really good, but her thoughts were so loud that she didn't spread her legs when he palmed her thigh.

"Is something wrong?"

She looked down at him. He was toying with the waistband of her panties and worrying his bottom lip. Damn, he was charming.

"I'm just still surprised."

His face reddened. "Yeah—it's— My best friend is a priest." He shrugged. "It's the guilt, you know."

She was intimately familiar with the guilt tradition of the Catholic Church, so she could *almost* understand. But she still had plenty of questions.

"But you can do everything else without guilt?"

He smiled up at her, looking boyishly sexy the whole time. "Nothing that brings you pleasure could ever make me feel guilty."

Just then, she forgot that none of this was really real. And she could see herself falling for Jack again. If she was smart, she'd use his chastity pledge to keep him at arm's length. Close enough for Annalise to believe that they were in love, but far enough to protect her heart.

But she wasn't in the mood to be smart, not when she had this little window of time with a sexy, charming man all but offering to let her use him for pleasure.

She could have her cake and have him eat her, too. The way he was looking at her right now, she could ask him for the moon.

"Anything, huh?"

His dimples deepened when she asked that. "Anything."

Before she could think better of it, she reached over to the top drawer and grabbed her favorite toy friend—the only thing that had made the last couple of sexless years bearable.

"What's that?" Jack asked, but he didn't look disgusted. Mostly curious.

He held up the clitoral stimulator she'd purchased after breaking things off with the twat/urologist and turned it over in his hands. She felt her skin flush at the prospect of having to explain to him how it worked. And she almost grabbed it from his hands so she could throw it back into the drawer and try to make him forget that she'd taken it out.

But then she remembered that she wasn't trying to convince this guy she was perfect. She wasn't trying to convince him to get married or spend his life with her. She was just going to have to keep him on the hook for a few more days. And he said that he would do anything to please her.

She decided to go for it, but he beat her to the punch. He'd figured out how to turn it on and off and had figured out what to do with it without her having to tell him. "So you put this over—"

"Yep."

"And then it—" He put his finger in and his gaze widened. She giggled; she couldn't help it. He joined her and said. "Wow. Robots really are going to take all of our jobs."

"You do bring some things that the machines can't reproduce." She leaned down and kissed him.

"I do." He got rid of her panties with a smoothness a celibate guy shouldn't have had and proved a quick study in using his new robot overlord in making her squeal and moan.

Her head fell back and she squeezed her eyes closed. And then he used his fingers, and she actually saw stars when she came. But the cherry on top was the look on his face—total adoration—just before he kissed her.

CHAPTER SEVENTEEN

NOW THAT SHE KNEW they weren't going to be having penis-in-vagina sex because of Jack's religious views, which had so many loopholes they looked like Swiss cheese, it strangely felt *more* intimate.

The only sounds in the room were their breathing and the drip from the bathroom faucet. The dripping usually didn't bother her because she slept like the dead, but the slap of the water droplets against the ceramic was deafening right now.

She wasn't supposed to want him to stay. He was supposed to be temporary, and she wasn't supposed to start feeling real feelings for him. But he'd gone and made her original plan impossible. It was as though he was made for her, which was stupid. People got in relationships with people who fit them well enough and then they re-made themselves to fit even better—or they broke up.

Even Jack couldn't be perfect; he was just better at hiding his imperfections than any guy she'd ever met. No one who looked as good as he did, smelled as good, and knew exactly how to touch her clit could be all good. There had to be something about him that made him a monster, and she meant to find out what it was.

Maybe if she got the ball rolling, he'd let something slip. Just enough so that she would stop the free fall into love/trouble with him.

"I haven't had sex with anyone, in—like—two years." That was not something she should have said to someone she'd just started dating.

"You haven't?"

She met his eyes then, afraid that she'd see the fear that she was hearing wedding bells swallow up any postcoital tenderness he'd had going. But she didn't see that. His gaze was as open and curious as it ever was. And maybe she wasn't imagining the hint of regret. Nothing but kindness and compassion on his face. Jesus, if she was the kind of girl who fell in love, she would be done for. As it was, her chest filled, and her eyes stung as though tears were about to fall. She gasped, afraid that he would see her losing it.

That would be the best way to lose him. At least then he would never know that she'd lied to him about her original motivation for dating him. No matter if she told him that she'd wanted to say yes to that first date before her boss demanded that she show that she wasn't a heartless shrew, she never would have actually had the courage to go out with him if it hadn't been forced.

She should be grateful to Annalise, and maybe even to Giselle, for forcing her into giving this glorious man—who was in her bed and wanting to just talk to her—a chance.

"How's a girl like you still single?" His words could have stabbed her in the throat. They echoed the voice of every guy she tried to go out with after Noah, when she'd been trying to be the girl a guy would want to marry. The ones before she'd given up on finding anyone who wanted something real and lasting. But the way he said them was soft and curious, and that made her want to give him a real answer.

"I'm just not the kind of girl most men want to marry."

He laughed as though she'd just said something unbearably stupid. "That's rich. Pull the other one, Duchess."

She slapped at his chest, and that only made him laugh more. Although she liked that he thought she was being ridiculous, she wanted him to take her seriously. So she crawled up on his chest so they were face-to-face and said, "Stop laughing."

"I'll stop laughing when you give me a real answer."

"Why don't you answer your own question?"

"Why am I still single?" She nodded at him and he bit his lip for a moment—so sexy—before continuing. "I keep having the perfect girl walk out on me."

Then Hannah started laughing. She couldn't even *imagine* any woman in her right mind walking out on Jack.

His arms tightened around her, and then she felt like a pinned butterfly specimen, his focus back on her. "Don't laugh at my deepest pain."

"Then you can't laugh at mine, either."

"Agreed." He nodded, solemnity washing over his face. "Tell me."

"It's not that guys keep leaving me. I actually broke up with my last boyfriend. He made it clear that we weren't serious, but I finally pulled the trigger."

"Not a surprise." Only a hint of his earlier humor remained.

"It's just that guys only want sex from me. Not forever."

"And that's not something you have to worry about with me."

She liked that he could have a sense of humor about this. "And sex with you is pretty spectacular."

"Not that you would know."

"Still—"

"Whatever, we were talking about deep, emotional pain." She'd much rather be talking about sex with Jack, specifically when and if they'd be having it, but she forced herself to go on. She'd decided on the strategy of finding out what was wrong with him by revealing what was wrong with her, and she would not be deterred. "Or they think I need improvement."

"What could you possibly need improvement on?" She loved that he sounded incredulous.

"I swear too much."

"But you're so articulate when you swear."

"And I eat too much."

His hands coasted down her sides, and he grabbed her ass in his big hands. Then he settled her over his cock, which was coming back to life. "I love watching you eat. You get this look on your face when you like something, and you make the same noise you make when I'm making you come—just quieter."

She didn't know she did that and was mortified at the thought. Making sex noises during dinner? No wonder Noah had thought she was trashy. "I do?"

"Yeah. It's fucking great."

"Jesus, no wonder most guys think I'm just a sex vending machine."

"Most guys are too flipping stupid to notice."

"But you're not?"

"Nah, I'm a journalist." She smirked at him, not quite sure she was following his line of reasoning. "I get paid to pay attention."

"If I'm having an I'll-have-what-she's-having moment every time I'm enjoying food, then I don't think it would take much to notice."

"We'll have to agree to disagree." He touched his mouth to her cheek, which was sweet. In contrast to his erection, which was not quite as sweet. "So, what put you off dating for so long?"

"I guess, after my last relationship, I just felt like it was all so pointless."

"I'd say that what happened fifteen minutes ago wasn't pointless." Nothing about what they were doing together seemed pointless.

"I don't usually come when it's casual." She was really just ripping herself open for him tonight.

"That sex toy definitely brought a certain formality to the proceedings." At that, she had to laugh. Jesus, why couldn't he just be a pussymonster all the time? Why did he have to be so funny and cute? "But I get that. You should be able to take your time."

"See, most guys—" She paused when he grimaced. "Present company excluded." That earned her another kiss, this one closer to her mouth. "Most guys don't want to wait. They jump right to the sex, past the banter, and there are definitely no tacos or puppy pics."

"Then what the hell are people doing on the apps?" His acting naïve, like a babe in the woods, was sexier than it ought to be.

"Mostly trying to get you to WhatsApp or Kik so that they can send dick pics and say inappropriate and abusive shit without getting called out on social media."

"That's dumb." He furrowed his brow as though truly disturbed by modern dating rituals. "Why would anyone think that would work?"

Hannah shrugged. Oddly enough, telling Jack what other guys did and having him react like he was personally offended on her behalf had made her want to throw him on the floor and ride his face. So, she'd failed in this instance to get him to reveal his big bad—the one that would prevent her from falling in love with him.

Too bad he rolled her underneath him and disabused her of the notion that she was anything but screwed. *Figuratively.*

CHAPTER EIGHTEEN

JACK TRIED TO FIND the perfect lighting for an intimate selfie, and he was failing miserably. This was stupid. And his penis was so ugly. Perhaps it was the ugliest penis on the good green earth.

And the last thing he wanted to be doing right now was hammering another nail in the coffin of the nascent relationship he had with Hannah. He hadn't intended to spend the night with her, but he'd justified it to himself—he hadn't gotten off. It had been all about her. Still, he wasn't just hungover from spending the whole night wrapped up in her scent, talking to her. Guilt ate at his gut along with the black coffee he'd sucked down as soon as he'd hit his apartment.

He hadn't showered yet because he liked the smell of Hannah on him. But it made him crave having the real her in his space. He should definitely shower. Somehow, taking a picture of his dick while Hannah was in a sense *there* felt even worse than just sending a dick pic.

Now that he knew her better, he could predict that she'd feel betrayed by this after what they'd done last night. He'd seen how hard it was for her to open up to him, and he'd been so flattered that she'd chosen him. Despite the fact that he should have walked away, he just hadn't been able to.

He'd always been the perfect boyfriend because he'd been able to sublimate his own needs to his lady's. Last night, his own needs had almost devoured his integrity until it was just a nub—sort of like how his penis looked from too close.

Why did *anyone* think sending an unsolicited picture of their genitalia was a good idea? Even though she'd seemed to want to see his penis, this seemed like an asshole move. If he were another guy, the kind of guy who thought dick pics weren't gross, what would he be hoping to get out of sending a picture?

Not to mention that he couldn't get an angle on it that didn't make his cock look either gargantuan or tiny.

This was bullshit, but it was what he had to do. He needed to do something that would make Hannah realize that he was just like all the other guys who had disappointed her before. Even though his two weeks weren't up, and he would have to fill in his word count with GIFs and shit that he didn't have to do to lose her, he couldn't avoid it any longer. Not after they'd slept—just slept—together and she'd all but told him that she was in love with him.

After last night, he probably had a customized guide on how to lose Hannah. Her ex was a blithering idiot because he'd had all that was her and given it up because he'd wanted something different. All that rejection had cut Hannah deep—no matter how much she tried to cover it up with being a badass.

Jack was in love with everything she was, and he didn't want her to lose a single part of it. The irony was that, if he didn't want to hurt her anymore, he had to make her break up with him right now. He wished he could avoid hurting her at all, but that would just make him the sucker he always had been with previous girl-friends.

He'd given up jobs and cities for his exes, and he had nothing to show for it. He couldn't allow himself to believe that Hannah was any different. Even though he didn't have it in him to psychologically torture her, he couldn't give up the chance to do what he really wanted to do in order to be with her for real. Not right now. For the first time, he was putting his career first, and he was so close to success.

The hope that she would eventually forgive him still lingered in his brain. After last night, he knew it was bullshit to hope that she wouldn't slit his throat and salt the ground that absorbed his life-blood after she found out the truth. It made him want to throw up.

Hell, he was so far in love with her that he'd probably never escape.

Maybe he needed to try portrait mode.

After about thirty minutes of experimenting with lighting—the sunlight coming in through a dirty window in his living room—he had a shot that didn't make him want to hurl. Sending it, however, was another story.

HANNAH WAS STILL IN bed when her phone buzzed on her night-stand. She hated the anticipation and excitement that made her toes curl into the sheets thinking about what Jack had sent her.

He was perfect, and whatever waited on her phone was going to be perfect, too. Jack Nolan was a goddamn unicorn—the kind of guy her friends had always told her not to hold out for. He was the kind of guy she'd described wanting to well-meaning relatives and friends, garnering her the description of "too picky."

That morning, lying in her dim bedroom, thinking of herself as some sort of magical sex goddess because of the sheer number and intensity of orgasms Jack had seemed to be able to call forth from her body on a whim, she felt vindicated. She hadn't even had to give him anything in return. And, given the talking after, the talking that had lasted almost until sunrise, she was shaken.

This wasn't supposed to be about love. Dating Jack was supposed to be about getting a promotion, not meeting her perfect match. But it was making her realize that maybe she'd been too hasty in giving up on finding someone.

The way that Jack was with her—most of the time—made her think that she'd just been dating the wrong men. Noah had been the wrong man, and nothing that she could have done or changed about herself was going to turn him into the right one. Jack could have been the right one if she wasn't using him and he hadn't started acting weird.

She hesitated to pick up the phone because there was a part of her that knew she could be wrong about Jack. After all, she'd thought she'd been in love with Noah and that he'd been in love with her, too. She'd convinced herself that he wanted her to be the best she could be and that was why he was always telling her—in all of his various ways—that she wasn't quite up to snuff.

What if he was texting to say that he'd had a nice time but didn't see this going anywhere? What if her pubic hair was actually an issue, and he didn't want to see her again? What if it was a reminder to pay her cell phone bill, and he'd never get in contact with her again?

All of these thoughts crowded her head until she slapped around the nightstand for the phone and grabbed it. He'd sent an image, which he'd done before when he was still wooing her with cute puppies.

When her phone recognized her face—which was still weird to her—she almost dropped the phone on it. He'd sent her a picture of his dick. A well-lit picture of it, framed so as to convey its actual size.

She was torn between wanting to throw the phone at the wall and saving the picture to an album all on its own. The odd thing—aside from his sending her a picture of his junk after she'd said that she didn't like pictures of junk—was that he hadn't sent the photo with a caption.

If he was going to intentionally disrespect her, he could have at least sent along a joke.

It seemed so unlikely that the man who went downtown at the slightest indication that she wanted him to would be so inconsiderate as to send her a dick pic after she said she didn't like them. And even though she had to admit that his penis was much more enticing than any she'd seen in pictorial form before, it made her slightly less attracted to him.

Despite his flirtation with another woman in front of her, which she'd chalked up to his maybe being nervous about how much he liked her, his character seemed unshakable. But, then again, she only really knew him biblically. And she didn't know why he'd sent this to her the morning after giving her so many orgasms that she'd forgotten all about how she was just faking their entire relationship. There were no bubble ellipses to tell her that he was planning to explain himself, either.

So she was left to figure out what he was trying to say by her damned self. And to try to claw back the sex buzz that his dick pic had killed. Because she wanted it back.

Maybe there was some sort of lesson here. Maybe her thing with

NOT THE GIRL YOU MARRY

Jack was just about lust, but she needed to be open to meeting someone great. Maybe not all guys were rotten to the core with toxic
masculinity.

Shit. She didn't know what had happened to make Jack turn into
a typical fuckboy. And she didn't know if this was just a fluke or a
joke or what, but she knew she needed to get in the shower and
make a plan of attack for tasting cakes.

In the end, curiosity about this perplexing man's motivations
won out.

> Hannah: To what do I owe the pleasure?
> Jack: Welp, my cock has been like that 👍 since last
> night.

She was kind of flattered by that—the idea that he'd been
distractingly turned on for almost twelve hours. But she was also
frustrated that he had some sort of pact with a priest that prevented her from doing anything about it. And a little concerned for
his health. Weren't hard-ons that lasted four hours or longer dangerous?

> Hannah: IDK whether to take that as a compliment or not.
> (And I totally offered to take care of that for you)
> Jack: Oh, it's a compliment. I would have eaten your
> pussy again for sure.

Dear Lord, he had a dirty mouth for a guy who abstained from
sex. Her abdomen went liquid, and her skin heated so much she
wanted to kick off her blankets.

Hannah: Such a gentleman. But I don't know if I could
have handled any more.

Jack: Your taste turns me on so much that I would be
even harder than I am right now.

It was way too good to be true. Still, she snaked her fingers underneath her panties. Sure enough, her vagina had no compunctions about mansplaining or flirting with other women.

Hannah: You should do something about that

Thinking about him touching himself while she was touching herself—and how it was the closest they were going to get to having actual sex—turned her on even more. His celibacy was going to make her obsessed with his getting in his pants. If they'd done the deed last night, it might have been boring or uncomfortable or less sexy than foreplay. But now that it was forbidden, she couldn't stop thinking about him sliding inside of her.

Jack: Are you telling me to jack off? 🙏

Hannah: 😊 if you must.

Jack: Oh, trust me, I must.

Hannah: As long as you're thinking about me . . .

Jack: I can't think about anything else, Duchess.

So she was on his mind? Maybe that's why he'd started acting weird? It was scary to *like* like someone. Hell, she was scared of how much seeing that he thought about her in text was making her feel.

Hannah: Well, now I have a situation.

Jack: A flood in Ms. Havisham's basement?

Why did he have to be so flipping funny? It turned her on and made it harder to view him as just a piece of meat that would get her a promotion.

Hannah: Swept away all the cobwebs.

Jack: Stop turning me on with literary references and spread your legs.

She wasn't about to tell him that they were already spread and she was close to coming.

Hannah: Why would I do that?

Jack: So you can rub your clit, pretend your fingers are my dick, and we can get off together . . .

Jack: Are you touching yourself?

Hannah: Yes. You?

Jack: Pretending I'm deep inside you

She was pretending the same thing and so, so close. And the fact that he was moving so fast when he specialized in slow meant that he must be close, too.

Hannah: Already?

Jack: Remember I've already sucked your clit until you started sounding angry about it? Keep up, Duchess

Hannah: What position are we in?

Jack: I want to take you from behind, but I want to see your face the first time. Hmm.

Both. She definitely wanted both. But face-to-face was a lot. And this wasn't supposed to be a lot. Despite how much she wanted to kiss him while they boned. Shit. She *needed* both.

Hannah: We'll just have to do it more than once . . . if you're up for it. Making up for lost time and all.

Jack: If you can be a smartass, you're not doing this right. If I were there right now, I'd spank you.

As a rule, she was not into that kind of thing. But from Jack, she could totally get down with a little slap and tickle. But he didn't necessarily need to know how much that turned her on.

Hannah: 😈

Jack: That's two.

Cheeky.

Hannah: I'm so scared! (And turned on, keep going)

Jack: Where were we? Ah, I'm inside you've already come once so you're very wet and very tight and I'm listing saint names in my head to keep from making an ass of myself.

She rolled her eyes for real at his reference to saint names. It was his religious vow of celibacy keeping them from doing this for real right now. But then again, this was maybe better. He couldn't know for sure how much he was affecting her.

> Hannah: Think about how they were martyred so I can catch up.
> Jack: On it.
> Jack: Dammit, Hannah. Even thinking about your pussy has me feeling like a rookie again. All that pretty, wet pink.

Mansplaining and weird behavior aside, this man knew exactly what to say and how to say it to get her close.

> Hannah: That's the stuff. Right there . . .
> Jack: Put two fingers in before you come. Almost as good as me there with you.

She didn't read that last text for several minutes after she came. She had to close her eyes against how much he pushed her buttons, even when she was doing the pressing.

NOT FUCKING HANNAH WAS going to be the death of him. Sexting with her made him come so hard that he had to catch his breath. And her 🖤 🖤 🖤 response when he sent her a picture of his abs smeared with evidence of what she'd done with him told him that other guys were probably just doing this whole sexting thing very, very wrong.

He was so strung out on finally getting to come with Hannah that most of his humiliation from telling her that he was saving sex for marriage the night before was gone. Patrick would never stop laughing at him when he told him that.

Not that he was going to tell the father that he'd used the church's teachings on premarital sex to avoid having sex with Hannah when they hadn't ever mattered before. Jack was pretty sure that was a sin, and he was guessing that there weren't enough Hail Marys and Our Fathers to make up for it.

But it was the only thing he could think of in the moment that would save him. Not that it would save him from falling for Hannah. Nothing could stop that. Not after he'd slept in her bed. Not after she'd told him things he got the feeling she never talked about. Not after that morning.

Guilt at lying to her ate up his afterglow. He was so screwed.

CHAPTER NINETEEN

HANNAH ALWAYS HAD POINT on the company Halloween party, which she'd never been nervous about. She always had the perfect venue, theme, decorations, and music planned by late June. And this year was no different in those respects. But there was more riding on it this year. If this went well and she could convince Annalise that Jack had fallen in love with her, she would be a VP.

Uncharacteristic butterflies roamed free in her belly. After spending the night with Jack and the ironically sexy sexting that came the morning after, she was fairly certain that Annalise would interpret whatever was between them as love. But a little bit of uncertainty remained.

So much was riding on tonight, and she needed it to be perfect. If tonight went well, she was almost guaranteed a promotion.

And she could finally stop being the perfect girlfriend for Jack Nolan.

All of their most important clients and soon-to-be clients were sure to be wowed by the private tour of the Art Institute's Egyptian collection followed by cocktails and canapés in the Modern Wing.

Everyone was dressed in costumes from antiquity, which made for a stellar icebreaker and lots of men in very short skirts. All wins for Hannah.

But that didn't stop a pit from forming in her stomach as she hung out at the back of the tour, waiting for Jack to show up in his costume. Even though she should be paying attention and rubbing elbows, she was checking her phone every five seconds.

He was late.

Still no message about running late, totally uncharacteristic. Not that she knew what characteristic was. They'd just started dating two weeks ago. He'd done a bunch of annoying guy stuff—mansplaining, introducing her to both of his parents, and fighting his brother. And he'd sent her a dick pic.

He'd probably just been on his best behavior until she'd offered sex. Now he'd taper off. He'd show up late tonight without giving her a heads-up. Next week, he'd tell her he'd call her, and then "something would come up." In a few weeks, hopefully after the engagement party, she'd realize that he hadn't called or texted for a week. And she wouldn't be able to follow her previous advice to Sasha—if a guy isn't calling, it's best to leave it alone. She was woman enough to admit that Jack had wiggled his way underneath her defenses. Not that she'd tried very hard to keep him out.

She liked him. *Oh fuck.* She really liked him. Just in time for him to ghost her.

Luckily, she was saved from freaking out by Sasha finding her and pulling her over to deal with a problem with the caterers—they had gluten-free options and vegan options, but no gluten-free *and* vegan options, and one of the guests was having a conniption because she'd consumed mayonnaise with egg in it.

It was times like this when she felt like her job was stupid and

Noah had been right to suggest she do something more substantive and serious with her time.

All it took to fix it was telling the caterer to set aside some of the gluten-free toasts to pair with the vegan topping, but sometimes she couldn't believe that she had to tell people these things.

Worse yet, she was so hot from spending time in the kitchen that she swore she could feel her heavy kohl eyeliner slipping down her face and her wig listing to one side—not exactly the image of the cool, competent professional she was trying to portray for her boss and all of their firm's most important clients.

By the time she made it back to the party, the tour was over, and everyone was drinking in the vestibule of the Modern Wing. She checked her phone and still nothing from Jack. This was ridiculous. They'd been on a bunch of dates, and they'd had everything but sex. She could text him to see where he was when he wasn't where he was supposed to be. Doing that wouldn't make her a harpy. It didn't make her "crazy," and it wouldn't make him break up with her.

Where are you?

The message was delivered and then read, but still nothing. Not even the three dots. *Shit.* That jerk-off was going to stand her up. Without a goddamn word. Or an apology for freaking out after they'd gotten intimate. Not even a transparent excuse. He was going to bounce—and all she had to show for it were some orgasms.

Picking just the wrong moment, Giselle swanned toward her, wearing a costume that would have fit in on the set of an HBO period drama set in ancient times. Without doing anything, the woman managed to make Hannah feel even shabbier.

"Where's the boyfriend?" Giselle asked in a voice that made Hannah gnash her back teeth together.

She feigned looking around for him even though she knew he wasn't there. Even though by Monday everyone would know that he'd stood her up, she wasn't about to give Giselle any satisfaction in that regard right now. "Not sure. I was dealing with an emergency in the kitchen."

Giselle pressed her lips together. "Hmm."

"Where's your hubby?" God, the word "hubby" was awful, but it somehow seemed to fit the other woman's husband. "Cowering in the corner somewhere?" That probably wasn't necessary, but Hannah was feeling pretty raw and didn't really have the patience for Giselle's particular brand of psychological warfare right now.

Her coworker just changed her champagne glass to her left hand so that her giant engagement ring flashed in the light. Her aim was so good that Hannah was temporarily blinded. "He's getting me another drink. Husbands are handy for that. Not that you would know."

Hannah looked at her closely, squinting her eyes, as she took a sip.

"What are you staring at?"

"Checking to see if you have a forked tongue."

Giselle let out the closest thing to a laugh that her evil core would allow. "Shouldn't you be sucking up to Annalise or the Chapins right now?"

Hannah resented the accusation that she was some sort of suck-up. Not that it wasn't true. After all, she'd acquired a real live fake boyfriend at her boss's behest to prove that she wasn't averse to romantic love. That was real dedication.

And in this moment, when she was worried that all of her dedication wouldn't pay off and that all she'd be left with was a heart a little more cracked than it had been, she was too tired for more combat with Giselle.

"Don't you ever get tired of being such an underhanded bitch?"

Giselle paled under her carefully applied makeup, no doubt copied from an academic text on ancient face painting. Even though she absolutely loathed the woman, she had to respect her attention to detail. "Don't you ever get tired of being . . . you?"

Well, now Hannah knew she'd gotten to her. And still, it didn't matter. Giselle was going to get the promotion, and it wasn't even going to be a contest. Hannah wished she had told Annalise to stuff her promotion the moment she'd agreed that picking up some poor guy and dating him would prove her dedication. At least she would still have her pride. She would be able to reply to Giselle with something sharp and funny and mean. Something witty, instead of, "Yeah, honestly, I do."

It was exhausting to have to be on her guard all the time. She'd thought she didn't have to be that way with Jack. Too bad she was probably wrong.

Knowing she'd just admitted defeat, she decided to go look for Sasha. After all the times she'd helped her bestie pull herself together after a good sob over a guy, the least that same bestie could do was help her fix her makeup after a solid ten-minute cry in the bathroom.

She felt stupid, and her whole body felt as though someone had pounded it with a meat tenderizer. She'd avoided dating because she'd wanted to avoid this numb feeling that followed someone rejecting her just for being herself. And not only had she opened herself up to him, broken so many of her rules for him, but she'd started to believe that he could actually like her back.

Such bullshit. Dating—love—was bullshit.

Tears burned the back of her throat, and she wasn't sure she could make it through the evening without falling apart. She was never like this, and it just made her feel like crying more. She hated crying, and the fact that she was about three seconds from bawling at a work function was deeply embarrassing. Jack had embarrassed her, and it burned in her gut.

If he hadn't been serious about her, why had he introduced her to his family? That still made absolutely no sense to her.

It didn't matter now. He was done with her, and she was going to make herself done with him. She wasn't about to get a promotion, but she wasn't going to show any more cracks in public.

She spotted Sasha's wig—she was doing kind of an ancient Greek Barbarella thing with a beehive—and moved across the crowd. Even though she was cracked and crumbling and close to tears, she managed a couple of handshakes and smiles with the heads of marketing for her most loyal clients.

Just when she'd finished chatting up the head of marketing for the Hawks, the one who had gotten her tickets at center ice for her and Jack, she spotted him.

She hadn't seen him before because he'd been hidden behind Sasha's wig. He was holding a drink and laughing. Both of those things brought a haze of red over her vision. He'd been ignoring her texts and drinking and laughing with her best friend while she'd been mourning both her promotion and their—whatever *this* was.

And he was just standing there—laughing?

HANNAH'S MURDEROUS GAZE WAS like a spiked heel digging into his nuts. Tonight, he was trying "lack of basic consideration and respect" on for size, and it didn't fit him any better than flirting with other women or making things too serious, too soon.

Because he knew her well enough by now to know that behind her obvious anger there was some hurt on the side. He hated himself for doing this to her, but he was determined to follow through. He'd screwed things up by lying to her, and losing her for real was his penance.

She made her way over to him and Sasha and put her hand through his elbow. He knew he looked like a jackass. Although he'd followed instructions and worn his Mark Antony costume, he hadn't shaved in about three days and had made sure to smear some wing sauce on his toga. Chris had suggested that he go to the gym and not shower before the party, but that seemed excessively slovenly.

Instead, he decided to show up forty-five minutes late, not respond to any queries about his ETA, and then not look for her when he finally did show up. Jack had always been an ace communicator in relationships because he'd been taught basic manners. And he hated when a woman didn't communicate with him.

Except no communication might be preferable to the rage that Hannah was communicating to him perfectly right now. She hadn't even said anything, but the way her nails dug into his arm was plenty evocative of the way she'd probably like to skin his balls with her fingernails. And the feral smile she gave him when he looked down at her told him that this was the night. She was done with him.

"What are you two talking about?" Her voice was bright but almost brittle. *Translation: Where the hell have you been? And why didn't you let me know that you were going to be late?*

Seeing how angry she was now, he wished he had gone this route first. She would have broken up with him before they'd even slept together, and he could have told her the whole truth. She would have laughed at his stupidity and then continued dating him because he would have put on a charm offensive to rival any romantic-comedy movie. Grand gestures galore.

"I got caught up with the boys." It was partially true. After the gym, they'd gotten beers and his friends had given him more advice on how to drive Hannah to dump him in the most efficient way possible. Chris and Joey were an endless font of that kind of information, had Jack thinking that they might be lost causes in the relationships-with-human-females department. And it had him feeling really bad about being a dude.

"And broke your phone?" Her tone was sweet, but he was pretty sure she was laying a trap for him.

He could feel her emotional investment in him in the form of her anger, and he had a feeling that there would be no going back. He felt as though he were being torn in different directions.

He pulled his phone out of the one pocket conveniently sewn into his rented toga and pretended to be seeing her text message for the first time. There was only one of them, which surprised him. He expected multiple messages, increasing in anger. At the very least, he expected her to threaten his future ability to have children. That's what the girl he'd met at that stupid speakeasy would have done.

This Hannah was not that girl at all.

The moment he'd laid eyes on that girl, he'd been able to see a whole future with her. That wasn't uncommon: he'd had the same kind of trippy romantic projection with all of his former girlfriends. And none of those relationships had worked out, despite his best efforts.

That Hannah was different because she'd looked right through him. She'd seen past his try-hard Boy Scout exterior and straight to the heart of him. He knew this because if she hadn't seen it, she wouldn't have let him buy her a taco, much less see her naked.

All of his other girlfriends had been sweet. And Hannah was, too. She just hid her sweetness under a layer of tart that made her sweetness all the more satisfying. But something had changed between the night they'd met and when he'd almost had sex with her. Seeing her tonight, with all her sweet and tart broken up together, he realized the gravity of his mistake—she'd been serious about letting him in, while he'd been using her.

"Must have had my ringer off."

"Oh." Just one loaded word before she turned back to Sasha and started talking about some wedding that they were planning together.

He tuned them out, letting his mind wander and taking in the party. He was supposed to be arm candy tonight, which was rich. This was the sort of place where his mother would feel comfortable. His father would stick out like a sore thumb. Jack and Bridget had become as adaptable as possible—they could pass for neighborhood kids at the corner bar, but they could also clean themselves up for fancy parties with their mom's friends and colleagues. Maybe Michael had never bothered because he'd been older when their mom left, hadn't needed as much mothering.

Tonight, he felt out of place. Not just because he'd made some half-hearted effort to not fit in, but because he hadn't felt this sort of desperation to please someone since right after his mother had left. And even though plenty of water had flowed under the bridge of his parents' divorce, he still felt like he wasn't enough and had to try harder. That was why it was so much more difficult not to try at all.

He was ripped from his self-psychoanalysis by Sasha's mentioning Senator Chapin. The same Senator Chapin who had cost his dad and Michael a government contract. The same Senator Chapin who was allegedly taking bribes and pulling strings he had no business pulling in city hall. Unfortunately, Jack hadn't been able to get anyone on record saying that Senator Chapin had rigged some appropriations legislation so that one of his biggest donors would be sure to win a government contract.

"You're planning Senator Chapin's daughter's wedding?" He injected himself into the conversation, even though he was playing arm candy.

"Yes, and Hannah is going to get a promotion because of it." Jack liked how proud Sasha was of her friend and how they seemed to take ownership for each other's successes.

For her part, Hannah just rolled her eyes and shrugged, obviously trying to downplay how important this was to her.

"That's a big deal." Jack tapped his glass to Hannah's. "You should be proud of yourself." She stiffened at his patronizing tone, and he could feel her pulling away from him. That was the whole point of dating her, but he couldn't help wanting to pull out of the death spiral he'd initiated.

"It's not a big deal," she said. "Sure, it's a big wedding for important people, but I've planned bigger events, and Sasha is helping me. She's the real expert."

"Hannah is being modest. She's the one who planned tonight's event, and she's the most detail-oriented and organized person I know."

"But you're the one bringing the romance level way up," Hannah shot back, trying to outflatter her friend.

This was what Jack liked about women most—other than boobs and the fact that they smelled really nice. Bridget and her friends were always earnestly trying to build one another up. He and his friends, on the other hand, were constantly busting one another's balls. It could get exhausting. Just once, he'd like Chris or Joey to tell him how much his haircut made his cheekbones look good.

"And you're the one making sure that all the bride's demands are met."

Jack's mouth quirked up. He'd bet Hannah could cajole a caterer or a florist into doing just about anything. Hell, his dad could probably use her to shake down subcontractors. He shouldn't think about her at the same time he thought about his family anymore. It wasn't fair to either of them. He needed to focus on finishing out this story and moving on to covering politics.

"How much is the budget on this wedding?"

Sasha must have had plenty of champagne, because she jumped right in despite a look from Hannah. "Oh, we couldn't reveal it."

"It's nothing we can't handle." Hannah must have thought he was questioning her ability to handle it. God, he hated having her mad at him. It seemed like he couldn't say anything that night without it sounding crass or dismissive or patronizing. He'd flubbed up by being late and unkempt, but he wished that Hannah would just lay into him about that instead of acting like he'd suddenly turned into the enemy. The enemy being other men, the men she'd dated before who had let her down. He didn't want to be that guy, wished he had another choice—

Then he saw Senator Chapin across the room, with his wife and presumably his daughter. And he had an idea.

"Can I get an introduction?" He interrupted Sasha and he felt bad about that. But he was eager to put his new plan in motion before he could think better of it.

Hannah looked him up and down. Her gaze lingered on his stained toga and unshaven face. "Are you drunk?"

"No." That was true. Part of the plan for the night had been to get very drunk in a way that would infuriate Hannah, but he'd scuttled that as soon as he'd seen her. "I just might want to have an in for a story at some point."

Hannah scoffed. "Like 'How to Run for Senator and Win'?"

That hit him in the gut, though he supposed he deserved it after telling her how she should feel about her job. "Yeah, I'm trying to break into the political beat."

Hannah paused and bit her lip. "Can I least get the grease off your toga first?"

He nodded, and she grabbed his hand, tugging him toward a dark hallway and into the bathroom.

"If you wanted a quickie before talking to the senator, you could have just asked." He couldn't resist making the joke. He might have decided that lying was off the table, but teasing and flirting were still very much on it. And after he'd explained things to her, sex would be very much on the table as well.

"Shut up."

She had grabbed a bottle of club soda off a tray, and then doused the stain with it. While she worked, he had a chance to look at her. Her wig was off-kilter, probably from running around making sure everything was going smoothly all night and wondering where the hell her date was.

He reached out and straightened it, and she looked at him through the blunt bangs. He let his palm run down her cheek and wiped away a little bit of out-of-place eyeliner with his thumb. That afternoon, Chris had been complaining about how a girl he'd gone on a date with the night before had showed up in "full porn-star makeup" and went on to detail how makeup was just a tool women used to trap men. His best friend was an idiot, to be sure. And Jack couldn't disagree more.

Maybe it was having a younger sister he'd had to help teach how to apply makeup so that the nuns wouldn't send her home for harlotry, but he got that it wasn't about fooling anyone. Makeup wasn't about anything having to do with catching a man. Even with tons of black gunk smudged around her eyes, Hannah couldn't hide from him. And the golden green of her eyes shone even brighter with all that dark around it.

The way she looked at him, as though his bad behavior had been forgotten, forced him to kiss her. And she opened up to him as though he'd been playing this whole thing the right way from the very beginning.

All of his worries about his new plan blowing up in his face fled, and her lush mouth filled him with the resolve to do whatever he had to do to keep her.

She pulled back, and her swollen lips quirked up in a smile. "Wipe your mouth."

He looked into the mirror over her head and saw that her red lipstick was smeared over his face. He looked debauched and almost ruined. At least he looked how he felt.

God, he was such a maudlin asshole tonight.

"All done." He looked down and, sure enough, the stain was gone.

"You're magic."

She shrugged again. "Would have been done sooner if you hadn't kissed me."

"I'm not going to not kiss you when I want to." He put his hand on her lower back as they left the bathroom. An older woman saw them leave and appeared to be scandalized. He winked at her. "I'm going to kiss my girlfriend whenever I want."

HOLY SHIT HAD HER night turned around. Not only had Jack met and clearly impressed the senator, but Annalise was halfway in love with him. As soon as Jack went to the bar to fetch them drinks, her boss had caught her eye and fanned herself in the face. Apparently, Jack could charm even the ice queen herself.

That was probably why she'd never stood a chance once he'd turned his attention on her. It was why she hadn't lied and told him that she had to stay and clean up after the party, even though they had a crew set up to do that. It was why—instead of telling him she was tired or had a headache—she was half in his lap in the back of a car. Why his mouth was on hers and his hands were under her skirt.

Truth was, he could have stood her up tonight and she probably would have forgiven him. She might have had a little heartburn about it, but she would have accepted any excuse. He hadn't snuck around her defenses; he'd blown them to bits. If she had any sense of self-preservation, she would be questioning how much she felt for him. She'd be pushing him away, not taking him home with the full intention of doing everything but sex with him.

At some point, they'd have to talk about communication if she was really his girlfriend and he was really her boyfriend. But for now, his kisses were too heady, and she was just champagne drunk enough to ignore this evening's indiscretions.

"You taste like champagne." He sounded as though that pleased him, and it sent a shiver down her whole spine. He caught that and ran his hand up and down her back. "You should have brought a jacket."

"I was so busy thinking about the party that I forgot that it would get cold." She hadn't needed to wear anything over her costume when going into the party.

"Next time, I'll bring you one." She liked the sound of all of that way too much. She liked that there would be a next time, but mostly she liked that he wanted to take care of her.

For so long, she'd been fighting letting anyone in. With Jack, she felt like she could just let go. So he'd made a few mistakes. She'd made enough in her past that she could forgive him. And if he ever found out that she'd said she'd go out with him to advance in her career, he might get mad. But she had to believe that what was real right now was the chemistry that fizzed between them when they locked eyes. The fire that raced over her skin when he touched her. The way he smiled at her that made her heart race.

Instead of telling him any of this, instead of scaring him as much as he terrified her, she kissed him until they got back to her place.

CHAPTER TWENTY

USUALLY, JACK WAS HAPPY when he was drinking beer. Maybe the happiest he ever was. And that wasn't because of the beer. But when he was drinking a beer, he was usually around his friends or his family—people who got him and understood him. He was around the people whom he didn't have to watch his words with. Being with his dad, Michael, Bridge, Chris, Patrick, and Joey never felt like a chore to him.

That was why he usually didn't drink beer at work events. Work felt like scotch or something brown and smoky that he could have one drink of before he made an exit.

Maybe he felt unhappy because he didn't want to be drinking beer in a dive bar whose scotch could not be trusted to celebrate the fact that one of his colleagues had just gotten a job with the *New York Times*. He knew that the powers that be at the site weren't going to spring for Gene & Georgetti, but a place where anyone without socks was likely to catch dysentery was a new low, even for *HM*.

He didn't like feeling jealous of his coworkers, and he knew it wasn't a good look. But he was mature enough to admit to himself that he wanted what that guy had. And maybe he wanted more than what that guy had because he was still wanting his mommy's approval. If he worked at the *Times*, it would be something that both his parents could brag about. The fact that he even thought about that made him want to reexamine his life choices. The fact that he was still after the same thing he'd been after since he was fourteen years old was probably what made the terrible beer turn sour in his gut.

The only source of sustenance—peanuts that had probably been in the same brass bowl for about a decade—didn't give him much hope that he could settle his stomach anytime soon.

God, he was tired. He didn't want to work on his assigned story, either. So making noises about a deadline wasn't likely to get him moving out the door in the near future. Not even to escape the eighties power ballads pouring out of the ancient jukebox.

And maybe he was so jealous because of the huge contrast between what a guy who'd been hired a year after him had accomplished and his assignment—manipulating and using a woman who had blown his damned mind.

In fact, the only place he wanted to be right now was between Hannah's sweet thighs. Ever since he'd slept in her bed, he hadn't been able to concentrate on anything else. And after the dick pic and her nonreaction to his showing up late and disheveled to her work party, he hadn't been able to come up with any new ideas for pushing her away.

Because he didn't want to push her away. Everything in him only wanted to pull her in closer.

If only he had the courage to tell Irv to get his fluff piece from some other idiot and to tell Hannah the truth. Staring into the piss-colored brew, he even had a brief fantasy of going to work for his dad. Not even supervising like Michael, but doing the loud, noisy, dirty work he'd always hated. But maybe he'd only hated it because it had been the loud, the noisy, the dirty, that his mother had rejected and pushed away when she'd walked away from all of them.

And even though he'd started working on the school paper to spend more time with his girlfriend, he'd stayed with it because his mom had approved of his intellectual pursuits. The times she'd visited campus and taken him to lunch, she'd actually asked him about what he'd been working on and listened to his answers without pursing her lips.

He'd truly loved it, too. But he hated what he was doing now, and he couldn't stomach hurting Hannah. Although she was a tough nut to crack, being around her made him feel easy, deep inside. When he woke up in her bed, he felt like he belonged there. Like every other woman he'd ever been with had been a practice run for Hannah.

But he'd given up on his own ambitions for a woman before. And he wouldn't forgive himself if he chucked his job and Hannah still walked away from him. He refused to be the kind of sucker he'd been for every other woman he'd ever risked his heart on.

Didn't make it any easier, though.

He hadn't called her, which he knew had to hurt her feelings, but that wasn't an intentional move. He just didn't know what to say to her that would make what he was doing okay. Lying made him want to punch himself in the nuts. And telling her the truth would probably make her punch him in the nuts.

So his nuts were toast either way.

Concern for his nuts didn't stop him from checking his phone to see if she'd called him. Disappointment kicked him near, but not quite directly in, his junk when he saw that he'd only missed messages from his dad and brother.

Before, when he hadn't been deliberately trying to be a jackhole to women, he'd never not known what to do in a dating situation. He'd lived by the guiding principle of doing whatever it took to make his lady happy. And now, when he was trying—and somehow failing—to make a particular lady so unhappy with him that she would dump him, he was bewildered. For a moment, he wondered if this was how most straight men felt most of the time. And it rocked him back on his heels until his beer was empty.

He ambled over to the bar, calculating that he had one more beer's worth of fake smiles and small talk in him before his façade cracked. He'd put in his order when he got a hard smack to the middle of his back that told him he wasn't going to get out of this without talking to his boss.

"How's the story going, kid?"

"Fine."

"She dump your ass yet?"

The truth was that he didn't know. Maybe the sex stuff after the Halloween party had just been a kiss-off, but that wouldn't make a good story. He had to come up with something in the way of a status report. "Nah, but I'm on the right track."

"You're too pretty." The tone of Irv's words denoted that they were not a compliment. "With the outline you gave me of what you've already done, she should be trying to run you down with a car."

Given his newfound empathy for the masses of idiots who didn't know how to date, he begged to differ. "Nah. I think that she's probably just so used to the kind of shit that I've been doing that she's letting it roll right off her."

His second beer arrived, and he ordered Irv another one. If he was going to listen to his boss tell him how pretty he was, he needed a bit more of a buzz on.

"I think you need to step up your game, kid."

When he'd first started working at the magazine, he'd thought that Irv calling everyone "kid" had been charming. Tonight, it was grating. And he didn't want to talk about this article anyway. It was bad enough that he actually had to write it in the first place.

He wanted to shift to the kinds of stories he *should* be working on. "Listen, I've done some more digging on that political story I mentioned. I talked to my dad's buddy, and he has a guy who's willing to talk—"

Irv totally just cut him off, which wasn't new. But the anger brewing in him, the urge to hit something or yell, was brand-new. "I think you need to do some truly heinous shit to make this work—like cheating or asking her if she wants to 'open up' the relationship. I hear that's a thing that all the kids are doing. Maybe you can even tell her that you've been married all along. That'll definitely do the job—"

"You want me to lie to her?"

"Kid, you've been lying to her the whole time."

Wasn't that the sad truth. Except for the first night they'd met and a handful of text messages, everything about them had been a lie. Other than the sex—he hadn't been able to keep the truth of how much he wanted her out of that. But sexing her up wasn't going to prevent her from doing him grievous bodily injury when she found out—or after she read the article.

His mind scrambled for a way to get out of this stupid story. "Can't I just fill in the rest with generic advice? I really have chemistry with this girl, and I want to see where it goes."

Irv paused for a moment, and then guffawed. "I pay you to do a fucking job. If you don't want to do your fucking job, I have thousands of résumés in my e-mail from people who'll do whatever the fuck they're told."

He'd never heard his boss say anything that cold before. Suddenly, he realized why the seemingly avuncular man had been brought in to steer the digital ship. Irv was ruthless; he got people to do what he wanted, but he snuck up on them.

Jack's only response was a nod.

"Good." Irv hit him on the back again. This time, Jack listed a bit to the side, as though some of his muscles had been pulled out of his body during their conversation. "We're actually going to do something with a streaming service, and I need your pretty face on the news."

Jack struggled to process the pivot to a pivot-to-video this conversation had taken. "I'm up for that?" He had a hard time believing it given that Irv had just threatened to fire him.

"Of course," Irv said, apparently ready to forget all the shit he'd just said. "Team players get to do real news. On-screen."

So he had a clear choice to make. He could either tell Hannah the truth, not write the story, and get fired, or he could write the story, which would tear Hannah apart, and get to do real news.

Shit.

CHAPTER TWENTY-ONE

Wednesday, 10:17 p.m.

Jack: hey

Hannah: sup?

Jack: what r you doing?

Hannah: about to go to sleep.

Jack: what r you wearing?

Hannah: r u sexting me!?

Jack: trying to 😴

Hannah: I'm about to go to sleep

Jack: send n00ds?

Hannah: are you drunk?

Jack: no

Hannah: if I send you a nude, it will be a nude cat . . .

Jack: I like pussy.

Hannah: I recall

Jack: yeah, you do

Hannah: stop being a jerk. Going to sleep.

Jack: asking for n00ds makes me a jerk?

Hannah: yup

Jack: sleep well

Thursday, 12:45 p.m.

Jack: whatcha doing?

Hannah: working. Aren't you?

Jack: I'm bored.

Hannah: my grandma used to say that if you're bored, you're stupid.

Jack: wow

Jack: you're a little mean, aren't you?

Hannah: listen, Jack. Last night you asked me for naked pictures . . .

Hannah: now you're interrupting me at work

Hannah: what are you trying to do here?

Jack: just trying to talk to you . . .

Hannah: I'm at work now

Jack: so am i

Hannah: I don't have time to talk at work

Jack: because planning parties is so important 😑

Hannah: I don't think I like Jack-on-text

Jack: ☹️

Hannah: can we put a pin in this?

Jack: I guess

Hannah: want to grab a quick bite after work?

Jack: so, I only get a quick bite?

Jack: I like long, lingering bites.

Hannah: I'm still at work. Why are you talking about sex?!

211

Jack: I'm a dude.

Hannah: let's pause this

Jack: whatever. Ur no fun

Hannah: That's certainly not what you thought the other night.

Jack: you're still thinking about it, too?

Hannah: of course.

Hannah: That's why I didn't block your number after you asked for nude pics

Jack: noted

Hannah: so, dinner tonight?

Jack: let's play it by ear

Hannah: fine

NOTHING—OTHER THAN MAYBE ORAL sex from one Jack Nolan—made Hannah happier than cake. She liked all cakes—white, yellow, chocolate, cheese, even carrot as long as it didn't have raisins. And she wasn't even particular about frosting. Buttercream and cream cheese were the superior options, but she would never turn her nose up at a fudge or meringue.

Hannah would let nothing stand in the way of her enjoyment of cake, not even a certain senator's daughter whining about her fictional gluten allergy. Her father had let that one slip after one too many swigs of scotch last week while tasting signature drinks at one of the possible wedding reception venues.

And now Madison was trying the patience of Hannah and Sasha's favorite baker in town. It had taken every string Hannah could pull to get Ali to create a cake for the engagement party on short notice, but Ali seemed to be souring on their deal (cake in exchange for

Beyoncé tickets) with every reference to how any trace of wheat flour would cause Madison digestive issues.

"This coconut cake is gluten-free," Sasha said as Hannah stuffed her mouth with a piece of the gluten-rich chocolate option to keep herself from making a smartass remark. "Really, any of the options could be."

Madison scrunched up her face and looked to her mother for guidance. For her part, her mother looked bored. "Just make a decision, Maddy."

Madison bit her bottom lip and looked as though she was trying not to cry. For Christ's sake, it was just cake. It didn't matter what she chose. People were going to get drunk and eat the cake. It was the most important day of only Madison's life; everyone else there would just be in it for the party and possibly a photo op with the senator.

Her hesitation to make any real choices made Hannah wonder if she really wanted to get married at all.

The bride-to-be's indecision was going to drive her nuts. Hannah reminded herself that she *wanted* to be planning weddings because it would be good for her career, not necessarily her sanity. But at this point she didn't know if she would make it through planning this engagement party—and it was just a test run.

Huh. Maybe a test run of the cakes would make Madison's ultimate cake choice easier.

"Why don't you get a selection of all the cakes for the engagement party and then pick what you and the guests actually like best for the wedding?"

Madison's eyes lit up, and Hannah knew that she'd made the right decision. Sasha thanked the baker, who gratefully packed up leftovers for Hannah and Sasha to bring home.

Thursday, 6:45 p.m.

Hannah: leaving work now. Still on for dinner?

Thursday, 7:34 p.m.

Hannah: I'm getting hangry.
Hannah: like scaring small children hangry

HANNAH WAITED FOR JACK to respond to her texts about dinner for a good half hour before breaking out the cake samples. Sasha would understand when she came home from her date to find nothing but crumbs—this was an emergency.

After today's success with getting Madison to pick a cake, she actually felt really good about her chances of earning her promotion the right way. And Annalise believed that she and Jack were in love. But his not responding to her texts when they had plans was not a good sign that they'd make it as a "couple" through the weekend. And then it might not matter that she was actually good at her job.

She was eating red velvet cake with the richest cream cheese frosting she'd ever had, but she wasn't really enjoying it. It was hard to enjoy one of the bonuses of her line of work because she wasn't sure it was the right line of work for her anymore. If she had to have a boyfriend to get a promotion, then what was the point?

And she was starting to think that she'd rather have the boyfriend be her real boyfriend than have the promotion. Which was a real problem. She'd thought she would be able to keep herself from growing feelings for Jack. He was too perfect—not just for her, but for any flesh-and-blood woman. But then he'd started showing cracks, acting like a normal guy, and it almost made him seem more attainable. More human.

But it was silly. Almost all of his behavior since their first date had the stench of ambivalence all over it. If she'd been seeing him for real, she really hoped she would have dumped him by now—no matter how good the sexy times were. But she had the sneaking suspicion that she would have let him do all the stupid stuff he'd been doing because they had chemistry like she'd never had with anyone else.

And that made her feel like a real fool.

Thursday, 10:18 p.m.

Jack: still want to get dinner?

Hannah: had takeout two hours ago

Hannah: And cake. You missed out on cake.

Hannah: going to bed. G'night

Friday, 10:18 a.m.

Jack: you still want me to come to your thing 2morrow night?

Hannah: you still want to?

Hannah: I thought this was turning into a booty call for you?

Jack: u mad at me?

Hannah: kind of.

Jack: why?

Hannah: I feel like Jack-on-text is like every other guy on Tinder.

Hannah: I like Jack in person much better

Jack: you like me in person?

Hannah: stop fishing

Hannah: if you want to come, please pick up a tux today before five

Jack: I have a tux.

Hannah: a 1920s vintage one?

Jack: that sounds uncomfortable

Hannah: if you want to see me festooned in sequins, pick up the tux like I told you

Jack: I like it when you order me around

Hannah: of course you do. 😏

Jack: so, I'm forgiven if I pick up the tux

Hannah: see you tomorrow night

Jack: send pictures of the sequins

Hannah: I'm busy. Have a caterer to menace.

CHAPTER TWENTY-TWO

JACK HADN'T BEEN TO confession since the time he had to go before his First Communion. But he couldn't just lay everything out for Patrick during their weekly basketball game. He didn't want Chris, Joey, or Michael to hear about how guilty he felt and about how much he felt for Hannah.

Any one of his friends and family would help him move. They'd bail him out of jail. They'd help him bury a body. But they would give him a rasher of shit if he told them that he was so in love with Hannah that he couldn't see straight and that he was thinking about tanking his career—again—just for a shot at being with her.

Patrick would get it because he'd made the same type of hard choice when it came to becoming a priest, and Jack had been there for his friend when it had come time for him to make that choice.

He got in the little confessional booth and waited until Patrick's silhouette appeared through the metal mesh screen. "Bless me, Father, for I have sinned."

"Nolan?" Patrick's surprise was certainly unpastoral. "What are you doing here?"

"Aren't you supposed to ask me how long it's been since my last confession?"

"I know it's been at least twenty years, because I was waiting in line behind you the last time."

Jack laughed. His friend was right. And he'd been waiting a long time. That last/first confession had happened around the time his parents were divorced. The priest had taken a long time trying to convince him that it wasn't his fault, that he had nothing to do with his mom not being there when he got home from school, or the fact that his father never laughed anymore.

"Seriously, what did you do?" Patrick asked.

"I lied to Hannah."

"That's not new. You've been lying to her since you met." Maybe Patrick couldn't keep his judgment tamped down because they'd been friends for so long, but still.

"You're kind of shitty at this, Padre."

"Don't swear in the confessional."

"Aren't you just supposed to give me a thousand Hail Marys or something and send me on my way?" That wasn't really what Jack was expecting; he certainly deserved to crawl across a floor of nails for what he'd done to Hannah—what he was thinking about doing to her.

Patrick sighed. "Why is this just bothering you right now?"

"I think I could be falling in love with this girl."

"You can't know that, dude."

He certainly felt like he knew it. The idea of losing her made him feel like shit. "I think I know myself."

"I beg to differ." Patrick had the nerve to sound bored.

"What the fuck does that mean?"

"Language. House of God. C'mon."

"Sorry."

Patrick paused before continuing. "You say you're in love with this girl, but you hardly know her."

"I know enough."

"You know you have a healthy amount of lust for her."

"About that, I should probably confess to more than the lying—"

"Jesus Christ, Nolan." Patrick must be disappointed in him if he was taking the Lord's name in vain while performing his priestly duties. "You slept with her?!"

"No. Kind of." Jack decided to come completely clean, with the likely effect of making pre-priesthood Patrick very, very jealous. "There was some sodomy—some mouth sodomy—and some very impure thoughts exchanged via sext."

He wasn't going to say anything about the sex toy thing because that might blow up his friend's brain.

"You have to tell her the truth," Patrick said. "And I'm not just saying that's the way to get right with God. You're barely even Catholic anymore." True. Jack just wanted someone with some authority to tell him how to fix this. Patrick being the smartest guy he knew and having God on his side, he thought this was the right place to come. "But you have to tell her the truth if you want a chance of finding out if you're in love with her."

Damn. Patrick was right. "What if I tell her the truth and she never wants to see me again?"

"There's a chance that will happen, but it's not like you have anything to lose here if it does. If she won't listen to you and accept an apology, then what do you really have now?"

"I'll lose my job if I tell her the truth." Patrick knew that Jack had made most of his academic and career moves because of whatever woman he was dating at the time, so that was a big deal to him.

"I wouldn't say this to any of my parishioners, and definitely not to any of my other friends, but maybe think about yourself and what's best for you for once?"

Part of Jack wanted to do that. If he could turn off his feelings for Hannah and go through with the story, he would take that opportunity right now. He didn't like feeling as much as he did about Hannah and not knowing whether he could make things work.

On the one hand, he was afraid that she was just like every other girl he'd ever been involved with. He was afraid that he would never be enough for her, no matter what he gave up to keep her. Just like he hadn't been able to keep his family together by being a good little boy. Maybe he was done being a good guy altogether.

But still, selfish didn't fit him. It wasn't the man he was raised to be, by either of his parents.

"I can't tell you what to do, but I can tell you this—" His friend paused and breathed. Oddly, even though Jack wasn't a real believer anymore, a sense of calm came over him just sitting there for a beat waiting for his confessor to speak—to give him his penance. "You have to figure out if this thing with Hannah is different from your things with Maggie, Katie, and Lauren. If she's the other half of you and not just a way for you to work out your mommy issues."

How the hell was he supposed to figure that out? Next time he went to confession, he was definitely going to a priest who hadn't known him since he was in diapers.

JACK DIDN'T WANT TO talk to Hannah's ex. There was a good chance that he would tell Hannah that Jack was researching a story, and Hannah would assume that he'd only been dating her to get information about the senator. Of course, she would be right in assuming that he was using her for a story. But talking to Noah Long was his best shot at getting what he needed to break the story on Senator Chapin.

Even after Irv's smackdown at happy hour, he wasn't about to quit working on this story. He didn't become a journalist so he could humiliate a woman he could really fall for. And he had a gut feeling about this story. It could be his ticket out of working puff pieces. It had to be.

Nolan men never quit when they had a gut feeling like this. And they never hesitated to make their own opportunities.

He'd been sitting outside the senator's local office for a few hours when Noah finally emerged.

Jack didn't make a habit of comparing himself to other guys—he'd never had a reason to. But he found himself wondering how he measured up against Senator Chapin's aide. He couldn't not. Hannah had sworn off dating for years after things ended with this guy.

He'd never been into a dude before, but he knew for a fact that Noah was handsome. Noah's parents were both professors at historically black colleges in Georgia, and he had been valedictorian at Morehouse. He'd worked in advertising for a couple of years before entering the foreign service, which had landed him in Senator Chapin's office.

Noah Long was the total package, unlike Jack. Jack was still feeling his way through life, still trying to make a career he loved happen.

"Noah." He stopped in front of Hannah's ex on the sidewalk. "Could I have a word?"

The guy pasted on a slick smile that didn't reach his eyes and straightened his pure silk tie. "Do I know you?"

"No, but I'm reporting a story on your boss."

Noah's slick smile disappeared. "Then you know that you can call my assistant during regular business hours to set up an interview."

"This isn't the kind of thing I think you want to talk about in the office." Jack needed to stand his ground now.

"Seriously, where do I know you from?" Noah narrowed his gaze. Jack toyed with telling him that he was the guy who was reaping the rewards of his stupidity when it came to Hannah but thought better of it. It would be best if Jack remained a faceless reporter to this guy. From Hannah's oblique references to the guy, it seemed like he had his head up his ass enough that he wouldn't even remember Jack's name. Hell, he hadn't even asked his name.

At the same time Jack said, "I'm Jack Nolan," Noah said, "You're Hannah's new boyfriend."

Jack wasn't about to deny it. Even though he wouldn't feel like Hannah's boyfriend until she knew the whole truth about how they'd started and why he'd acted so strangely, he liked hearing it, and he wanted it to be true. "Yeah."

Noah scoffed, and Jack's fist clenched reflexively. "Good luck with that." That this guy didn't see that Hannah was pure gold pissed him off for sure.

"That's not why I'm here to talk to you." Jack needed to get this back on track. "I've gotten some documents that seem to insinuate that the senator's involvement with the building contracts and permits for the new federal building downtown aren't completely on the up-and-up."

"Listen—"

Jack wasn't about to let this guy put a spin on the situation before he'd even asked the question. "I can either get your comment now or when your boss is forced to resign." Jack shrugged, trying to appear nonchalant. "You seem like a pretty smart guy, and you probably care enough about your future in politics to want to distance yourself."

His gambit didn't work. Noah's spine seemed to stiffen, and he said, "I can see why you can get past Hannah's lack of class."

"We're not talking about Hannah right now." Jack didn't want to have to punch the guy in the middle of the street. "We're talking about how you're working for a guy trying to fleece the people he's supposed to represent and what's going to happen when that all goes public."

"You and she are just alike." This asshole really wasn't going to let this go? Maybe he was still obsessed with her. Jack knew that he would be if he couldn't convince her to date him for real after telling her the truth. "Everything is good or bad, pure or evil with her. And she has less tact than most toddlers."

Basically all of Jack's favorite things about her. "Hannah's honesty might be off-putting to someone who wouldn't know the truth if it hit him in the nuts. But her honestly and loyalty are two of my favorite things about her."

Jack should be telling Hannah this, but it felt good to say it to *someone*. And making this douchebag feel the pain of losing Hannah all over again was just a bonus.

He hoped he wasn't imagining the pain crossing Noah's face. "Are you going to comment on the allegations, or what?"

"No comment."

What a douche. Hannah was better off without him. It remained to be seen whether she was better off without Jack.

CHAPTER TWENTY-THREE

HANNAH DIDN'T KNOW HOW Sasha didn't kill at least three brides a year. They were planning the social event of the century for the next evening. Caterers, florists, and a big band all had to be confirmed and/or supervised, and Madison got a wild hair up her ass to go wedding dress shopping. And then she got an appointment at the most exclusive bridal salon in Chicago and insisted that Hannah and Sasha come with her to "run interference" with her mother.

Wasn't that what friends were for? Over the past couple of weeks, Hannah had gotten the impression that Madison didn't have that many friends. And that hurt Hannah's heart. She didn't know what she would do if she didn't have Sasha and their other college girlfriends in her life. Thinking about how lonely Madison must be to force her wedding planners into hanging out with her was the only thing that got her onto a pink couch, surrounded by fluffy white dresses, when she ought to have been reaming out a rental place for trying to short them on forks.

Hannah would never admit it to anyone, but she loved wedding dresses—the satin, the tulle, the glitz. She used to dream about wearing one and meeting a man who really loved her at the end of the aisle of the basilica at Notre Dame.

Over the past couple of weeks, spending so much time with Jack while surrounded by the wedding industrial complex, she'd allowed herself to start dreaming of a wedding again. She couldn't pinpoint exactly when it had happened, when the daydreams had come back, when the guy at the end of the aisle in her daydreams had turned into Jack Nolan.

But, even though this had all started out as fake, simply a way to prove that she wasn't a sad, bitter spinster-in-waiting, her feelings for Jack had certainly become real.

The wide-eyed bridal gown consultant hustled across the sales floor and back again, into the back room and back out, until her knees were buckling from the weight of all the dresses in her arms.

"I want to wear blush," Madison said.

Mrs. Chapin sniffed. "Over your father's dead body."

"Maybe an off-white," Sasha suggested.

Hannah should say something, but her eye kept snagging on a cream-colored dress that seemed to have walked right out of her dreams. It was simple, but she could almost feel it floating around her feet as she walked toward Jack. Danced with him at their wedding.

She shook her head, trying to clear it out. Even if she and Jack were really going to be together after the engagement party, after she came clean about using him to get ahead at work and confronted him about his strange behavior, it was way too soon to be thinking about marriage.

When Madison spoke to her, she realized she'd lost the thread of the conversation. Madison was holding the dress that Hannah saw herself wearing in the wedding she was not going to have to Jack. "You don't like this one?"

Hannah flushed. "I do." She tried to cover. "I think it would look stunning on you."

Madison gave her a knowing smile. "No, I think it would be perfect on you."

"You should try it on." Oh sure, now Mrs. Chapin was down for some frivolity?

"Yeah, it would look fabulous with your skin tone." *Et tu, Sasha?* When Hannah gave her a pointed look, she shrugged and said, "What? It's true."

"We're not here for me. We're here for Madison." She was going to be firm on this. "And we should really be checking on the florists—"

"I insist you try on the dress, Hannah. It's my appointment, and I can do what I want."

Hannah looked around to find all the women in the room seemingly firm in their conviction to have her try on the stupid dress.

Her hands shook as the consultant helped her put on the dress. As though fate had decided to laugh at her, it fit perfectly. She was almost too nervous to look in the mirror, afraid she'd completely fall in love with the idea of being with Jack for real.

But she looked up when the consultant gasped. And then she gasped. The dress was absolutely perfect, better than she'd dreamed. And that was a huge problem.

The things she dreamt about were never better in reality. The life she'd planned out in her head with Noah hadn't even come close to happening. And she'd been so careful to try to keep Jack out of her heart. A few yards of chiffon and some expert beading that made her tits look fantastic shouldn't make her feel *anything*.

But seeing herself in the dress made everything real. She touched the fabric at her waist, ran her fingers over the seams. She couldn't discern a specific pattern, but the whole was greater than the sum of its parts. It all worked together.

She and Jack might not have gotten the most auspicious start, and she couldn't quite see her way through how coming clean with him was going to go. He could very well never want to see her again if she told him she'd used him. And—outside of his very talented mouth—he hadn't been anywhere close to perfect since their first actual date. But the way she felt with him was the way she wanted to feel—she felt like she belonged with him. She could be herself with him, which was something she'd never experienced with anyone else.

"Hannah?" Sasha had come looking for her. She must have been staring at herself in the mirror for a long-ass time.

"Be right out." She had to get out of the dress before Sasha came in, but the bridal consultant must have been helping Madison, the real customer. So her best friend walked in on her and slapped her hands over her mouth.

"Hannah, it's—"

"I know." Her eyes filled with tears. "Help me get this thing off."

JACK WOKE UP WITH Hannah straddling his hips with her long, sexy legs. He'd been dreaming of her, so it took him a moment to realize that the dream had ended and her smooth thighs were rubbing up against his jeans.

After running down more leads on his corruption story earlier that day, he'd been at loose ends. He'd taken the L up to the Loop and wandered around Millennium Park, even doing a stupid-tourist thing of staring at his own face in the Bean. About halfway through, he'd realized what an idiot he'd been and come back to his apartment to write.

He hadn't meant to fall asleep as he waited for Hannah, but he hadn't been sleeping much since his conversation with Irv. Luckily, he'd had a brief reprieve from the how-to game when a celebutante had gotten in a coke-fueled car crash and all of the site's articles had to be about that for three days.

God bless the celebrity news cycle.

So, even though talking to Patrick and running down leads on the story about the senator hadn't quite yielded a solution yet, he'd called Hannah and asked her to come over after she'd gotten done with some work stuff she had to do for the Chapin engagement party the next night. He hadn't seen her in almost a week, not since he'd woken up in her bed, wrapped in her smell, and decided he'd do whatever he had to do to keep her. Not since Irv had threatened to destroy his professional reputation if he didn't destroy his burgeoning relationship with Hannah.

They'd texted and talked on the phone, and he'd half-heartedly tried to be an ass. But neither of them, it seemed, could stand not to talk for even a day. And that wasn't the same as tasting her skin and feasting on her gorgeous mouth. Nothing technology could come up with compared to having her weight pushing him into the couch.

Hannah smiled down at him, and he forgot all about his career. This was dangerous because he was supposed to be telling her the truth. But that would require his putting the brakes on what was happening now, and he just wasn't prepared to do that when she put her hands on his face and pressed her mouth to his.

Not when he was trapped between waking and sleeping with a

dream of a woman rubbing herself against his cock and moaning into his mouth as he got harder.

When she finally gave up his mouth, he said, "That's some wake-up call."

"Is it okay that the doorman let me in?" She nuzzled his jaw, sounding as soft and sleepy as he felt. He wrapped his arms around her, holding her tight to him.

"I wake up with a hot woman in my lap, I'm too smart to complain about that."

She pulled back again, a look in her eye. "Question is, what are you going to do with me?"

"You have tonight off?"

She nodded. "You?"

He really should be working. Or telling her everything, but he still didn't know if that was the right thing to do. The only thing he did know was that he needed more time to figure it out and he wouldn't figure it out unless she was right there with him.

It wasn't him who decided that tonight they would just be a real couple and that he'd figure the rest out tomorrow. It was the way she sighed when he grabbed a handful of her fine ass and moved her body up his so that he could take control and kiss her properly.

Her sigh was just magic and fire like that.

ALL HER RULES WERE out the window now that she was officially Jack's girlfriend. Jack's girlfriend could not be expected to hesitate or have doubts about slipping into his apartment and waking him up by grinding on him—not when she hadn't seen him in almost a week.

Luckily, he'd seemed amenable to the idea. His hands roamed

over her back, slowly. They had all night together, and he took advantage. His kisses were soft, but not weak. They were leisurely, which just made her want more of him. He was hard beneath her belly, so she knew he was tamping down his urgency to be inside of her, but that did nothing to make her less impatient.

When he moved his mouth behind her ear, tipping her head to one side, she said, "I don't need all this."

"Huh?" He still sounded sleepy and so damn cute that she wanted to eat him up.

"Foreplay." She moved her hips, making him groan. "The foreplay is the fact that I haven't seen you all week."

He cupped her jaw and made her look him in the eye. He had the nerve to look amused. "What if I need to taste you all over, Duchess?"

She smiled back at him, sure there was one good way to provoke him. "I just wish you would get to the good parts."

"I never should have gone down on you." His chest moved as he laughed. "Now you just see me as a mouth with legs."

Running a finger over his lips, she said, "I like the abs, too." He laughed again, and she moved her hand to his chest. "But this is the best part."

He sobered, and they stared into each other's eyes for a beat. Maybe she shouldn't have said that. It really was too soon to know if she felt all of the things that she wanted to say that she felt. But then he made it all okay when he smiled again. "Then I think I need to remind you about my mouth."

Then he grabbed her thighs, settled her on his face, and did just that.

After he'd made her come, fed her, and made her come again, they'd watched movies until they fell asleep on his couch. She was clean from the soap in his shower, wearing his T-shirt and sweats, and completely wrapped up in him. His steady heartbeat under her hand grounded her and felt like home.

Nothing had ever felt like this before. If this wasn't love, then maybe Annalise was right, and she didn't know what love was after all.

CHAPTER TWENTY-FOUR

NOAH HAD ONCE CHOSEN to chide her in front of a room full of people because she'd described her Halloween costume as a "flapper" rather than a figure of the Harlem Renaissance. Just more evidence that she hated her own blackness, according to him. She was sure that if someone asked him about his costume tonight, at Madison Chapin's engagement party, he would say he was dressed as Langston Hughes.

He caught her eye and lifted his glass of champagne, as if she cared that he thought she'd done a good job planning the party. She knew she'd done a *fantastic* job planning this party. She'd turned the ballroom at the Drake Hotel into a time machine destined for the 1920s. Everything was dripping with expensive, fragrant flowers. And champagne and signature gin and whisky cocktails flowed like water. The center of the room had been cleared off as a dance floor, and an honest-to-God big band played on the stage.

Madison and her fiancé were already hammered, doing the Charleston among their friends. Senator Chapin and his wife were glad-handing guests, who were no doubt doing double duty tonight as donors. Noah stood slightly behind the power couple, ready to jump in and produce the forgotten name of an acquaintance at a moment's notice.

Hannah stood near the entrance, waiting for Jack. He wasn't late yet, but she'd been very clear that he needed to show up on time and in the tux she'd made him pick up. He'd tried to protest and say that he had his own tuxedo, but she needed him to look like he belonged.

Somewhere along the way, she'd forgotten to be sweet and biddable with Jack. But he'd rolled with it thus far. Whereas any other guy would have bristled at her telling him what to wear and how to fix his hair—slicked back like a silent-film star—she'd been able to hear Jack's smile over the phone. And not a smile like he was amused by her and was deciding to indulge her. It seemed he truly liked that she was extremely picky and always thought of everything.

The fact that he really saw her and liked what he saw was a balm to her frayed nerves. She'd been so busy planning this massive event—people really had no idea what kind of hours a party of this size involved—and Jack had been so busy with an article that he couldn't tell her about—that they'd only had last night. She'd barely hesitated before sneaking into his condo, and she was glad she had. They'd had a nice, normal night, and she felt like they were a real couple.

It had to be the fact that she was so tired that let her mind wander back to the things he had texted her after canceling their late dinner on Thursday. Her face heated, and she grabbed a gin cocktail off a passing waiter's tray. She'd have only one since she was on duty, but she had to cool down in the increasingly crowded room. And gin would quiet the riotous thoughts in her head, which was increasingly crowded with thoughts of her intrepid journalist.

He showed up right then, stood next to her, and slid his warm palm across the exposed skin on her neck. She started and then lifted her gaze to meet his. He looked absolutely devastating, as though he belonged in a tuxedo all the time. With her free hand, she smoothed back a strand of hair that had escaped his exactly-to-her-specifications hairdo. He grabbed her hand and kissed the center of her palm.

Of course, that made her want to drag him into a coat closet. But that would ruin her perfect night with her perfect boyfriend. A night when she was going to get her dream job from the boss she'd admired in front of her least-favorite coworker and her smirking, condescending ex-boyfriend. She wasn't about to let her libido ruin it.

HANNAH WAS PERFECT, AND he really hoped that she didn't break up with him once the story dropped. He'd finally had enough to call one of his buddies from school who worked for the *Washington Post*.

From there, serendipity had taken the reins. Turned out, one of the reporters at the *Post* had already done some work on the story. But Jack had provided some missing pieces. Together, they had the whole picture, and Jack was going to have a byline in one of the country's great papers.

His editor planned to run it in the morning. As soon as it ran, he could tell Irv that he was out of a how-to guy. And a crack political reporter. And to shove his "How to Lose a Girl" story where the sun didn't shine.

He only hoped that the fallout wouldn't interfere with Hannah getting the promotion she'd worked so hard for. As insurance, he was going to do everything he could tonight to remind her that this thing

ANDIE J. CHRISTOPHER

between them was real. In fact, he was going to prove to her that it was realer than it had been the first night in that stupid speakeasy.

Kissing the palm of her hand was cheesy, but that was the only way he could get his lips on her right now, and he would take it. "You look beautiful."

She had her hair in some 1920s style with a silvery headband around her forehead that matched a dress that caressed her body like he would later that night. Once he'd told her the truth about why he'd been doing such stupid shit and promised that he'd never lie to her again.

"Thank you." Then she blushed, and he knew that she didn't need fancy words and charm from him. Just the truth. The fact that he hadn't been giving her the truth made him more uncomfortable than her saying, "You look pretty, too."

"Pretty?"

"Yeah, pretty." He would have argued that he was handsome, but she led him over to one of the three bars that she'd had set up—he'd never seen them at any of the weddings he'd been to in the same room—and the spangles on the dress shifted and glinted in the light. He was so obsessed with the way her ass looked as it shifted under the sparkly shit on her dress that he lost the will to argue with her.

He couldn't deny how impressed he was with Hannah's work. Not that he hadn't been impressed by her before, but her competence amazed him anew when he took in the whole room. She'd turned it into a cross between a sparkly fairyland and a gangster's hangout spot, and it worked.

She handed him a drink and clinked her glass with his. Before taking a swig, he stopped.

"What are we drinking to?"

She paused for a moment, squinting her eyes and scrunching her nose in a way that was so cute he wanted to kiss the hell out of her right then. "To us?" he asked.

Shaking her head, which worried him, she said, "To the future."

They clinked glasses and then drank, even though the toast made a knot form in his stomach. More than anything, he wanted them to have a future. But he couldn't guarantee that she would want the same thing after tonight.

For a few moments, he let himself believe that this was the beginning of something new and different, something without lies. The real thing with her that he'd wanted even before they'd met. She smiled at him, and he felt full of her. Then he couldn't help but kiss the corner of her painted-red mouth.

He was all set to properly kiss the hell out of her when her friend Sasha tapped her on the shoulder, with an apologetic look thrown his way.

"There's a brewing emergency."

Jack didn't know why he had the sinking feeling that the backward glance Hannah threw over her shoulder would be the last time she looked at him like she liked seeing his face.

CHAPTER TWENTY-FIVE

MADISON CHAPIN AND HER fiancé had disappeared right before the senator wanted to give a toast. Never one to miss an opportunity to turn a social event into a campaign rally, he'd invited a bunch of press people.

"How are you holding up?" Hannah asked Sasha as they left the party to search the service hallways and storage rooms for the young lovers.

"I'm great." Her best friend's voice was brittle. "I'm just really glad you're doing this with me, and not Giselle."

"Why is Giselle even here?" Hannah had been frustrated when her nemesis had shown up along with Annalise and her husband. As though she'd expected Hannah to screw things up and wanted to be here to enjoy it. "Shouldn't she be at home terrorizing her husband?"

Sasha opened a door in the hallway, finding the janitor's closet empty. "Do you think they snuck up to their hotel room?"

"Eh. They don't seem like the type of couple to do that."

"Yeah, you're right. I can't even imagine them in the thrall of lust." Sasha had to stop reading so many old-school romance novels. Trying to respect her love of historical romance, Hannah had tried to turn her on to Sarah MacLean and Joanna Shupe, but Sasha always went back to Kathleen Woodiwiss and Bertrice Small. Her purple prose reflected that. "You and Jack, on the other hand; seemed like he was about a minute from dragging you away to show you his throbbing member."

"Ew."

"Like I'm wrong?"

She was only sort of wrong.

"Just don't say 'throbbing member.'"

"If it's not throbbing, you might want to have that checked out."

"More like blue balls," she muttered. As much as she appreciated sweet Sasha making sex jokes, Hannah was really starting to worry. The reason Annalise had been hesitant to put her in charge of a wedding was that she wasn't a true believer in love. She'd worried that she didn't have enough appreciation for romance to make someone's wedding dreams come true. Sure, she'd always known how to sex up any event, but she hadn't really been able to empathize with someone who had been planning her wedding since she was six. She simply hadn't believed that she'd wanted that anymore.

But that wasn't the case. Someone had chosen her, and Hannah had started allowing herself to have white-dress fantasies at that stupid bridal salon about her and Jack. Hell, she'd started believing it before the bridal salon. And everything had clicked into place with him in that tux. If Madison Chapin blew up her own engagement party, preventing Hannah's promotion now that she truly knew how to bring the romance, she'd probably have to kill her.

The ping of metal hitting tile echoed through the hall, and Sasha and Hannah wordlessly followed the faint sound after exchanging a wide-eyed look in the dim light. Soon, the melodious ring of Madison's Disney princess voice rang out.

"It's over."

Shit. This is not good. Even if the breakup had nothing to do with her, the senator would not be pleased with this turn of events, and Annalise would, in turn, place the blame entirely on Hannah's shoulders. She'd been working for the woman long enough to know that her job was about a lot more than flower arrangements and caterers—it was about making sure that everything went smoothly.

As they approached the arguing couple, Sasha scooped up the discarded diamond solitaire worth more than the condo they shared.

On the fly, Hannah decided to play dumb. "Your father's about to give a speech. He needs you out on the stage."

Without looking at them, Madison's fiancé said, "We're not getting married anymore."

"No, we aren't." Madison crossed her arms over her chest and lifted her chin at her and Sasha. "You have to tell my parents."

Sasha looked at her, the panic plain on her face. She'd dealt with jittery brides before, but never one who wanted her to tell her father—a sitting senator—that the engagement party / photo op he'd been counting on was about to have a bad ending. A bad ending of *Titanic*-sized proportions.

Hannah was really more experienced with situations this tense and unruly, and she took a deep breath, summoning all of her patience. There was too much riding on this event. "No, Madison. You're both going to go out there and pretend to be deliriously in love."

"But—"

"I don't care if you can't stand the sight of him, if you just found out he cheated on you, or you just woke up today and decided to blow up your pretty little life."

"He didn't cheat."

Her patience running thin, Hannah nonetheless asked, "What did he do?"

"He's marrying me for money."

"Oh, honey." Hannah's heart hurt for Madison. Over the past couple of weeks, she'd spent enough time getting to know her that she felt as though they were becoming friends. But they weren't quite at the friend level where Hannah could tell her that she'd pegged the fiancé as an empty suit the moment she'd laid eyes on him.

Madison was rich and pretty and interesting, but her fiancé seemed to have little going for him other than perfect hair and capped teeth. She'd thought that Madison had been on board with the whole dynastic-marriage thing. She quieted her voice before she asked, "Did you think you were a love match?"

"No." Madison looked down. "But I thought it might make . . . well, I thought it might make someone jealous if I started dating someone else, and it didn't work."

"So you decided to get engaged to this douchebag? To make another person even more jealous?" *God bless Sasha.* Always surprised when people did bad things to each other.

"Yeah, and it didn't work."

"I mean, why not go all the way? Get married to this fool to make some other guy seethe?" Hannah had no idea why she sounded and felt so angry at this woman. Other than that she was stupid and immature and making a mockery of love.

Except she'd done the same thing to Jack that Madison had to her fiancé. She shouldn't even be thinking about him right now, but looking at Madison and taking in her stupid scheme made her realize that she had to tell him the truth—that she'd only originally dated him to get a promotion. That what they had had become a real relationship, that she wanted to be his girlfriend, but that it hadn't started out that way.

She wanted to go tell him right then, but she had to wait until she'd dealt with this.

"You need to tell the guy you're really in love with how you feel."

"I can't." Madison sounded so forlorn that Hannah couldn't help growing some empathy for her.

"But you don't want to screw up your dad's campaign, do you?"

"No." Both Madison and her fiancé spoke in unison.

Hannah grabbed the ring out of Sasha's hand. "That's why you have to put this ring back on and pretend for a few more hours. Tomorrow, you should tell your parents that you don't want to marry this guy. And tell the guy you're in love with how you feel."

"Okay." Madison took the ring and slipped it back on.

Hannah clapped her hands like a schoolteacher ready to get her students on the move. "Let's all go and do some acting."

Tomorrow everyone could tell the truth.

THE LAST PERSON JACK had expected to see tonight was Lauren's sister, Giselle. He'd met her only a few times while he and Lauren were dating. And, frankly, the cool blonde had dead eyes. It freaked him out.

As she stalked toward him as though he were a prey animal, it dawned on him that she must work with Hannah. And it didn't take too much of a leap to assume that Giselle was the work nemesis Hannah had complained about over text. Still, he didn't want word getting back to Lauren that he'd turned into a jerk, even though that didn't matter at this point. She was happy, and she'd moved on.

Of course, if he didn't play his cards right, word would get to Lauren that he'd lost the girl he fully intended on moving on with because of his stupid job. That thought had him eyeing the exits.

Instead, he decided to man up. He nodded toward the bar, and Giselle gave him a feral smile. She looked just like her sister, except more . . . brittle. Jack couldn't help but flinch when she grabbed his arm.

"What are you doing here?" Her question came out as a shriek, which reminded him of another reason he'd avoided Giselle while he was dating Lauren.

"I came with a date."

She narrowed her gaze at him, which he tried to ignore as he ordered himself another one of the special martinis and a glass of champagne for Giselle.

"Bride or groom?"

"Huh?" He handed her glass over and threw a five into the bartender's tip jar.

"Are you here with the bride or groom?"

"Neither."

"So you're a party crasher?"

He smirked at her. If he remembered correctly, and he did, Giselle had always thought her sister could do better than a lifestyle reporter from a blue-collar background. Didn't matter that his dad was a successful contractor; Giselle James-Stevens had always been concerned with the next rung of the social ladder. It gave him great satisfaction when he said, "I'm here with one of the party planners."

"Sasha?"

Other than wanting to provide a comprehensive report to her sister, he couldn't see why she was grilling him about his dating life.

Still, he wasn't going to be rude on a night this important to Hannah. "Hannah Mayfield."

Giselle's face pulled into a mask of disgust, and it made Jack's normally affable nature dissipate in an instant. He didn't have time to ask why she looked as though she'd just swallowed some funky spunk, because his boss seemed to appear out of nowhere.

"Jack!" Irv's voice was like a crack of thunder. "You're supposed to be working on my story."

Irv calling it his story further pissed him off. It was Jack's story, and one he no longer wanted to tell. "I'm entitled to a Saturday night." And he certainly hadn't expected to see his boss at an engagement party. "What are you doing here?"

"The senator wanted press here."

"And you didn't send one of your political reporters?"

"Not when I can drink top-shelf for free." Irv ordered a scotch, neat. "But it could be you drinking Macallan 18 on your beat if you play your cards right."

Giselle had somehow managed to screw her face on right and extended her hand to Irv. "Giselle James-Stevens."

Irv looked down at her hand as though it was a dirty rag before reluctantly taking it. As irritated as he was, Jack chuckled. He was sure Giselle didn't usually get such an icy reception from a heterosexual man.

"This the girl?"

Jack shook his head, hoping Irv would catch his silent plea to shut his freaking trap. But no luck.

"What girl?" Giselle sounded confused, which was probably another new experience for her. The last thing Jack wanted was for Hannah to find out that he'd been using her for a story from someone she referred to as "the Wicked Witch of the North Side."

"Jack's been doing a story—dating a girl but doing all the stupid shit that young guys do these days to make her break up with him." Irv took a drink and continued with a rueful laugh. "But she hasn't dumped him yet. No self-respect, broads these days."

Giselle's eyes got wide, and Jack legitimately wanted the floor to open up and swallow him whole. Then an evil smile crossed her face and she turned to them. "It was so nice to meet you, Irv. And Jack, it's always lovely to see such an old friend. But I really must go find Hannah and congratulate her on such a fabulous party."

Jack knew things would be over with Hannah if he didn't get to her first and find a way to explain things. Things like the fact that he'd never looked out for his career first when the choice was between a career and a woman. Things like he shouldn't have done that this time. And things like the fact that he was most definitely in love with her and would do just about anything *not* to lose her.

He wasn't sure where Hannah was at that moment, but he could move faster than Giselle in her heels and tight dress. Plus, she'd probably get distracted talking to some business douche who worked with her husband. He could find Hannah and tell her everything before Giselle got to her.

But just as he was about to excuse himself, Irv blocked his path of egress. "So, we've got to talk about this Senator Chapin story—"

"Irv, I—uh—" Jack hesitated. He wanted to tell Irv that that ship had sailed, but it would have to wait. He couldn't lose Hannah now that he'd figured out a way to keep her.

"You want the story, don't you?" He didn't have time to explain that he already had the story. It was Irv who'd lost it by not realizing that he was the man for the job in the first place.

"Of course I do." The ballroom was packed to the gills. He wasn't sure he would make it to Hannah in time.

"I was able to get one of their donors to talk on background . . ."

"And?" This was a waste of time.

"You'll never believe what he used campaign funds for—" Irv stopped when the music stopped and the senator, his wife, his daughter, and his daughter's fiancé got up on the stage. Everyone went quiet, and they couldn't exactly discuss the senator's downfall without being heard.

And then all hell broke loose. As soon as Senator Chapin opened his mouth, one of the reporters down by the stage shouted, "Is it true that you used campaign contributions to fund this event?"

Jack's attention swung away from Irv to the politician with his mouth opening and closing like a guppy. Another reporter—one who hadn't taken his eye off the ball because of a girl—used that opening. "And have you seen the story that the *Washington Post* just published about your interference with city contracts?"

After that, cacophony took over, and he pulled out his phone to see that the story had dropped early, about half an hour ago.

SENATOR CHAPIN INDICTED ON CAMPAIGN FINANCE CHARGES

By Jack Nolan

Senator Alexander Chapin was charged with nine felony counts today in the federal district court for the Northern District of Illinois. Among the charges were bank fraud, money laundering, and campaign finance violations. The charging document states that Senator Chapin allegedly paid for his daughter Madison's lavish engagement party at the Drake Hotel with campaign funds. The party is scheduled for this evening. Ms. Chapin and her fiancé met through his father, also implicated in the money-laundering scheme.

Senator Chapin has yet to resign from the Senate, but he has been removed from all of his committee assignments . . .

Before he had time to tell Hannah the truth about why he'd asked her out. Before he had a chance to tell her that he wasn't going to write the "How to Lose a Girl" story because he was hopelessly in love with her and didn't want to lose her.

Irv was gone, and he was standing alone at the bar. The lights had come up, and the partygoers seemed mostly shell-shocked.

That's when he spotted Hannah, standing next to the stage, ushering the betrotheds offstage. He started to move toward her but froze when he saw the flash of Giselle's red dress closing in on her.

Goddammit.

FUCK.

The last thing Hannah needed was Giselle mayonnaise on top of her shit sandwich of a night. Although she'd averted the minor crisis of a public breakup, it looked like the party was over for Senator Chapin.

She doubted that Annalise's gratitude over her saving the engagement party would make up for her extreme disappointment that she wouldn't be able to cash in on this couple making it to the altar. The closest thing to a royal wedding in the States would have meant a fat check and probably a trip to the Amalfi coast for her boss. Not to mention the bragging rights. And, despite the fact that none of this was her fault, she knew that for a good, long while, Annalise would see a missed Italian vacation every time she looked at her. Hopefully, she'd be more worried about her friend the senator going to jail. But Annalise could be pissed about more than one thing at a time, and she'd probably want to spread her anger around.

Hannah let a disappointed sigh loose once she'd pushed Madison et al. toward the back door. It seemed that Giselle, who was now standing in front of her, looking extremely satisfied with herself, had dodged a bullet by not booking this job.

"I met your boyfriend."

Just freaking great. She'd probably already told him that Hannah had just been using him to earn brownie points with Annalise. So, in addition to losing out on a promotion, she was going to lose the only guy she'd let herself care about in years. That hurt even more than the prospect of losing oral sex with Jack, which was saying a lot about her feelings for the guy.

Giselle stood there, waiting for her to ask the question, which she did. "Did you tell him?"

That bitch had the audacity to look innocent. Hannah had never slapped a woman, but she had a nearly insatiable desire to go *Dynasty* on Giselle's ass right now. "Tell him what?"

"About the reason I started dating him?"

"Why would I do that?"

"I don't know. Just to be a bitch. Like, you got here tonight, and you hadn't been bitchy enough during the course of your day until this opportunity presented itself." Hannah quite enjoyed the way Giselle started every time she called her a bitch.

"I think you have a distorted view of how I spend my time." She laid her left hand across her chest, showing off the iceberg on her finger. "To think, I came over here to tell you something important. To protect you."

Hannah didn't bother trying not to roll her eyes. "What are you trying to protect me from?"

"From the fact that your boyfriend"—she said that word with an amount of sarcasm that Hannah did not appreciate—"the man you've been dating—has been using you for a news story."

"What?" None of this was computing. Had he been investigating Senator Chapin? That would have been inefficient. And kind of outside of his lane.

Giselle was ready to drive the point home, though. "Yes, Jack's been writing a story about how to lose a girl. That's the only reason he ever dated you at all."

If Hannah hadn't felt like she'd been punched in the gut, she for sure would have slapped Giselle then. Just because she was *so gleeful* while being *so bitchy*.

"When I saw you together at the Halloween party, I was wondering what my sister's ex-boyfriend was doing dating *you*." She said it as though Hannah was an actual dog. As though Jack had been dating human women and then just decided that he preferred something . . . *less*.

All this time, she'd thought that Jack had actually liked her. And she'd started to believe that she'd made a mistake giving up on love. She'd started to believe that she *was* the kind of girl someone lovely like Jack would want to marry someday.

But she'd been wrong. She was the girl he'd *used for a fucking news story*.

Jack had been ready to humiliate her for his job. She had very little moral ground to stand on, because she'd done virtually the same thing to him. But she had a few pebbles to cling to, because she hadn't been ready to humiliate him in public.

Suddenly, it all made sense—the way he'd morphed from Mr. Perfect into a regular asshole, doing asshole things. How uncomfortable he'd seemed while doing those asshole things. Introducing her to his mother on their second date, and the rest of his family on their fourth. The mansplaining and the dick pic.

He probably wasn't even saving it for marriage—that complete and utter asshole! He probably thought it was all okay because he didn't get his dick wet.

Oh God, was his family in on the joke? Because that's what he'd done. He'd made a joke out of her. She felt nauseous, the hors d'oeuvres and gin cocktail roiling in her stomach. She'd toasted having a future with him less than thirty minutes ago. And he'd looked her in the eye.

Her office nemesis faded out of her vision. Even though the party had devolved into chaos once the press had peppered the senator with questions, everyone in the room seemed to disappear except for Jack, who was standing next to the ice sculpture with a short, paunchy guy Hannah didn't recognize.

Luckily, people were still crowded on the dance floor, looking at the stage because Senator Chapin had disappeared in that direction. No one was paying attention to what Jack was doing. Good. Maybe she could murder him in plain sight and get away with it. Doubtful, but a girl could dream.

For his part, Jack likely knew what he was in for the moment he saw her. No doubt the fury flowing off of her was tangible. He moved around the man he'd been talking to and approached her.

She grabbed another gin cocktail off of a server's tray and took a long drink before coming face-to-face with him.

"Hannah, I—"

"Did you try the signature cocktail?"

He shook his head slowly, obviously confused at the turn in the conversation. She moved quickly, dousing his face in the drink. He wiped his face and licked the gin off his lips. She would have enjoyed it because it was a sexy movement. But then she remembered that everything between them had been a lie. "Delicious."

She gave him the finger. "Sit on it and rotate, Jack."

"Can you let me explain?" Of course he'd want to explain. Because no guy dumping her had ever wanted to be seen as the bad guy. And Jack was very invested in everyone around him thinking he was a good guy. Hell, he'd even fooled her into thinking that he was good—if inept.

"No, you don't get to explain why you used me for a story."

She flagged down a server with a full tray of signature drinks and pointed to the table next to them. She picked up one of the whisky drinks and hit Jack with it just as he opened his mouth.

"Can you just be reasonable?"

"I think I'm being very reasonable." He took a step toward her and she took a step back, grabbing two more drinks to wield as weapons. "You're still alive, so that means that I'm being reasonable."

"Can't we just discuss this like adults?"

No hesitation, just another gin drink to his face. "No. I don't want to discuss how you used me to get ahead in your career." Adding another whisky drink to his ensemble—this time staining his white shirt—she said, "I don't want to discuss how you made me come a bunch of times, even though you were using me for a *fucking* listicle. So generous of you."

He held up his hands as she grabbed another gin drink from the tray. "It wasn't a listicle, I swear."

"So you were going to go into detail about how you used me to prove a point?" Her throat was getting hoarse from the yelling, and Annalise was floating over, so she knew her tantrum wouldn't go unnoticed.

She paused for a moment too long, because Jack almost got into the bubble she'd created for herself brandishing signature drinks. Hannah wheeled around, but her back was to the ice sculpture. He got closer, and she was about to start crying. Desperate to hold on to her rage, she grabbed the ice pick the sculptor had left.

"Hannah—"

"Come any closer, and I'll pop your balls like fucking balloons."

He looked from her face to the ice pick, as though he was considering the risk. As though she might be worth deflated testicles. There was a long beat of silence between them, when tears threatened again. But she kept his gaze. He might have destroyed any chance she would even think about trying to be in a relationship again, but he hadn't destroyed her. She refused to give him that.

"Hannah, what are you doing?" Annalise's voice was hushed but tight.

Still, she didn't break eye contact with Jack. "We're breaking up, Annalise. You were right. I'm not the relationship type."

"That's not true, Hannah." Jack sounded earnest, but he'd sounded earnest a whole lot during the course of their farce of an affair. "Why would you ever think that?"

The urge to strike back at him was too great. When she'd come over here, she'd wanted to make a scene and make him leave. But now she wanted to hurt him. Just for pretending to be the good guy right now. Not to mention, she wanted to save just a bit of pride—hard as that might be after throwing multiple drinks and threatening serious bodily injury.

"I only dated you on a bet."

Jack shook his head as though he didn't believe it.

"It wasn't a bet—" Annalise felt the need to interject.

"It wasn't?" Hannah finally looked at her boss. "You didn't want to give me this wedding, so you bet me that I couldn't get anyone to date me for more than two weeks."

"So, you used me, too?" She didn't even look at Jack when he spoke. This wasn't about him anymore. Not really.

"You didn't think I could do it, and that I would just happily go back and be your good-time girl, didn't you?"

Annalise backed away from her, and Hannah realized that she was still holding the ice pick. She glanced back at Jack and put it down on the table. "Yeah, I used you, too. It was all fake."

She turned to leave and ignored Jack's "Hannah, wait—"

In the background, Annalise said, "Maybe take the rest of the night off, and we'll talk about this on Monday." She'd be getting her ass fired on Monday, but she was actually more upset about everything that had happened with Jack right now.

She threw up two middle fingers at Jack and walked out, passing a bunch of guys in FBI windbreakers as they walked in.

CHAPTER TWENTY-SIX

YOU FUCKED UP." THAT was a rude awakening, especially coming from her best friend.

Hannah sat straight up in bed at her best friend's cursing. Sasha hated the f-word. When they'd first become friends, in college, Sasha had refused to say the swear words when doing rap songs in karaoke, which Hannah had found impossibly charming—especially since that gave her permission to curse very loudly. Getting woken up from a dead sleep with her roommate cursing at her was less so.

"How did *I* screw up?"

Sasha sat down on the foot of her bed and offered a steaming cup of coffee, the only reason Hannah didn't ask her to leave. She wasn't exactly up for being around people or being told about all the things she'd done wrong.

All the ways she'd been stupid about Jack.

She merely wanted to lick her significant wounds in private and build the armor back up around her heart. This time, she'd turn into titanium. But she couldn't do that with Sasha making her see how she'd been in the wrong as well. "He's the one who used me to get a news story."

"Just like you used him to get a promotion?"

The hot coffee scalded her tongue and throat, but that wasn't why she choked. Sasha was right. She had lied to Jack. Even though she'd already liked him more than she would ever admit before she'd decided to use him to show Annalise that she wasn't a total shrew. She'd gone ahead with it anyway.

Part of her wondered whether things could have been different, whether she could have been honest with Jack from the start. But she knew she never would have done that. Telling Jack that she needed him, after one kiss and a bunch of texts, would have required her to be vulnerable to him, and it would have required her to trust him. Before Jack had wheedled his way into her life—and her heart—she hadn't been able to do either of those things.

And, since he'd taken her trust and smashed it into a million pieces in a very public way, she wasn't sure she'd ever be able to trust anyone enough to give them her heart ever again.

"I didn't mess up, Sasha." She blew on the surface of her coffee and took another sip. "Jack just proved me right. My only mistake was that I ever trusted him at all."

Sasha sighed heavily and looked up at the ceiling as though she needed guidance and strength from above. "You didn't see it at all, did you?"

"See what?" Hannah grew incensed. Her best friend was frustrated with the wrong person here. She should be frustrated with the patriarchy, not her. "I saw last night that a man I really liked—" There was no need to say that she'd fallen in love with him, even if it was totally true. "I'm so humiliated—all that stuff he did. For his job. And then I threatened him with an ice pick."

"Listen, I'm not certain Jack hadn't already planned to tell you—" Sasha paused for a breath but continued before Hannah could get ramped up enough to argue with her. She needed much more than a few swallows of coffee to have this conversation. "It was all very weird and mortifying in a way that we need to process."

Oh Jesus. Sasha's degree in psychology rearing its ugly head again.

"I don't know that he was ever going to tell me. And the humiliation isn't even over. Jack is writing a story about how I fell for his game and then he strung me along and abused my trust for two weeks."

Sasha shook her head and her brow furrowed in a way that it always did when she was very determined. "I saw the way he looked at you, Han."

"We hadn't had sex yet. He was only looking at me that way because he didn't get what he wanted."

"Shut up." Hannah was stunned speechless. Her flawless, naïve, Irish Catholic rose of a best friend was cursing and telling her to shut up? Unprecedented. "Stop making this about sex. The way he was looking at you wasn't about sex. Not at all."

"Of course it was about the sex. It's always about the sex." And it was all her fault because she'd gone boots up for Jack at the very first opportunity despite the best advice of the woman sitting across from her right now. "That's all men ever want. I thought he was actually interested in a relationship. How dumb is that?"

"Not dumb at all."

"You were the one telling me I was doing everything wrong."

Sasha sighed. "I was the one who was wrong."

"What?" Hannah wasn't sure she was hearing her friend correctly. Sasha, who had never once admitted she was wrong about anything—especially dating stuff—despite her march of heartbreak through the past few years of app-based dating.

"I was wrong about Jack."

"No, I think last night proves that I was right about him all along."

"Stop lying." She had no idea where this blunt, bold woman had come from and what she'd done with her best friend. And she liked it. Although she would like it better if her blunt boldness was directed elsewhere. "You liked him from the start, and I saw the look in your eye after I got home the first night at the speakeasy, from the first time he texted you a picture of a cute dog. Just admit it. You *liked* like him."

Maybe she could admit that to herself, but she wasn't about to swallow her pride and admit that to her friend. Not when it was too late to do anything about it. "Does it even matter now?"

"It matters." Hannah's eyes filled, and she looked down into her cup, hoping it would hold answers. Sasha grabbed her forearm as though she was afraid that she'd lose her attention. "It matters because it's about how you feel, not the lies you told each other. It matters whether you liked him, because you matter."

"He made me feel like I did." She did not want to talk about this right now, when it felt like her chest was an open wound. "When he looked at me, I felt like he really saw me. Like he didn't see any room for improvement."

She hiccupped and paused, but Sasha didn't fill the silence. Her best friend, the one who had seen her through everything, knew how big a deal it was for her to spill actual honest-to-God-romantic feelings about someone.

"It just hurt so much that it was all a lie."

"How do you know it was a lie?"

All the confusion and pain she was feeling channeled itself into frustration. She didn't want to yell at Sasha; she wanted to scream at Jack. But he wasn't there, and her best friend was. At least until she finally found someone because she'd finally found her backbone and Hannah was truly alone. "He told me it was a lie! He was using me for the article!"

Hannah slammed the coffee cup on the nightstand and walked into the bathroom, not expecting Sasha to follow her. Unlike her, Sasha came from a bathroom-doors-always-closed family.

"I'm going to pee," Hannah said, expecting her friend to leave.

Sasha just took a sip of her own coffee and stood there. "So pee."

"You're going to harass me about this until I agree with you?" Hannah pulled down her boxers and called her bluff.

Sasha surprised her by pointedly looking down and saying, "You never waxed."

"Your point? Other than to harp on my grooming habits?"

"He looked at you like—I don't know—the most wonderful thing he'd ever seen. He looked at you as though he never wanted to look at anything else."

"You were seeing things."

"Dammit, Hannah!" That stunned her into silence. "The problem was that you *weren't* seeing things. You weren't seeing the way he looked at you, and you weren't there to hear him talking about you at the Halloween party."

She wanted to ask what he'd said about her, even though she didn't really want to know any of the things coming out of Sasha's mouth. It would be so much easier if she could just believe that Jack was an asshole—a worse asshole than Noah had ever been. At least he'd been honest with her. It would be so much simpler if she could just continue to believe that she was broken and that no one would ever love her as she was—that she was to be used and discarded unless she kept herself aloof forever.

"I swear that I'm not seeing this through my rose-colored glasses. Those glasses are broken, I promise." *When had that happened?* Before two weeks ago, Sasha had always been the most cockeyed optimist to ever look a cock in the eye. "But that man loves you."

"Love is dead." Hannah had said the same thing before, but there wasn't any power behind it in that moment.

"It wasn't before you flipped double fingers at him in front of a sitting senator."

"Who was about to get arrested on corruption charges. And virtually every power player in Chicago." Still, a big part of her wanted to believe Sasha. But she didn't want to feel hope. Hope was dangerous. "I think I drowned love in the bathtub with that move."

"What I don't get is why you don't feel like a guy like Jack would fall in love with you. Like, as your due?"

"No one's ever been in love with me."

"That you know of."

"No. I know it."

"And why do you think that is?"

That was a good question, one Hannah had pondered in therapy and out. But she'd never said it out loud, with Sasha in the room. Before now. "I mean, a guy like Jack is going to fall in love with someone who's more like you than me."

"You mean someone nice?" Sasha's mouth quirked up at the side.

"Can you grab more coffee so that we can finish this conversation with my ass covered?"

Sasha seemed to understand that it was important, so she nodded and left the room.

When Hannah got to the kitchen, Sasha was opening a bottle of sparkling wine and pouring it into champagne flutes.

"Do we have something to celebrate?" Hannah asked. "Did I miss something important between the bathroom and the kitchen?"

"I just didn't think scotch was a good idea as a brunch beverage."

"Makes sense." Hannah swiped one of the glasses off the counter after Sasha poured. "And the mimosas are always bottomless here."

"Exactly." Sasha grabbed her own glass; Hannah sat down and sighed. "Tell me why you don't think Jack would ever fall for you. I guarantee that I'll find any of your explanations stupid, but I'll listen."

"It's simple really. What if it's me? What if I'm just not enough?"

"Are you freaking—"

"I'm not kidding or joking or crazy, Sash." Hannah took a fortifying sip of the second necessary beverage of the day. The crisp champagne and sweet orange juice were a non-doctor-recommended balm to her sore throat and raw heart. "You don't know what it's like, because you don't have to. When I was with Noah, I wasn't black enough because, like, seventy percent of my friends are white girls. And I grew up in an almost all-white town. And I went to maybe the whitest school in that very white town. And I refused to be who he wanted me to be—to forget my family and friends who loved me and become some hotep's idea of a Stepford wife for him."

"He didn't want that." Sasha scrunched her forehead again. "He just wanted you to swear less."

"He also wanted me to hang out with you less." Hannah stood up and started pacing. Maybe this would be easier if she didn't have to look at Sasha's face while she did it. "He wanted me to be someone else—like he wanted to date a woman with straight hair and a small nose so that all his white friends would think I was attractive, but he wanted me to fit into *his* life."

"So he was the wrong guy for you. I don't see what this has to do with Jack."

"I was a diversion for Jack. Even without the article, he would have dated me for a few weeks, then scraped me off. I think he liked the novelty of dating someone *exotic*."

"You're from Milwaukee. You're not exotic."

"Minneapolis." Sasha had consistently gotten it wrong over the course of their friendship. She'd lose it if someone thought she was from Long Island rather than Westchester but couldn't keep her midwestern cities—outside of Chicago—straight to save her life. "And it doesn't matter because it's over now. But maybe Jack picked me because he knew he was never going to fall in love with me."

"That's not right." And now her nose was wrinkled.

"Then why do you think he thought, for one second, that it would be okay to date me for sport?" Hannah was at the point where she was fluttering her hands. "If he really liked me, he wouldn't have done that to me."

"Oh, come on!" Sasha stood up. "You did the same thing to him. And both of you accidentally fell in love."

"It doesn't matter." And then she decided to lay out all her real fears, the ones she'd never shared with anyone.

"Of course it matters!" Sasha quirked her head to the side like a confused puppy, and Hannah would have laughed if they weren't having the most serious discussion of their friendship. "You deserve to fall in love. Just like everyone else in the world. Why do you think you're the exception?"

"It's—complicated."

"No, it's not. You're the most lovable person I know." That was a crock of shit, and Sasha had to know it.

"I mean, I swear a lot. And I'm very impatient."

"So? It's kind of weird that I never say the f-word." Sasha shrugged. "And you know how to get things done better than anyone I know."

"But I'm not ladylike. Or polite." Everything about Sasha was polite, and Hannah felt like every conversation she'd ever had with Noah's mother had been one long correction of her manners.

"Okay, so someone's not going to love you because you're expressive and a little bit wild." Sasha was clearly just indulging her now.

"Men want to have a one-night stand with wild. They don't want it raising their children."

"That's not true. Remember Stacy?" The girl who lived next door to them junior year had practically majored in sex with basketball players.

"How could I forget the wrath of Sister Paulina?" Their school had a policy against premarital sex, which most people ignored. Unless they got caught. Like Stacy had been when the star point guard had knocked her up.

"They're still happily married, and they have three more children."

All of this was beside the point. The point was that Jack was not in love with her. He barely even knew her. It had certainly seemed like he'd been in lust with her when his face had been parked between her legs at her leisure multiple times, but that had to be dead by now.

"Stacy is a specific case in a specific time."

"Yeah, Stacy is a ditz who didn't get an IUD when you offered her a ride to the Planned Parenthood along with the rest of us." As a public-school attendee, Hannah had been shocked to learn that many of the women in her dorm had not had comprehensive sex ed in their parochial schools. So she'd carted as many of them as she could fit in her Prius to the women's health clinic to get them sorted out. "You are a kind, loyal, genuine person who is always willing to put yourself out there for a friend. And that's what Jack sees when he looks at you."

Hannah found herself getting choked up, and she couldn't meet her friend's gaze.

"You're going to take the compliment this time, Han." She always hated getting compliments; they made her terribly uncomfortable. She was much more used to being admonished.

Which made her wonder how she'd been able to withstand being around Jack for two weeks. He hadn't articulated his compliments, but just getting to be around him felt like approval. And, coming from him, it had been so easy. How? Maybe because she'd known it was only temporary. That he would eventually see her as clearly as Noah had and break up with her. Or that she would break things off before he could see that.

The fact that she'd been able to spend time with Jack, to let him see her without blowing it up and sabotaging it, made Sasha's words sink in in a new way. Maybe Noah hadn't seen her clearly at all, and perhaps she had something to offer worth keeping.

"I'm—" Actually, she wasn't sure. She'd always *felt* like the exception to her general view that everyone was lovable, and she couldn't remember a time—no matter how many honor rolls or perfect report cards she earned—she'd ever felt as though she was enough. Nothing had made her dad come back. Nothing had protected her from bullies in school. Nothing.

She wanted to just parrot Noah's words again. *I'm just not the girl you marry.* But for the first time, standing in her kitchen, hungover from grief at losing a relationship that hadn't even been real, she realized that it didn't make sense.

So she didn't say them. Instead, she let the idea that someone as great as Jack had seemed to be when they'd first met could like someone as abrasive, aggressive, and other as her.

"I love you, Hannah." Sasha's eyes filled with tears. "You've been my best friend from the first time we met."

"When I told you that I hated you because you were too perfect?" She'd always assumed they'd become best friends because they lived next door to each other in the dorms and because Sasha was nice enough to forgive her for being a terminal bitch.

"Yeah." Sasha sniffed. "I knew we'd be good friends then because you were real. I knew you'd never lie to me just to be nice. And it was so different. I need that in my life."

"But men don't like real."

"They obviously don't like fake, either!" She threw her arms out. "I'm alone, too."

"But that's because you keep dating idiots."

"I'm beginning to think you were right all along." And then the tears came back, and Hannah rounded the peninsula to hug her friend. She hated when people made Sasha cry, even when it was her. "That dudes are all terrible. What could be better proof of that than the fact that you—my caring, beautiful friend—are alone?"

"No, I'm wrong. You're the brave one, to keep trying even though no one can see what a treasure you are." Then they both broke down in sobs.

"You're the best."

"No, you're the best."

Then Sasha had to ruin it by saying, "Jack thinks you're the best."

Hannah sniffed the bubble of snot that had formed at the end of her nose and pulled back. "You've got to let this go. He used me for a story, and now we're over."

"Even if you can't see it now, I think he's going to make you see it."

"You really think he's going to get over the fact that I used him to get ahead in my job?"

"I think he's already over it." Sasha poured them both another glass of champagne. "He was over it before he wiped those drinks off his face."

Sasha had a point. She and Noah had never had a fight like that, even when they were breaking up. He'd pulled away, and she'd tried to pull him back—over and over—until finally, she'd just loosened her grip and let him go. She'd stopped trying to be what he wanted, and he'd stopped trying to nudge her into being what he wanted. The end of a war of attrition.

Last night, with Jack, she'd felt like they were both clawing to keep the great things between them. The chemistry, yes, but she knew that she'd never meet a man with the same integrity Jack had. Or she'd thought he'd had. And she might be trying to minimize her hopes that somehow this would work out, but she'd seen something like sadness mixed with determination in his gaze.

If he'd merely been using her, it wasn't like he would have been hurt that she was using him. It would have been the convenient way for them to say goodbye. No harm. No foul.

But there was harm—to her and to him—and her primary objective when she'd accepted that first date with him had certainly been fouled.

She wasn't about to get a promotion. The engagement party she and Sasha had planned was a disaster the engagement itself hadn't survived. And they would be lucky if either of them had jobs when the dust settled.

Sasha would land on her feet. Her parents wouldn't allow for any other outcome. Hannah—maybe it was time to go to law school, despite how much she didn't relish the idea. She'd figure it out. She always did.

Still, humiliation returned anew to Hannah's gut. In her attempt to prove to her boss that she could handle weddings, she'd royally bungled her first assignment. If she even had a job left, she would have a long row to hoe to get back to where she'd been.

On the bright side, the cops hadn't shown up because of anything she'd done this time. The engagement party wasn't in the papers because of anything she or Sasha had done.

She gestured toward the rapidly emptying champagne bottle. "Are you sure we shouldn't be trying to figure out how to make Annalise not fire us both?" Still, she tipped the glass up to her mouth.

"I'd say that feckless bitch Giselle should figure it out if she wants to be a VP so badly."

Hannah choked on her mimosa, but that didn't stop them from finishing the bottle.

CHAPTER TWENTY-SEVEN

YOU LOOK LIKE HELL, bro." Bridget punched him in the arm. He never should have taught her how to throw a punch.

Jack grunted in response. He didn't need his sister to tell him how he looked. Not only had he woken up in his liquor-soiled, rented tux that he definitely wouldn't be getting his deposit back on; he hadn't slept more than an hour or so. And there might even have been some eye leakage involved when he'd finally come down from the adrenaline of last night.

He'd considered begging off of Sunday brunch with his mom and sister, but he couldn't do that to Bridget. Michael had refused from the jump to indulge their mother's illusion that she was still parenting as long as she saw them all once a week, but he and Bridget both dutifully attended the command performance every weekend.

At this point, it was tradition. Plus, this time he had a national byline, which he should be really proud about. He'd woken up to several calls asking him if he was happy at the magazine, so it didn't matter whether Irv fired him.

But he couldn't seem to get himself to care. He was never going to see Hannah again. Even though he'd set out to have her leave him, he hadn't truly wanted her to. But it had really happened, and there was nothing he could do to fix it.

"No pithy comeback?"

Jack wasn't in the mood for a back-and-forth with his sister. If this had been the old days, when they were all living in the same house, he would have given her a noogie until she screamed and cried. But he was too tired to even return her arm punch.

For Christ's sake, his whole body ached. He felt like he had the flu. Couldn't his baby sister see that and take it easy on him?

The universe hated him, because as soon as they got to the table where their mother was already seated, she said, "What the hell happened to him?"

"He was probably up late, making luuuurve to his new girl-friend."

Before he could make them stop by telling them the truth, his mother clapped her hands and said, "I *really* like that girl."

Jack pulled out his chair with a little too much force, and that finally made his female relatives stop clucking over the girl who had ripped his heart out and stomped on it in front of half the city of Chicago.

They both just stared at him, as though meeting him for the first time. He guessed that was true for his mother; she'd never met the surly son of a bitch he felt like at that moment. In front of his mother, he was always on his best behavior. But it didn't matter anymore. Being the perfect son hadn't made his mother stay. And being the perfect boyfriend hadn't made any of his girlfriends stick around. Flubbing everything up intentionally had made things blow wider and faster than Irv could have ever hoped for before he chucked him. Nothing mattered.

"She dumped me."

"What did you do?" Of course his sister blamed it on him. She was so far up her own ass about her breakup with Chris that even her own brother wouldn't get the benefit of the doubt. Not that he deserved it.

And he didn't know exactly how to explain what had gone down with Hannah. Sure, she'd gotten the last word and broken up with him. The fact that she'd threatened him with an ice pick indicated that there'd been some feelings on her end. But she'd used him, too.

When her boss had gotten him a towel, she'd said, "I'm sorry you got pulled into this. I was merely being facetious when I suggested that she find a boyfriend if she wanted to plan weddings."

Even after the very public dumping, hearing that her boss had made a joke at Hannah's expense pissed him off. It pissed him off now, even in the very sober aftermath. In a stroke of amazing timing, the waitress came to take their drink orders.

His sister and mother ordered bottomless mimosas, the better to grill him with, he guessed. And he decided to join them in their inevitable afternoon hangover. "Me too."

"It must be bad if you're forgoing the Bloody Mary."

"She dumped me."

"We know that," his mother said. "The question is, what did you do?"

"I was using her for an article about how to lose a girl like all my idiot friends do, and she found out."

"You what?" His female relatives shrieked in unison, turning every head in the restaurant their way. He was apparently destined to be a spectacle this weekend.

"Yeah, I know it's stupid."

Bridget snorted. "I mean, at least you sped things up this time."

"What do you mean?" Jack had always been the perfect boyfriend. None of his previous breakups had ever been even a little bit his fault.

"You usually just smother a woman with your shtick until she gets sick of it."

"That's not fair."

His mother piped in. "You are—kind of aggressive in your affections."

"So, paying attention and doing what my lady likes is a bad thing now?"

Bridget rolled her eyes. "So defensive, big brother."

"I'm not being defensive." He definitely sounded defensive. "Mom, wouldn't you have stayed with Dad had he paid attention to you? If he had known you wanted to go back to school and offered to make that work?"

His mother sighed deeply and looked down at the table. "Is that what you think?"

"Yeah." They hadn't ever really talked about their reasons for getting a divorce. It had kind of just happened and then his mom wasn't around after school anymore.

"That's not what happened at all." His mother looked gutted. For once, Jack didn't have the energy to manage her emotions.

"News to me." Bridget took a swig of her newly delivered beverage.

"Your father and I . . . we just . . . didn't work anymore."

"That's because you stopped working." Jack had no idea where that angry declaration had come from. "Relationships are work. You left Dad because the only thing he had time to put work into was his business."

"I married your father when I was eighteen years old." She shook her head with a faint smile on her face. "We were so in love, but we didn't know what we were doing . . . what we really wanted out of life. And after the three of you were born in four years and were such holy terrors, it just got so hard. We forgot that we were in love with each other."

"But why did you leave us with Dad?" This had been a source of pain for Bridget for a long time. As the only girl, she'd often felt isolated and especially affected by their mother's absence.

"Your father could provide you with a stable home, and he didn't have the need to get out." She made a circular motion with her hands. "Sean never wanted to see the world the way that I did. Not back then."

"It's still selfish." Jack had never said that out loud, but he'd thought it for a long time, wondered if that was why he was hopelessly attracted to women who would leave him without looking back. "You had kids. You don't get to travel the world when you have kids."

"Not unless they have a father like Sean." He'd never heard his mother talk this way about his father. Almost as though she—admired him. "I mean, if you're honest with yourselves, who is the more nurturing one of the two of us?"

His father had always done most of the cooking, the cleaning, and the school drops—even before his mom had left. She was always ready after school with art projects and unique and sometimes not-kid-friendly snacks she'd picked up at some international grocery store after school, but his mother had never been like the other moms. She hadn't noticed when piles of laundry collected in their rooms. She'd always been off in her little dream world.

If he was truly honest with himself, it had been sort of a relief when she'd left. His life had become much more predictable.

"And I stayed in touch. Saw you all every week."

"But that's not parenting."

"For men it is. Why should it have been any different for me?" She made a dismissive gesture with her hand that made Bridget roll her eyes.

"Because you're our mother." Jack felt himself getting angry, but he didn't know what for. They hadn't had this argument before, and for some reason it felt important to have it now.

"Yes, and your father was a better mother than I ever was."

Bridget's gaze narrowed on their mother. "You sound like you're still in love with him."

"We've been seeing each other again." His mother just dropped that on the brunch table as though it was her AmEx card to pay the check. Without a thought or hesitation.

Jack wished he could have prepared himself for that, because it shook him to his very core. Everything he knew about his bitterly divorced parents falling apart around his ears. On the one hand, it made more sense that they were talking on the phone again. On the other hand, they'd been apart so long that it was kind of gross. For the past fifteen years, his parents had acted like they hated each other. And now they were dating? *Yuck!*

"You're dating Dad!" Bridget was clearly as perturbed by this as Jack was. But where he was speechless, Bridget was livid. "How? Why?"

"Since my divorce was finalized. And I wouldn't call it dating, dear." Their mother smoothed her gray hair out over one ear. "We're too old to call what we're doing dating."

"So you have, like, an arrangement?" Jack finally found his words. He didn't want to know this. He really didn't want to know this.

"Yes. For years. We're not a good married couple, but we're still good when it's just us."

"Shit, that's gross, Mom." Bridget rarely called their mother "Mom," so she must really be upset.

"Language, Bridget."

"You know I lived alone with Sean Nolan and his two spawn for over a decade. So you know what kind of language I was exposed to." Bridget was starting to yell, and Jack should probably intervene and smooth things over, but he was too rocked by this new information to do anything.

"Well, not everything is about you, Bridget."

"She knows that—" Jack's interjection was weak. "This is a lot of information for brunch, and I thought we were here to talk about my problems."

"You know how to solve your problem, Jack."

"No, I don't." Jack had no idea how to get Hannah back. She'd probably visit mayhem upon him if he showed up at her house with roses. And she would definitely eviscerate him if he tried some grand public gesture.

"Yes, you do." His mother seemed insistent that he was smarter than he actually was.

"I actually agree with her." At least Bridget wasn't yelling anymore.

Jack shot his sister an *Et tu, Brute?* look.

"You said it before. You paid attention to her for almost a month.

More than any other man she's dated, probably." His mother gave him a pointed look. "You know her because you made it your business to know her. How would she want you to fix this?"

"She'd want me to drop dead about now."

"So she has a quick temper. Does it last?"

He thought back to how she'd rolled with everything he'd done to try to lose her—except the lying. One thing he knew for sure about Hannah was that she valued honesty and integrity above all else. The one unforgivable thing he'd ever done to her was lie about the story. If he'd told her flat out about the assignment, she probably would have gone along with it and even upped the production value. He smiled to himself.

There wasn't going to be some rush-to-the-airport scene where he could declare how much he loved her and ask her for a second chance. Even if there was, Hannah would run him the hell over with her car before stopping to hear him out.

"I need to give her some time to cool off?"

"She might just use that time to plot different ways to kill you." Bridge had a point. "Maybe you should get in there right away."

"If she needs time, she needs time." His mother would certainly know something about that, Jack thought, wincing anew at the morning's other revelation.

"She liked hanging out with Dad, Michael, and Bridget," Jack said. "I think it made her feel like I was thinking about a future with her. And her jackhole ex-boyfriend never made her feel like that."

"I think she enjoyed herself at the gallery opening." His mother was right. Until he'd tried to make her jealous by flirting with another woman in front of her, she and his mother got on like gangbusters.

Now that he thought about it, when neither of those things

fazed her, that might have been the precise moment he fell in love with her.

An idea began to form in his head for how he might approach getting her back without sustaining grievous bodily injury. It would take the cooperation of his mutant-version-of-the-Brady-Bunch family, but it all started with finishing the article about how to lose Hannah and sending it to just one person.

He finished his second mimosa in one swallow and motioned for another. This was going to be painful.

CHAPTER TWENTY-EIGHT

HANNAH WALKED INTO ANNALISE'S office fully prepared to be fired. And to be yelled at, which she hated even more than the idea of being out of a job. That was because she had a plan for what she would do if she got fired: find another job or hang out her own shingle. Her only plan if Annalise started yelling was to try not to cry and probably fail. Her hard-ass-bitch shell had cracked, and she was at a loss for what—if anything—to do about it.

She'd always liked to cry in secret, but she could feel that a bout of yelling would get those juices flowing. Ironic given her penchant for breathing fire at vendors who refused to bend to her will. Just remembering that gave her spine some steel. At this moment, she was too raw from realizing that she was in love with Jack, and that he'd been using her and lying, to keep her emotions in check. The pain of realizing that he was closer to being the perfect guy that she'd met at a stupid, pretentious bar than to the cad he'd turned himself into for profit was stabby and vicious. And she needed to rechannel that pain into what her whole fling with Jack had originally been about: saving her career.

The first step—getting fired like she had the goddamn ovaries to take whatever Annalise threw at her. She was definitely, probably going to lose her job, but she wasn't going to break down in front of someone she'd looked up to until recently.

After her conversation with Sasha, she'd really thought about what Annalise had asked of her. It was clear that she'd never intended to promote her—and likely that she looked down on her for her confirmed bachelorettehood. She'd probably told her that boyfriend equaled promotion just to exert control over her, and that was pretty disgusting.

She'd worn her chicest black dress that morning and didn't even stop at her desk to drop her purse. If this went how she thought it would, she wouldn't be there for very long anyway.

After multiple mimosas, she and Sasha had come up with a plan for how to play this. Although she'd tried to convince her best friend that at least one of them should keep her very good job, Sasha would not be dissuaded. Sasha had been on the "screw Annalise" train long before Hannah had boarded sometime after mimosa number three. Heartbreak over losing Jack seemed to have softened her edges—the really weird thing was that Hannah didn't hate it.

Still, she needed to pretend to have her sharp corners and brass knuckles to deal with this meeting.

She didn't knock, just slid in the glass door while her boss stared at her screen.

"Good morning."

"Is it?" Hannah hadn't been expecting sarcasm, but okay.

"No, it's actually a pretty rough morning." That wasn't a lie. She was terribly hungover.

Annalise motioned to the chair across from her desk. Apparently, this wasn't going to be a short conversation. Hannah sat down and felt her boss's disdain settle like a blanket over her.

They stared at each other in silence for a long beat, and Hannah fought not to shift around in her chair.

"You have nothing to say for yourself."

"Not really. I think threatening my ex-boyfriend with an ice pick at an event I'd planned really spoke for itself."

"You're definitely fired."

"I figured that." She went to pick up her bag in a move that Viola Davis would be proud of, when Annalise held up a staying hand.

"Your ex-boyfriend?"

This bitch was really going to insert herself into the situation again. "I think you've meddled in my love life enough, Annalise."

"I never thought you'd actually find a boyfriend."

"And you never intended to promote me." Hannah didn't need to question it.

Annalise took her dark, thick-rimmed glasses off and sat back in her chair. For the first time, Hannah noticed how brittle her boss seemed. Sort of like a de-winged hummingbird that couldn't stop moving even though she couldn't get anywhere.

"You were good at planning parties for professional sports teams. And they liked to look at your tits." She shrugged one of her shoulders. "And you're a smart girl. I thought you would fail and realize that you were really doing what you were meant to do."

She shouldn't have asked the next question, which she definitely asked. "And what was I meant to do?"

Her former boss made a *pfft* sound. "Look pretty. Do the dirty work."

Two weeks ago, Hannah would have believed that was all she

was good for. In that moment, confronted with someone who saw her the way she'd seen herself for years, something had changed. She knew that she was meant for more than looking pretty and doing someone else's dirty work. She no longer doubted her own ambition.

And she wasn't crying. She'd probably cry later when trying to figure out how to pay her student loans on time while she and Sasha were getting their ideas off the ground, but not as she made her very Viola-like exit.

AS SHE WALKED OUT of the office, she flipped off Giselle, who blanched at the rude gesture. Then she winced again when Hannah mouthed the c-word in her direction. This reaction filled Hannah with so much satisfaction that she ran into Noah's tall frame as he exited the elevator.

"Are you okay?" He grabbed her arm, and Hannah waited for her body to react to him now that she wasn't wrapped up in an oxytocin overdose named Jack Nolan. Still, there was nothing except a hint of irritation that he'd ruined her perfectly good exit.

"I'm fine. Except for the fact that I just got fired, I'm fine."

He laughed, and it was the annoying sound he always made when he thought she was being cute. "Lucky you didn't get arrested."

"Wouldn't be the first time." She looked up at him and noticed that his smile was strained. Funny, knowing someone that well. "What are you doing here? Shouldn't you be seeing about bailing your boss out? And wouldn't he have fired us even if he hadn't gotten hauled away in a paddy wagon?"

He looked back toward Annalise's office for a beat and then back down at her. Grabbing her arm and steering her toward the elevator before she could extricate herself, he said, "Let me take you for coffee."

They were both silent on the elevator. She didn't know what Noah was thinking about, but Hannah was hoping that he wasn't here to give her a list of reasons why the party sucked before the *Post* story dropped and the senator got arrested. She didn't think her ex was that much of a jerk, but she hadn't thought that Jack would lie to her repeatedly throughout their entire relationship, either.

Once they exited the building and Noah led her toward a coffee shop, she breathed easy. He cared too much about what people thought of him to get really mean in public. But he still kept her in suspense while he ordered her coffee for her.

"I might have changed my order." She hadn't, but still.

Noah shook his head. "Always difficult."

"This is well-trod ground." She knew she was difficult, and she wasn't about to change that—not with her ex and not right now.

Noah ignored her and smiled at the barista who handed over their drinks. Then he pointed at a table in the corner with her cold brew.

When they were both seated, he said, "I'm going to marry Madison."

She wouldn't have been more surprised if he'd told her that he was joining a Catholic monastery. "Madison Chapin?"

He smiled again, but this time it wasn't the smile that he'd indulged her with when he'd thought she was being ridiculous. It was damned close to the smile that Jack had laid on her after the first time they'd done sex things. *Holy shit.*

"Yeah." He sounded shy. He'd never sounded shy about anything with her.

"You realize she's a white girl, right?"

He took a drink of his black coffee. "Yeah, and I'm in love with her."

Not once, in the year they'd dated, had he said he was in love with Hannah. And, strangely, she wasn't hurt by the fact that he was in love with someone else and could say the words. She wasn't jealous that she'd never heard them from him, because they would have been a lie. He'd liked certain things about her a lot—mostly the way she looked and how good the sex was. But he'd never truly *seen* her.

He'd wanted her to become more reserved and proper and go to law school so that they could be a black power couple.

And now he was in love with a white girl. A senator's daughter who'd been kicked out of the United Kingdom after blowing off her third day of study abroad.

Amazing. All there was to do was laugh. And laugh harder. Noah stared at her as though she was afflicted or speaking in tongues. She fought to catch her breath so that she could explain, but tears were starting to leak out.

"It's just so funny." She wiped her eyes, probably rubbing runny mascara all over. "I spent my whole life wanting to be as white as possible—so I could be like the rest of my family. And then you dumped me because I couldn't just put on a dashiki, wear my natural hair, throw up a fist, and embrace my blackness, and now you're—"

"That's not quite fair—"

"And now you're with the Beckiest Becky to ever Becky!" The barista was definitely staring at them now, but she couldn't stop.

"I'm in love with her."

Holy shit. He was totally telling the truth.

Even though she wasn't jealous, she had questions. "You're the guy she was trying to make jealous with the fiancé?"

"They broke up."

"I know. This is just too good."

"After the engagement party." He smirked the smirk of a man who was now getting laid properly.

"But you worked for her father—"

"Not anymore." He shook his head and a muscle in his cheek twitched, changing the whole mood of the conversation. "He fired me after he found out. Apparently, he's a secret racist."

"At least he was racist enough to keep you out of the inner circle heading to jail right now." She hadn't wanted Noah to go to jail, not even when she'd thought he was a total shithead.

"You're not mad?"

Not at all. If someone had told her that she'd be able to see Noah with new eyes on today of all days, she would have laughed until she literally died. But now, with him looking kind of rumpled and vulnerable and in love? This was not the man who had torn her heart out and told her that she would never find anyone to take the broken bits of it for his own. She could feel empathy for this Noah who had no job and was up to his ears in love with the last person she would expect.

"Yeah, you're really in love with her." She paused, biting her lip. Wondering if he would nail her for how pathetic the next statement sounded. "And you were never in love with me."

"I loved you." She doubted that and was about to tell him so when he continued. "But I wasn't really ready to be in love with anyone."

She didn't try to interrupt him again, didn't try to make a snide remark or cut him down. Something in her gut told him that she needed to hear what he had to say.

"I was in love with the idea of what you could be. But I was really in love with the idea of what we could be together. I was an asshole."

Hearing him say that was unbelievably vindicating.

"I'm sorry I hurt you." He sounded truly sincere.

"You didn't just hurt me." Tears pricked her eyes, and she was too tired to fight them. One crawled down her face. "You told me that no one would ever want to marry me. And I believed you."

He looked down, and she could see the shame crawling over his body. She looked at him with tears running down her face until he looked up at her so he could see what he'd done.

"I'm sorry."

They sat there in silence. She wiped her face with a scratchy napkin and drank her free coffee because—free coffee.

"Do you still believe me?"

She thought it over again, along with the conversation she'd had with Sasha yesterday and the way she'd felt around Jack when he hadn't been purposefully being an ass. "No."

"That's good." Even when he was apologizing, he managed to sound pretentious.

That was the precise moment she realized she had never been in love with him—she'd just tried to please him. And that led to the realization that she was really, truly in love with Jack because it hadn't been that hard to please him. Even through all of his lies, she'd felt his approval for her—for who she really was—not any of the try-hard shit she'd pulled with Noah and all the guys before.

"You're thinking really hard."

"I was never in love with you."

That made Noah blink. Twice. "Harsh, but fair."

"It's sort of my brand." She shrugged and then looked him in the eye. "You're really kind of odious. I would have hated being married to you."

He smiled. "You would have been the worst thing that ever happened to me."

And then they both laughed and finished their coffees as though they hadn't individually blown their lives apart.

CHAPTER TWENTY-NINE

WHEN HANNAH OPENED HER door to Sean Nolan with a toolbox in hand, she wasn't quite sure what to make of it. Maybe he was here to avenge his son's honor and the wrench was the weapon with which he was the most comfortable.

Then he said, "I'm not here to try to get you to forgive my idiot son, but you shouldn't be paying more on your water bill because you—rightly—broke up with him."

"Pay what on my what?"

"You got a leaky bathroom faucet, right?"

"Yeah." As apologies went, Jack sending his dad over to fix things at her place was clever. Mostly because she was still having homicidal ideations toward Jack. She really felt as though she should resist, even though the drip was keeping her up even more than missing Jack and being out of a job.

"I'll get it fixed in thirty minutes." She opened the door wider and gestured for him to enter.

"I'll get you a beer." Jack's dad had just happened to show up while Hannah was binging on *Lovesick*. To his credit, he didn't seem too freaked out by the premise of the show—a guy gets chlamydia and has to tell all of his ex-lovers about it. Sean Nolan just shrugged and stuck his head under the sink.

True to his word, he fixed the faucet and left without once trying to convince her to give Jack another chance.

HANNAH'S SUSPICIONS ABOUT JACK'S intentions became deeper when Jack's sister, Bridget, called her and offered to write up an agreement for her and Sasha that would help them form their business.

"How did you know Sasha and I were starting a business?"

"Do you want to start an S corp or an LLC?" Bridget completely ignored her question. "The paperwork is a little bit different for the type of company, and I can explain the differences if you want—"

"I thought you were a prosecutor." Was Bridget even qualified to do this? Could it put her job in jeopardy?

"I ran a clinic for small businesses during law school, and this is easy-peasy."

So she was definitely qualified, but she and Sasha had just planned to hit up her father's attorney for help when the time came—meaning when they had enough money to pay him. "How much do we owe you?"

"This is my pro bono service for the year."

"You don't have to do this." She wondered if Jack had even told his sister anything about the breakup. "Jack and I aren't together anymore."

"I know." Bridget sighed. "My brother is a total idiot, and I'm not supposed to tell you otherwise. Not that I would. But you're cool and fun, and I hope we can be friends even if my brother is now dead to you."

"You got it."

"Good. Look at the descriptions of the types of companies I'm going to send to you in a little explainer and get back to me as soon as you can."

Bridget hung up before she could thank her again.

HANNAH WAS READY TO forgive Jack by the time his mother called and offered her and Sasha their first real job.

When she quoted the amount of money the museum was going to pay them to plan the opening of a new exhibit for children, Hannah was ready to forgive Jack a lot.

"Ms. Simpson, you really don't have to do this." Hannah didn't know why she was hesitating at this point. Clearly, Jack was systematically fixing her life in order to get her to forgive him, but there was just too much water under the bridge for them to pretend that they hadn't based their entire relationship on lies. The fact that he was dragging his mother into this made her feel a little yucky. She'd lied to Jack, too. "I'm sure there are much more experienced firms you could go with."

"Oh, I know." Jack's mom paused. "But your old firm is astonishingly expensive. And now that you're not there, very stodgy. Plus, I like you."

Hannah didn't think they were that much cheaper than Annalise and company, but she definitely agreed with the stodgy part. And Giselle was so clueless about children that she'd probably have them eating finger sandwiches—not even peanut butter and jelly ones. She wasn't even going to touch how Jack's mom liked her.

Still, she hesitated. Shouldn't she be cutting all ties with Jack? And even if she didn't cut all ties, it was about time she actually talked to Jack. His sending his family to make amends for her losing her job wasn't going to get either of them closure. In the end, though, she wasn't about to say no to this opportunity.

"Thank you. And thank Jack for me, will you?"

"Oh, I'm not supposed to say anything on Jack's behalf, but I suppose I should apologize." Hannah had the feeling that Jack's mother's apologies were rare, so she listened closely. "His father and I didn't do a great job when we got divorced making sure our kids knew that the divorce wasn't about them—and that we thought it was the best thing for them. I'm afraid that Jack felt abandoned by me and—indirectly, mind you—messed up his relationship with you because of that."

"You raised a good man, even if you weren't there at the finish line." Hannah knew it had to be hard for the older woman to admit that maybe she'd done something as huge as parenting wrong. "He was the perfect boyfriend when he wasn't trying to be bad, and I lied to him, too."

"Although you might have started out lying, I knew you were the right girl for him the night he brought you to Artie's exhibit."

"How did you know that?" Hannah snort-laughed. "Was me nearly flying into a jealous rage your first clue?"

"No, the fact that you didn't require him to be the perfect boyfriend." Hannah could almost see the other woman shaking off her wistfulness. "Anyhow, you'll plan the event. It will be smashing. You'll forgive my son, and I'll try to be at least a little bit grandmotherly with your children."

She hung up before Hannah could dispute the existence of future grandchildren, and Hannah called Sasha with the good news.

———

HANNAH PUT OFF READING his e-mail for as long as she possibly could. By the end, she'd forgiven Jack and was waiting for him to call. However long it took.

To: Hannah Mayfield
From: Jack Nolan

I'm sorry. I didn't turn the article in to Irv, and I won't—no matter what. But I'm sending it to you because when I did try to write it, it made me realize what a mistake it would have been. I'll do anything to make it up to you.

Xoxo,
Jack

It wasn't elegant or smooth. His words lacked the charm that he'd displayed the night they'd met, but she kind of melted at his clumsy apology. And she didn't hesitate at all in opening the attachment.

HOW TO LOSE A GIRL IN TWO WEEKS: AN APOLOGIA
by Jack Nolan

I am a fuck-up. Chances are that if you, like me, are a cis-gendered, heterosexual man, you are also a fuck-up. Before I met the girl of my dreams almost a month ago, I thought I had it all figured out. I was the perfect boyfriend, and my girlfriends kept dumping me because of something wrong with them. You probably think that you're the perfect boyfriend, too. You would be wrong. Very, very wrong.

(I need to interrupt this important message to let you know that all my ex-girlfriends left me because I am a fuck-up, but I digress.)

And, yeah, I saw my friends committing all variety of pedestrian fuck-ups and thought I was better because I knew how to communicate reasonably well, I tried to listen once in a while, and I knew how to plan a date well. But what I didn't know was how to show up and be vulnerable. And my failure to do so means that I'll probably die alone, pining for the aforementioned girl of my dreams.

I should back up and explain. Either because of my gigantic balls or my unfathomable hubris, I agreed to try out each and every one of the knuckleheaded stunts my friends have been pulling on the fine and upstanding bachelorettes of Chicago on an unsuspecting girl. All in the hopes of teaching my brethren to act right.

Now, I didn't just go on Tinder and swipe until I found a lady who caught my fancy. No, I had to compound my future screwup by trying all this shit on the only woman I could see myself spending the rest of my life with. The one who took one look at me and realized that I wasn't nearly the good guy I thought I was. The one who would bust my balls from Lincoln Park to the edge of eternity and leave me without a hint of regret. I thought that I could clean it all up afterward, once the truth came out.

Well, dear readers, pride goeth before the fall. And I fell hard. Everything I did to sabotage our burgeoning love affair, she took in stride. I mansplained, and she put her hand over my junk to silence me. (A seriously underrated voodoo trick if you need to shut up your significant other. Only with consent, please!) I introduced her to my mom, thinking that she'd run screaming if she thought I was a mama's boy. Nah, she rolled with it, and I ended up being the odd man out.

I introduced her to my hard-drinking dad and lunatic siblings, thinking that would scare her away. It didn't—she was more at home in the house I grew up in than I was. She belongs there as much as I do.

I showed up late to an event that was important to her, looking like shit, and she just cleaned me up and introduced me to every important person in her work life. She looked at me like she trusted me—even though I'd pulled an asshole move—and I fell in love with her right then.

I didn't want to lie to her anymore, but I couldn't bring myself to tell her the truth. You see, my boss threatened my job if I didn't finish this article. And my job was the only thing I had that made me feel like I was the man I was supposed to be. Without my job, I'd just be a smartass with mommy issues and a short but savage list of failed relationships. I'd put my career second for one too many women, and I wasn't about to do it again. And it was all because I hadn't been able to get my head out of my ass and see what I'd been doing since I asked Maggie Doonan to the freshman dance—I'd been trying to make my mom love me enough to stay with my dad.

And with my dream girl, the Duchess of my heart, none of that worked. Nothing I did to make her dump me made her dump me. And none of the sparkly dates or the killer moves in the sack were enough to make her forgive me for lying to her and using her to further my career.

So, for what it's worth, here's my advice:

1. If you want to lose a girl, tell her a lot of lies.
2. And then, double down on the lies.
3. Realize you're in love with her too late to make the lies okay.
4. Humiliate her in front of her ex-boyfriend, her nemesis, and her boss.
5. ACTUALLY, DON'T DO ANY OF THIS SHIT, YOU FUCKING LUNATIC!!!

Here's what I hope you do: I hope you learn from the mistakes in your past. Maybe get some therapy to work on all the issues you've been taking out on the women you've been dating. The next time you meet a girl you like, LISTEN TO HER. (Don't mansplain. It gives us all a bad name.) And then do the things she says she likes, and don't do the stuff she doesn't. Be honest, but not in an "I'm just being honest with you so that I can make myself feel better about being an asshole" way. Be really honest about the things you've been talking about in therapy.

Most importantly, if a woman takes your heart out of your chest and holds it in her hands, be extra good to her. She really deserves it, and it will fuck you up royally if you do something she won't forgive you for.

CHAPTER THIRTY

HANNAH AND SASHA'S FIRST event wasn't the opening of the children's gallery at the MCA; it was an event that Hannah had anticipated planning for herself for more than a year. But she hadn't ever expected to be an employee. She'd always expected to be the bride.

Madison Chapin and Noah Long were to be married—on a shoestring budget because Madison was no longer speaking to her felonious parents. And since she hadn't wanted to give up the twenties theme, even though she'd given up her original fiancé, they were having the reception at the speakeasy where Hannah and Jack first met. They were going out of business and happy to have the rental fee for the night before the new tenants came in.

It would be small, intimate, and so on theme that they wouldn't have to spend a lot of money on decorations. Just plenty of booze and no political donors.

Jack still hadn't called her, and he'd stopped sending his family over to help in the past two weeks. Maybe he was waiting for her to reach out. She wanted to text him so much that her fingers itched, but she knew that she would have to talk to him in person. It would be hard because she knew that it wasn't likely that he would want to give it another try with her. And she very much doubted that they could just pretend that they were starting fresh—that she'd said yes to a date with him because he'd bought her tacos and kissed her like he knew what he was about and that she believed that someone like him could really love her like she wanted to be loved. He'd just wanted to leave her better off than she had been before that stupid fight at the engagement party.

And she needed to stop thinking about it because she was a busy small-business owner with an event to plan.

She and Sasha had been up until three a.m. hot-gluing beads on the bouquets for Madison and her bridesmaids and making favors for guests. It reminded Hannah of the parties they'd planned together in college and how much fun that had been. How much simpler and more hopeful she'd been.

Unlike her feelings about making favors, returning to the original scene of the crime where she'd met Jack aroused complicated feelings. Sasha was handling everything at the wedding venue. They were getting married at a small community church nearby, and Noah's father was performing the ceremony. Apparently, the Longs didn't have a problem with Noah marrying a white girl. They hadn't liked Hannah because she swore too much and they'd met her when she looked rode hard and put up wet.

Which wouldn't have been a problem with the Nolans. She and Sasha had gone to dinner with Bridget the week before, and Bridget could recite a dirty limerick that would make a longshoreman blush.

Hannah really liked her and would have been happy to have her as a sister-in-law if things were different.

She had to stop thinking about him. Now was not the time.

Which was going to be hard because he was standing outside of the speakeasy with a bunch of guys—some of whom she recognized from the first night they'd met. They were all dressed in puffer coats, jeans, and work boots, but Jack stood there with the nerve to look as dashing as he had in a tux.

Hannah almost didn't get out of the car. She was poised to turn the ignition back on and drive around the block until they left. Although she'd been pining for weeks now for the man she was currently drinking up with her eyes, she was afraid to see him. What if he just wanted to make things right so they could be friends? What if doing favors for her, sending his family to show up when she needed help, writing that she was the love of his life, were just ways to assuage his guilt over using her?

It took her north of a minute, but she got out of the car on shaky legs and walked over to Jack. Hopefully not looking as terrified as she felt.

"What are you doing here?"

He smiled at her, and the fucking dimple slayed her again. She'd only been lying to herself when she'd claimed that she was only going out with him to prove to Annalise that she didn't hate love. The dimple and the smile and the stupid sparkly green eyes had sealed her fate from the moment they'd met.

And then he wiped his hand over his beard—which was new and very hot—and looked up at her with more sparkly green bullshit in his gaze and said, "Thought you might need some help setting up. Sasha said you're still a two-woman operation."

"Jack, you don't have to—"

He stopped her with a hand on her shoulder, and the heat from his touch rendered her mute. "I want to, Duchess."

Using her nickname gave her hope that this was real and that everything but the stupid bullshit he'd done to try to get her to break up with him was real. "We should talk."

"We'll talk later." He squeezed her shoulder and then motioned his friends over to the car. "Keys?"

She handed her keys over and watched four grown men haul favors into the venue.

JACK STARED AT HANNAH on and off until it was time for him and his crew to leave. The last thing he wanted to witness was Hannah watching her ex-douche getting married to another girl. And there was too much that they needed to say to each other that they couldn't say to each other during someone else's wedding.

So he went to Chris's place and waited for the four longest hours of his life, barely distracted by the Michigan–Ohio State game. He counted down the minutes until he could see Hannah again and tell her exactly how he felt about her without any lies or pretense between them.

Based on how she'd looked at him today, she had some stuff to say to him, too. As soon as the clock hit ten forty-five p.m., he was out of Chris's pad—leaving his friend snoring on the couch with half a slice of pizza balanced on his chest—and on his way back to the bar.

He waited for almost everyone to stream out, feeling like a creeper waiting outside of the bar. But then he descended the stairs.

His palms were sweaty, and his palms never sweat. He'd calm down as soon as she agreed to give him another shot. She had to.

When he walked in, she and Sasha were the only people left. Sasha saw him come in and winked at him. Good sign.

And then Hannah turned and smiled at him. Not the hesitant smile of thanks she'd given him before he'd left earlier in the day, but the full smile she'd given him right before she bit into dessert, or right after the first time he'd gone down on her.

Just thinking about the faint possibility of getting his mouth on her again had his heart racing and the front of his jeans growing tighter. He had to slow down and make her see that he saw her and wanted her and needed her. That part of him had been dying without her.

"You're here."

"Nowhere else I'd rather be, Duchess."

Sasha picked up her bag from behind the bar. "I'm—uh—going to head out."

Neither of them answered her. They just smiled at each other like total goofs until they heard her heels echo on the stairs. That made Jack look down at the box in his hand and offer it to her.

"I don't feel like I deserve a gift."

"Shut up and take it." He wasn't in the mood for her self-deprecating bullshit. To his surprise, she didn't argue with him. Instead, she ripped open the package to find a brand-new pair of gray moccasins.

She had them out of the box, her heels off, and the soft leather slippers on her feet before saying anything.

"You like them?"

"I love them."

He wiped his sweaty palm over his sweaty brow. "I think you've warped my mind. I think you look sexier in those than in the heels."

"Probably because when I'm wearing heels, I'm thinking about how much I'd like to stab someone with them just so they get a hint of the pain of wearing heels."

"I don't know, I kind of think you're sexy even when you're about to stab me."

She looked down. "Sorry about that. It was probably a little extreme."

He took a step toward her so that he could be in her space, smelling the sweet spice of her skin and the scent of her fancy shampoo—a smell that made his dick go hard. A Pavlovian hard-on.

"I deserved it."

"I lied to you, too." He offered his hand then, knowing that his girl hated to admit that she'd been wrong. "I'm sorry."

She met his gaze, and her unusual-colored eyes flashed up at him. His mouth tingled with the need to take hers, but he didn't want to rush this apology. Before he kissed her, he needed her to know exactly how he felt about her. This was about him wanting to be *her* perfect boyfriend rather than *the* perfect boyfriend.

She bit on her bottom lip, bare and pink after a full day of talking and working. "I really love you, and I need to kiss you right now." That seemed to get the job done.

"I l—"

He cut her off; he could hear it later. He'd demand to hear it a thousand times, in a thousand ways—mostly naked ways for the next few months or so—but he needed to kiss her and touch her right now.

As soon as his tongue touched hers, she wrapped her arms around his shoulders and pulled him closer. He drowned in her smell, savored the feel of her body up against his. But he needed more. She'd opened up an endless well of need—need she alone could assuage—and met him touch for touch.

He picked her up and plopped her ass on the bar. The way he'd wanted to the night they'd met. And then he opened up her knees so they climbed the sides of his body. But then he pulled his mouth from hers. There would plenty of making up for lost time when they finished talking.

"I love you." He already knew he liked hearing it best when he was just finished kissing her. It was soft and sweet and real. And he knew she didn't say those words like that to anyone else. That was his "I love you."

"We both messed up." He put his hand around the back of her neck so she wouldn't pull away from him. "I'm sorry."

"I didn't think someone like you would ever want to be with me if I was the real me." She ran a finger down his forehead and he shivered. "You were just so perfect the night we met."

"I didn't think you'd stick around for long, even if I refused to use you for the article, and Irv threatened to fire me if I didn't." He didn't like admitting that he'd been stupid enough to think that his job was worth more than the woman in his arms. "I'd given up jobs and opportunities for promotion before because of women. And they always left."

"They were dumb."

"Nah, I was just trying too hard with things that were temporary." He had to stop and kiss her again, needed to confirm to himself that she was still there with both her legs and arms around him. "And I was up my own ass about how I was always the victim."

"And I for sure thought you were going to leave me for someone more glamorous. Someone like Sasha or Giselle."

He pulled a face. "Sasha's cute, but not my type. And I already dated a glamorous blonde a lot like Giselle."

"I know. You dated her sister. The actress." She bit her bottom lip. "I looked her up. Hated her on sight."

"She didn't turn out to be right for me, either." She rested her forehead against his, and something clicked back into place inside him. "Turns out I like women who get mean when their friends are insulted."

"So, you like bitches?"

"I like loyal women who bust my balls and don't put up with my shit."

"I liked your article. I'm almost sad that no one else will get to read it."

"Liked it?" He'd been hoping that she'd love it so much that she had to call him, but he totally got that she'd needed time to cool down. And he'd thought that sending his family over would show her that he was serious about her more than busting in with flowers and getting on his knees.

"Did you get fired?" she asked.

He actually hadn't gotten fired, because Irv had changed his tune about his potential to cover politics after he found out that other outlets wanted to hire him. But he wasn't working at *Haberdasher's Monthly* anymore, either. "I actually got a new gig."

A look of concern crossed her face. "This is not the part where you tell me you're moving, is it?"

"Nah, I'm going to be a features writer for *GQ*—but about Chicago and the rest of the Midwest. Politics and lifestyle."

"I'd say you have an aptitude for both."

"If by aptitude you mean getting a sitting senator indicted and almost having my manhood permanently injured by ice pick in one night, you'd be right."

She laughed, and it was the best sound. The only sound he wanted to hear for a week that wasn't her asking him for more sex.

He had to know if she forgave him, if they could move forward. "Do you think you can trust me again? You give me what I need when you trust me." His eye twitched because if she couldn't trust him, this wasn't going to work. "I know I screwed up, but I need you to trust me again."

"I trust you. You're here with me now, and you knew how to fix it." She ran one finger across his forehead, moving his hair out of his face. "You made sure I knew that you were all in. You threw your family at me and made sure I knew that I belonged with them. With you."

That she got what he'd been trying to do made him want to pump his fist in the air.

"You didn't have to do all of that, though."

"I didn't?" he asked. "You threatened to deflate my balls, Duchess. I thought I needed to go all in."

"I didn't mean it." She smiled. "Well, I only meant it a little bit."

"See? I had to keep our future children safe."

She shook her head. "You do realize that our child's first word will probably be 'fuck'?"

"That'll be my dad's fault, though." They both laughed. "I'll always know where I stand, I guess," he said. "That's one of my favorite things about you. You're always straight with me."

"I promise not to actually bust your balls." She kissed his forehead then. "For our future children's sake."

Before they finally got down to the more fun business of the evening, he said, "Just promise to gently cup them whenever I'm really fucking up."

"I'll make sure it's in the vows."

CHAPTER THIRTY-ONE

THEY NEEDED TO BE alone, and soon. Now that he wasn't faking being a good Catholic, she was going to need at least a few days with nothing to do but him. As soon as the rental company picked up the rest of the glassware, Jack shoved her into his car and broke the sound barrier on the way to his condo.

They didn't even hold hands in the elevator, as though they both knew that once they started, they wouldn't stop.

But once they got inside his door, all bets were off. He groaned, and it hit her in the gut. Then he kissed her mouth, and her whole being lit up. She clutched at his shoulders as he took her mouth in the most ludicrously delicious kiss she'd ever experienced.

By the time he moved his mouth behind her ear, they were both panting. She clawed at the hem of his T-shirt because she needed it off—now. He raised his arms as though reluctant to take his hands off her hips. And as soon as he was shirtless, she stepped back to look at him. Which was a mistake, because he was more ripped than she remembered.

Christ, he must be doing those superhero workouts. That was

the only explanation for how big and muscled he was. His body was just stupid hot, and it rendered her speechless. And he was in love with her.

"Did I grow a third nipple or something?"

Her mouth was dry, but she managed an "or something." Then he laughed and stepped closer to her again. When she couldn't see all of what he was working at the same time, she looked up at him, summoning her most cynical smirk. "Are you on some weird, illegal steroids?"

He laughed. "No." One corner of his mouth tipped up, making his dimple pop and reminding her of how cocky he was. It should have been a turnoff, but it wasn't. She liked it. And looking at him, she acknowledged that a little bit of that cockiness was earned. She couldn't exactly hold it against him. She'd rather hold herself against him. "You like?"

As much as she wanted to play it cool and pretend that she saw a half-naked Adonis every day and that all of her ex-lovers had looked like they were very serious about Captain America cosplay, she couldn't. "I love."

The dimple got even deeper and he came back in for another kiss, one so mind-melting that she just up and forgot that she was soft in some places that she'd rather not be despite her religious attendance at SoulCycle classes and Pilates. She did that to be strong, not to be hot. Working out to feel good in her skin was one thing when she'd been on her extended dating hiatus. But now, when Jack was pulling apart the sides of her shirtdress and she was lifting her arms for him to take it off, she suddenly felt self-conscious. Which was ridiculous, considering that he'd seen her full-on hairy bush multiple times.

Somehow, this felt different. This was the first time she was having sex with someone who loved her—the first person who'd said those words. And the way he looked at her. Like she was precious, and he couldn't seem to take all of her in at once. The adoration in his eyes must have been what made her peel her tights off faster than the speed of light, and what made her stand still as he ran a finger over her sternum and down to the core of her as slowly as the last few minutes of the last day of school.

He looked at her as though she were ice cream, which she knew he loved because she couldn't seem to stop watching his videos; she'd watched them so many times in the past few weeks that she had them all memorized. But every time she missed his naughty mouth, she hadn't been able to help watching that one about homemade ice cream. He worked an ice cream cone just like he worked over her body. She'd never look at mint chocolate chip the same way again, but she didn't care.

"You like?" She wanted him to look at her like this forever, but she also didn't want it to start feeling awkward.

He reached around her and unhooked her bra. "I like so much I want more. Let me see all of you, Duchess."

She had the feeling that he was talking about more than just her naked body. And she didn't want to hold anything back. In that moment, she realized that the reckless way she used to love wasn't bad or wrong. She'd just been aiming her love at the wrong men. Something about being with Jack made it feel so right.

"I want—"

"Tell me what you want and I'll give it to you, Duchess."

"I want your hands."

"That's a given." He complied immediately, running his hands down her sides and into her panties, toying with the straps in a way that drove her insane. "What else?"

"I want your mouth."

"You have to tell me where." But he kissed a spot on her neck that must have controlled the tendons in her knees, because they seemed to drop out from under her. "You like it here, but where else?"

Feeling like she needed to wrest some control back, she went to work on his belt and his pants. "I also think your cock should get involved."

"Thank Christ." He lifted his eyes heavenward.

"Yeah, thank God the vow of celibacy was fake." She would have had a hard time waiting for all this now that she knew that he was hers.

"Hey, I kept you satisfied." So funny that he wanted to defend his honor instead of actually get to have sex with her.

"Yeah, I was worried about you." She laid a kiss on his chest, just above his heart. "I was worried that it might have fallen off from disuse."

"It's still right here."

She found the appendage she wanted underneath his boxer briefs—of course he wore fuck-hot black boxer briefs—and wrapped her hand around it. Turned out, the big-dick energy was totally authentic. When he didn't come back with one of his sexy, infuriating questions, she stroked him. Satisfaction whirled inside her when he groaned and took his hands off of her so he could push down his pants and boxers.

Until he was more naked than she was. And, God help her, he had that dip in his hips that she could never remember the name of,

NOT THE GIRL YOU MARRY

so she just called it the "fuck-me bone." He really was trying to kill her with his hotness.

She must have said that out loud because he laughed again. "Gladly."

"What?"

"Fuck you." He grabbed her hand and ran his index finger down her palm. It was almost as sexy as his hands in her underwear. "I will gladly fuck you once we get to the bedroom."

In retrospect, dragging him into his bedroom like some sort of deranged cavewoman was probably slightly unhinged. He might reconsider the whole being-in-love-with-her thing. But she would worry about that later. Like, after she'd had several orgasms.

As soon as they reached the bed, he pushed her down on it. She spread her legs so that he could lie on top of her, and she sighed when he rested his weight against her. That familiar safe feeling came back because he was all around her. They sighed in unison as all their parts lined up.

She looked up at him, stared into his eyes, and everything was perfect. Or it would be as soon as he put on a condom.

YOU ARE IN DANGER, his dick warned him as he sank deep inside her. Not that he needed his penis's opinion on the matter. His head and his heart had known that Hannah was trouble the moment he'd clapped eyes on her. And now she was all his, and there was no turning back.

She was in love with him, and that was a good thing—his dick didn't want to be anywhere but where it was right now for the foreseeable future. Having her be in love with him was a major help with that.

The bed and the ground seemed to shift beneath him, and the one thing he was sure of was that he would never forget being with her. In this moment he couldn't remember being with anyone else or what that felt like because he knew, right now, that he'd never had magic before.

When he didn't move, she dug her nails into his biceps, and her smile turned feral. It turned him on even more that she couldn't wait for him to move, that she let him know what she wanted so clearly.

"Please, Jack." Her breathy voice was so raw and real and authentic to her that he couldn't do anything else but move.

Normally not at a loss for words, he didn't have many in that moment. It was odd; he'd never had a problem coming up with creative and filthy dirty talk during sex, but Hannah blanked his brain of everything except the monosyllabic descriptions of what he was experiencing in that moment—*hot, wet, tight, mine.*

He had enough of his mental capacity remaining that he wedged one hand in between them and rubbed her clit between thrusts. During their first night together, when he'd gone down on her, he'd learned her enough to know that she needed constant stimulation. And if he was almost rough, it made her totally lose control. He loved that he knew what felt like a secret about her, something that perhaps no one else had taken the time to learn. He wanted to know all of her secrets and hoard them so that he could tell what she was thinking when he wasn't buried inside of her, so close to orgasm that spots covered his vision.

"Yes." He lost her eyes when she moaned that word and threw her head back. He buried his head in her neck and kissed the damp skin there. She tasted like sunlight, which was such a hokey thing to even think. But, with her, he couldn't seem to help himself. She made him horny with her sharp humor and husky laugh, but she made him melt with everything underneath that.

The orgasm careened up his spine, hitting him the moment after she found hers, whispering his name over and over again. And his last thought before he nearly blacked out from pleasure was how much he loved her.

EPILOGUE

IT WAS TIME TO take the next step. She'd been dating Jack for real for more than a year now, and they'd moved into Jack's condo together six months ago.

Things were great.

When they weren't lying to each other to get ahead in their careers, their careers actually went a lot better. Hannah and Sasha were making a living off of their party-planning business—Good-Time Girls. After Madison Chapin's wedding had made all the wedding blogs, they'd grown a reputation for planning weddings for quirky brides on a budget. And Hannah had kept most of her sports and arts clients because they'd all been paying Annalise's prices so they could get Hannah's expertise.

Jack had just written an article on the new female senator from Illinois, who ran on an anti-corruption agenda that got a lot of attention. This past week, he'd been in New York because he was the newest politics contributor at MSNBC. Several of the anchors kind of had the heart eyes for him, to be honest. Not that she could blame them. Jack Nolan could tempt even a nun.

But he was back in Chicago, and one thing was missing from their life. She just needed one thing to feel complete. That's how they "just happened" to wander past a dog shelter on her first Sunday off in months while they walked around Lincoln Park with hot cappuccinos after brunch with his parents and sister.

"Wanna go in?"

Jack hesitated. He did look tired, and maybe this wasn't the best time to bring a whole lot of change into their lives. But she saw the way his eyes lit up every time he met a new dog. And they'd been sending info about shelter pets to each other so much that they took up more real estate in their text chain than where to eat and sex stuff. Combined.

They needed to do this. "We can just look."

"But then I'll feel bad if we don't take anyone home."

He wanted a dog so badly *she* could taste it. "I just have a feeling that we'll find our new friend today."

Jack shrugged in that way he had that wasn't nonchalant. It was the same way he'd shrugged when she'd volunteered her ethnic background. After a year with the man, she knew that it meant he knew something was important to her, and he was on board.

They entered the shelter and signed in at the front desk. Although she'd been in earlier in the week to make sure the dog that Jack had sent her with three heart-eyes emojis and three exclamation points was still there, the person at the front desk didn't betray recognizing her.

She walked them back, and Hannah had to slow herself down because she was too excited to become dog parents with Jack. She was obviously insane to be this amped about something so normal and mundane, but this was huge for her. She'd never been with someone she thought she'd be with for a dog's whole life.

Gus, the one-year-old cream-colored French bulldog with a recent cleft palate repair, was a symbol of how solid she felt about her and Jack being together for the long haul. She could never put into words how much it meant to her that he loved her that much.

So he was getting a declaration of love in canine form.

Jack stopped right next to her, looked down at Gus, and then smiled at Hannah. Then, instead of saying a word, he dropped down on his knees—actually just one knee. The shelter worker smiled at her as though she had a secret, and the secret was *not* that they were getting a dog.

When Hannah looked back down at Jack, he already had Gus—who looked *very* familiar with Jack for having just met him—out of the cage and clipped onto a leash that had just appeared out of nowhere.

"Hannah—"

"Shut up." That just flew out of her mouth. She didn't want him to shut up, but he surely wasn't going to say what she thought he was going to say.

Seeing as how he was pretty close to perfect, he just paused and pulled a velvet jewelry box off of Gus's collar. "Will you marry me, Hannah?"

"You're not going to say all the other stuff about how I'm the woman of your dreams and stuff?" She wiped her face with both hands, her gaze jumping from Jack to their dog to the ring box.

"I thought I was working on borrowed time, since you already told me to shut up."

"I still want to hear the stuff. I just needed a second."

"Do you want to hear the stuff or get your ring and take our dog home?"

NOT THE GIRL YOU MARRY

The shelter volunteer cleared her throat. "I think she has to say yes first."

Jack repeated, "Will you marry me?" at the same time that Hannah shouted, "Yes!" and fell to her knees to kiss Jack and then their new family member.

Not the
Girl You
Marry

ANDIE J. CHRISTOPHER

DISCUSSION QUESTIONS

1. At the beginning of the book, Hannah has given up all hope of meeting someone and she isn't looking for love. Some people say that "you always find love when you stop looking." Do you think that's true? What role does hope play in finding love? What role does luck play in finding love?

2. Hannah is fiercely protective of her female friends, particularly Sasha. Do you think that she derives a sense of worthiness from her female friendships? How so?

3. Did it strike you that Hannah identified herself as biracial rather than black? Do you think that played into the failure of her relationship with Noah? How do you think her racial identity played into the development of her relationship with Jack?

4. Jack's dad gives Michael and Jack a very brief—but frank—sex talk. Did the content of that talk surprise you? Did it subvert the notion of toxic masculinity? How does Sean Nolan's attitude toward sex influence Jack?

5. Who would you cast to play Hannah and Jack in a movie version of the book?

6. Jack perceives himself as the ideal boyfriend at the beginning of the book because he's surrendered his needs for the needs of his partners in the past. Is Jack the perfect boyfriend? Or is his perfection keeping him from making a genuine, lasting connection?

7. Jack has close, intimate friendships with his male friends—particularly Father Patrick. How do you think those relationships shape him as a person and affect how he approaches his burgeoning relationship with Hannah?

8. How did you feel about Noah and Hannah's relationship as exes? Why do you think they started dating in the first place? How do you feel about where they ended up?

ACKNOWLEDGMENTS

First thanks go to Kristine Swartz for loving my words enough to publish them, making my characters shine, and serving as my part-time, honorary therapist during revisions. Huge thanks to Cindy Hwang and Erin Galloway for their enthusiasm about this book. Jessica Brock, Roxanne Jones, Jessica Mangicaro, and the Berkley sales team—I bow down to you for your mad skills in getting this book in front of as many readers as possible. Thank you to Emily Osborne, illustrator extraordinaire Colleen Reinhart, and everyone in the art department for making the cover so beautiful.

Thank you to my agent, Courtney Miller-Callihan. I'm so grateful to have you in my corner every day.

Adriana Anders and Kasey Lane, the Book Smart Tarts: thank you for the wine (Adriana) and the tough love (Kasey). Most of all, thank you for telling me that I'm a good writer and I have pretty hair when I need you to. To the Wicked Wallflowers, Jenny Nordbak and Sarah Hawley, thank you for shipping me with the best Chris. And Jenny Holiday, thank you for becoming my friend even though I accosted you on the subway.

ACKNOWLEDGMENTS

I have no idea what I did in a past life to be worthy of such wonderful friends. Kim Guzman, Kelly Montgomery, Barbara Gibson, Beth Skierski, and Elizabeth Dillion were the inspiration for Hannah's friendship with Sasha. Thank you for putting up with my shenanigans and being my friends for nearly twenty years. Thank you to Laurel Simmons, who is usually my first reader and would be my top choice as a romantic comedy sidekick.

Katie Dunneback, Tara Kennedy, and Michelle Sandiford. Thank you for always being there with a bottomless mimosa and for not commenting when I inevitably order the shrimp and grits.

Finally, thank you to my family. Mary Manka is the best mom and probably one of the best people in the world. And my aunts—Margaret Doonan, Jean Manka, and Maureen Manka—thank you for everything. Each of you helped shape the woman I am today. To my cousins Sean Doonan, Molly Calkins, and Acacia Hagenson, I love you all so much.

And finally, thank you to my grandparents, Bud and Wilda. Your wild and epic love story, Grandpa's belief that I was pretty much magic, and Grams's love of romance novels are the only reasons I write them today.

USA Today bestselling author **Andie J. Christopher** writes edgy, funny, and sexy contemporary romance featuring heat, humor, and dirty-talking heroes that make readers sweat. A graduate of the University of Notre Dame and Stanford Law School, she grew up in a family of voracious readers, and picked up her first romance novel at age twelve when she'd finished reading everything else in her grandmother's house. It was love at first read. It wasn't too long before she started writing her own stories—her first heroine drank Campari and drove an Alfa Romeo up a winding road to a minor royal's estate in Spain. Andie lives in the nation's capital with her French bulldog, Gus, a stockpile of Campari, and way too many books.

CONNECT ONLINE

andiejchristopher.com

🐦 authorandiej

📷 authorandiej

👤 authorandiej

Ready to find
your next great read?

Let us help.

Visit prh.com/nextread

Penguin
Random
House